MW01146484

WEEPING WALLS

by

Gerri Hill

Bella
BOOKS

2013

Bella Books, Inc.
P.O. Box 10543
Tallahassee, FL 32302

Printed in the United States of America on acid-free paper.

First Bella Books Edition 2013

Editor: Medora MacDougall
Cover Designer: Judith Fellows

ISBN: 978-1-59493-386-8

Other Bella Books by Gerri Hill

Artist's Dream
At Seventeen
Behind the Pine Curtain
The Cottage
Coyote Sky
Dawn of Change
Devil's Rock
Gulf Breeze
Hell's Highway
Hunter's Way
In the Name of the Father
Keepers of the Cave
The Killing Room
Love Waits
No Strings
One Summer Night
Partners
The Rainbow Cedar
The Scorpion
Sierra City
Snow Falls
Storms
The Target

About the Author

Gerri Hill has twenty-four published works, including the 2013 GCLS winner *Snow Falls*, 2011 and 2012 GCLS winners *Devil's Rock* and *Hell's Highway*, and the 2009 GCLS winner *Partners*, the last book in the popular Hunter Series, as well as the 2012 Lambda finalist *Storms*. Hill's love of nature and of being outdoors usually makes its way into her stories as her characters often find themselves in beautiful natural settings. When she isn't writing, Gerri and her longtime partner, Diane, keep busy at their log cabin in East Texas tending to their two vegetable gardens, orchard and five acres of piney woods. They share their lives with two Australian Shepherds and an assortment of furry felines.

CHAPTER ONE

"Mother, *please*."

"You've been avoiding me for weeks now, Paige Riley. I won't be put off any longer."

Paige sidestepped two men in business suits hurrying down the sidewalk like she was doing. She was late. And she was never late.

"Mother, what do you want me to say?"

"I want to know who that woman was in your apartment and why she was half-naked."

Paige stopped suddenly, pushing her sunglasses on top of her head. "First of all, she was not half-naked. She was all the way naked. And secondly…it's none of your business."

She ended the call quickly as she stared up into the cloudless sky.

Did I just out myself to my mother?

* * *

CJ Johnston had never been one to wear her feelings on her sleeve. But since she and Paige had returned from Hoganville— since they'd become lovers—she felt like Ice and Billy could see right through the aloof façade she tried to keep in place. While technically she was partners with Ice, not Paige, they were still all on the same team. If they went public with their affair…well, they didn't want to take a chance that Howley—or someone higher up—would break up the team. After Hoganville, after the dust settled, their team staying intact was questionable in itself. Whenever the FBI and mass suicide is mentioned in the same sentence, people, especially politicians, quickly distance themselves and begin pointing fingers.

While she and Paige got what amounted to a slap on the wrist, Howley got demoted. He was still their squad supervisor, but someone had to answer for the forty-four people who died in a synchronized suicide, not to mention the murder of fellow agent Avery, who was posing as the school's director, and Ella, the teacher at the school. It would still take months before DNA results were back on all the human remains found in the cave, but the fact that the senator's daughter—what was left of her—had been identified eased some of the apprehension from the end result. As she told Howley, if she had to do it over again, she wouldn't change a thing. Fiona had set things in motion. There was no other option. Even if CJ had known the rhyme Fiona taught her was a trigger phrase for a mass suicide, she'd still use it. After all, Belden, Ester Hogan's bodyguard, had had his meaty hands around her neck. She had no doubt he would have snapped her in two without a second thought.

She wasn't sure if anyone really believed their story of the "monster" or not, but she and Paige and Ice had all put the creature in their reports. For all the media coverage the raid on Hoganville garnered, though, there was never once a mention of any creature roaming the woods at night. And in the weeks since then, even with the excavation of the cave, there had been no sighting of it. Evidence that something had shredded and ripped bodies apart was there, obviously, but she had no clue as to how the medical examiners would explain it. And at this point, she didn't care. She knew what she saw, knew from what Don and Fiona had confided to them that the creature had always been there, and she knew without a doubt that she would *never* go back.

So after all of that, after Hoganville and after the run-in with Paige's mother—and Seth, Paige's supposed fiancé—she and Paige had agreed it was best to keep their relationship a secret. Which

CJ was finding harder to pull off than she'd thought. She could see the questions in Ice's eyes sometimes, but she ignored them. She and Paige had perfected the art of flirting long before this. Their nights out for beer with the guys were just as they used to be—only now, their flirting was real. Billy didn't have a clue, she was certain, but Ice was watching them. He seemed to be more captivated with their flirting than curious. Or so she hoped. If he came right out and asked her, she was fairly certain she wouldn't lie to him. He was her partner, after all.

She took another inconspicuous glance at the elevator doors, then checked the clock. Paige was never late. And while they didn't see each other every night, last night was not one of them. She'd left Paige's bed before dawn, getting home in time for a quick run before showering and heading to the office. And in the last two months, she had never once beaten Paige to work.

Howley came out of his office, a thick folder in his hand. She, Ice and Billy all started shuffling papers and tapping on their keyboards.

"Quit pretending to be working. You've all already submitted your last report. I know you have nothing." His gaze went to the three of them before landing on the empty chair. "Where is Paige?" He then turned slowly to CJ, eyebrows raised. Since Hoganville, he'd treated them differently. Almost as if he *knew* they'd taken their undercover assignment to pose as girlfriends and made it real. And they, in turn, went out of their way to argue and tease as much as they always had. She matched his stare now, her own eyebrows arching.

"Well?"

CJ shrugged. "I don't know." She glanced at Billy. "Where's your partner?"

"I haven't heard from her," he said.

"It's unusual for her to be late. Someone call her. We've got a case," Howley said, holding up his folder.

They all looked at CJ expectantly, and she furrowed her brow in a frown. "You want *me* to call her?" CJ pointed at Billy. "You're her partner. You call her."

"I don't care who calls her. Find out where the hell she is."

Billy had just picked up his cell when the elevator doors opened. Paige hurried in, looking flustered. "I'm so sorry I'm late," she said, smiling apologetically at Howley. She slid her gaze to CJ, and CJ gave a quick, subtle raise of her eyebrows. Paige held up her phone. "My mother thought it would be a good morning for a chat," she explained.

CJ smirked. "Well, you're never late, Agent Riley. We thought maybe you had a hot date last night. Maybe they stayed late this morning?"

Paige leaned over her desk, a flirty smile on her lips. "Why does everything revolve around sex with you?"

CJ leaned her elbows on her desk. "Maybe I'm in a bit of a dry spell and I'm living through you."

Paige rolled her eyes. "Dry spell? You run out of bars to hit up, tiger?"

When CJ would have replied, Howley held his hand up. "We don't have time for your bickering this morning, ladies. We got a case. Conference room. Now."

CHAPTER TWO

"Got a young boy, Hispanic, estimated to be about five or six years old. He was found, possibly strangled, on the grounds of an old abandoned house," Howley said, sliding stapled papers to each of them. "Five days ago. Still unidentified. No one has reported him missing."

"Undocumented?" Paige asked.

"That's the assumption."

Ice flipped through the pages, wondering why the FBI would be involved with a case like this. "Why does this fall to us?" he asked, giving voice to his question.

"Because it's eerily similar to a case from fourteen years ago. Cold case," Howley clarified. He picked up the remote and pointed it at the monitor on the wall. An enlarged map of the Houston area appeared. He zoomed out to the northeast. "There's a little community here just southeast of Cleveland—Pecan Grove," he said, pointing with the laser. "Off of Morgan Cemetery Road, we have a mobile home park. Shady Pines. All four victims lived there."

Howley slid his gaze quickly to CJ, then away. Ice, too, glanced at her. She grew up in just such a community, although much closer to the city. It was something she never discussed. He knew about her old man, knew he used to beat her. But CJ never talked about it.

"Fourteen years ago, over a span of two months, four young boys from this community went missing. Two age seven, one age eight and one age nine," Howley said. "Mark Poole was the first boy to disappear. He was seven. Paul Canton disappeared eight days later. He was age seven also. Butch Renkie went missing two weeks later. He was age nine. And the last boy, Bradley Simon, age eight, went missing three weeks after that. Only one body was ever found. Paul Canton, the second to disappear." He punched the remote and a photo of an old three-story house popped up.

"Jesus, that's like something out of a horror movie," CJ said.

"The house has been vacant forty-some years. It's old," Howley said, glancing at his notes. "Built in 1915. Anyway, the house is only significant in that both bodies were found on the grounds." He brought up another photo, this one obviously dated. "This was Paul Canton at age six. His body was found four weeks after he disappeared, one day after Butch Renkie went missing. The house has a chain-link fence around it, the windows are all boarded up on the first floor, it's locked up tight. There are a few breaks in the fence where someone could get in," he said. "Paul Canton was strangled. Body left on the grounds. The house was searched. Nothing. No leads. No witnesses to any of the abductions. And no subsequent boys went missing after Bradley Simon disappeared. Cold case."

"And now another body is dumped," Paige said.

"You think same killer?" Billy asked. "Fourteen years apart?"

"Or a copycat?" CJ offered.

"All of the forensic evidence is not back yet, but the ME's initial report says strangulation. The condition of the body is not identical, however. Our unidentified body has bruising and contusions on his pelvis and legs. ME hasn't posted cause of death yet."

"So you want us to poke around?"

"The locals are still working this new case, but they don't have jack," Howley said bluntly. "So yeah, you go poke around. The old case file, it's scanned. The file has been emailed to you. Read it. Get familiar with it. You've got two days."

"Two days?" CJ asked.

"Two days to see if the cases are linked. Two days to determine if we can work it or not." He shrugged. "If you find nothing, it stays a cold case. It's been fourteen years. I don't expect much, but you never know."

Ice tossed his papers down. "Two days isn't long," he said.

"It's long enough for me to foot your hotel bill." He flashed a quick smile. "Of course, it's Cleveland. Maybe we'll find a cheap motel for you to stay in."

"I've been through Cleveland before," Billy said. "It's a small town, sure, but it's not like it's just a dot on the map."

Howley slid them all another paper. "Those are your contacts. It's outside the city limits so the sheriff's department is working it right now. They know you're coming. Chuck Brady is who you need to contact."

"So there's not going to be a power play?"

"I think they'd hand it over to us in a second," he said. "Take the rest of the afternoon. Tie up whatever you need to. You leave in the morning."

They all pushed their chairs away from the table at once, Ice already making a mental list of what he had to do. They were following Howley out of the conference room when Howley stopped and turned back to them with a bit of a smirk on his face.

"By the way, with budgets as tight as they are, we've only booked two rooms. Buddy system."

"Oh, come on," Ice said. "Really?"

"Really."

"Me and Ice?" Billy shook his head. "I've stayed with him before. He snores like a freight train."

Ice looked at the others, expecting more protests. He was shocked by the look that passed between CJ and Paige. The last few weeks—hell, a month or more—they'd been acting weird. Sometimes when he watched them, he'd swear there was an intimacy in their glances, but other times they were the same old bickering fools they'd always been. The look they shared now disappeared so quickly, he wasn't sure he'd actually seen it.

"Seriously? It hasn't been that long since Hoganville," CJ said. "I'm not sure I've recovered from that yet. She's a neat freak," CJ said, pointing at Paige. "She's got all these rules."

"Like you're a piece of cake to live with," Paige countered. "You're a slob."

"A slob?"

"Did you or did you not leave your clothes on the floor by the bed?"

Ice watched as CJ opened her mouth to reply, then shut it just as quickly. He was again riveted by the look they shared. There was a familiarity in that look—a look he'd sworn he'd seen before with them—but maybe it was just the result of them having been through what they had in Hoganville. Dealing with everything they had, it had to have brought them closer together. But still…

Howley held up his hand. "Save your complaints. It's just one night. Come back with what you've got. We'll go from there." He paused again. "There's just one more thing. The old house where the body was found—the locals claim it's haunted. You might want to keep that in mind."

As soon as he was gone, CJ turned to them. "Is it just me or does it seem like we're getting all the shit cases lately?"

"I don't do haunted," Ice said as he shook his head. "No way I'm getting near that house."

"You think he's taking his demotion out on us?" Billy asked.

CJ rolled her eyes. "You think?"

CHAPTER THREE

Paige felt a wave of déjà vu as she folded clothes and placed them neatly into her large travel bag. It wasn't too many months ago that she had been doing this very thing, about to head off into the woods of East Texas with CJ and dreading the very prospect of it. But now? So much had changed between them that she was nearly giddy with anticipation. Not that they didn't spend most nights together anyway. Maybe it was the thrill of it. Maybe it was the fact that Ice and Billy would be there. Or maybe it was just the fact that they would be working a case together again. Since they'd been back from Hoganville, they'd worked cases together as a team, but she spent most of her time with Billy. She and CJ had taken it almost to the extreme of avoiding each other for fear the others would find out...find out that they were lovers.

She paused, closing her eyes for a second, still surprised that she and CJ had fallen into such a comfortable relationship. At first, she was afraid it was based too much on sex and that they would end up drifting apart when they ran out of things to talk about. So far, that wasn't the case at all. The sex between them was fabulous, yes, but their attachment went so much deeper than that. At least for her. But that was one thing they had yet to talk about.

She went back to her packing, wondering why they shied away from it. Both of them. While they'd talked about everything under the sun, from her privileged upbringing to CJ's horrific childhood, they never once broached the subject of where their relationship was headed or what either of them expected—wanted—from it. Perhaps they were afraid, afraid of what the other would say. Paige often wondered if what she was feeling was too much too soon. And she knew CJ's fear—that she wasn't good enough.

But still, she was afraid to go there. Was it lust? Certainly. But could she truly, honestly say that she'd fallen in love with CJ?

She took a quick breath, those words causing a tumultuous feeling in her stomach. She stared off into space, seeing CJ's face, these days almost always with a smile plastered on it. Had she fallen in love with her?

"Yes."

She laughed quietly, the sound loud in her empty apartment. What if she told CJ that? Would she freak out? Would she run? Or would she be relieved? Sometimes when they made love, it was all there in CJ's eyes. She didn't attempt to hide it. Paige sometimes thought she was reading too much into it. CJ had her past, her many, many one-night stands. Sometimes Paige was afraid of that, afraid CJ would drift back to that life. So she would look into CJ's eyes, looking for a sign that told her CJ loved her, cared about her. But when she found it, it frightened her. What if it really was too much too soon? And more importantly, what if it didn't last?

Well, now wasn't the time to contemplate it. The guys wanted to meet for beers before they were whisked out to the "boonies," as Ice called it. She knew CJ would have rather spent the evening alone—as would she—but they'd already missed last week's night out.

* * *

"Paige is coming, right?" Billy asked for a second time.

CJ flicked her eyes to the door then to her watch. "It's only ten after," she said.

Ice tipped his beer back, downing it. He loved this bar. Loved that practically everyone knew everybody, loved that the bartenders knew what beers they wanted and had them opened and on their way before they'd even sat down. He loved the atmosphere—cops talking about cases, who they busted and how, who saw what. He loved it all. Maybe because he was single and didn't have anyone to go home to, but he looked forward to their night out each and every week.

"Do you really snore like a freight train?" CJ asked.

Ice glared at Billy. "I do not."

"Do too, man. Which reminds me, I need to pick up some earplugs."

Ice tossed his coaster at Billy, hitting him square in the forehead. Billy scowled back at him, rubbing his forehead with two fingers.

"Is this how you two are going to be for the next two days?"

"Yeah, what's with that deadline anyway?" Billy asked.

Ice picked at the label on his empty beer bottle. "Cold case. They either match or they don't."

"Howley doesn't want us picking up this new case unless it's related," CJ added.

Ice slid his bottle to the middle of the table, the first dead soldier of the evening. He was about to order another round when Billy broke out in a grin.

"There's my beautiful partner now."

They all turned as the lovely Paige Riley headed their way. Ice didn't miss the quick look she gave CJ and again his curiosity was piqued. These next few days should prove to be interesting.

"Sorry I'm late," she said. "I couldn't decide what to pack."

"It's just two days," CJ said as Paige sat across from her.

"Yes, but shoving jeans and black FBI T-shirts into a duffel bag isn't really my style."

"And what makes you think that's what I did?"

The corners of Paige's mouth lifted in a smile. "Isn't it?"

"Well, they weren't all black T-shirts."

"Another round?" Ice asked, already raising his hand toward the bar.

CJ slid her empty bottle to the middle, joining his. "Did anyone have a chance to read the old file yet?"

"I just glanced through it, that's all," Billy said.

"Me too," Paige said. "They interviewed people from the neighborhood, kids and teachers from the elementary school, that's about it. No one saw anything, there were no strangers hanging around, nothing suspicious," she said.

CJ nodded. "I skimmed through it pretty good," she said. "Since I didn't have much packing to do," she added with a grin. "The only thing of interest found was a smudge on his belt. It was chalk. White chalk. Also found some under his fingernails."

"Like you'd find in a classroom?"

"Yeah. Only the kid never made it to school that day."

"So it could have been from another day," Ice said.

"Not according to his mother. That was a belt he only wore to church. They were taking class pictures that day so his mother dressed him up. Anyway, he was found two weeks after he disappeared. The chalk under his nails was fresh."

Billy raised his eyebrows. "That's it? That's all the evidence they found?"

CJ nodded. "That's it."

The waitress stopped by with four bottles of beer. Ice was about to hand her a twenty when Paige beat him to it. He nodded his thanks at her.

"So the killer is someone who handled chalk or could have had the boy handle it," Paige said. "I did read where all the teachers were questioned."

"Yeah. No abnormalities in their routine, no one ever missing or had time unaccounted for. All squeaky clean," CJ said as she took a swallow from her beer.

"Do we know anyone who worked the original case?" Ice asked.

CJ shook her head. "The file listed three agents as leads. The only one still in the Houston area is Ronnie Duran, but I don't know him. Any of you heard of him?"

"No, but it wouldn't hurt to pay him a visit," Paige suggested.

"*If* we find out the cases are linked and we work it," Ice reminded them. "But cold cases are a bitch."

"It'll be nice to get out of the city, though," Billy said. "You guys spent all that time out in the woods during the summer. Me and Ice were still stuck here."

"Oh, yeah, we just had a blast," CJ said sarcastically. "I highly recommend spending time in Hoganville. As an added treat, maybe you'll get to be chased through the woods by a crazed unknown and unnamed monster."

Ice laughed with the others, but he remembered all too well running for his life as said monster chased them back to Hoganville. Which of course reminded him of something else he was scared of.

"Do you really think that house is haunted? Or was Howley just giving us shit?"

CJ shook her head. "The agents investigating the case never saw anything out of the ordinary, but they only checked it one time. It was locked up. No evidence of a breach anywhere. No evidence of activity inside."

"So where did Howley get that?"

"Some of the people they interviewed mentioned that it was haunted." CJ grinned. "Apparently there were some murders with an ax."

Ice's eyes widened. "Back in the day?"

"Hell, I don't know," CJ said. "That's just what one of the locals said when they interviewed her."

"Let's remember," Paige said, "it's not the house we're investigating. As Howley said, the only significance of the house is that the bodies were dumped on the grounds."

"Let me just say that me and haunted houses don't mix," Ice said, unconsciously rubbing his shaved head.

"What are you afraid of, baldy?" CJ asked. "It's just a house. Surely you don't believe in ghosts."

"Whether I believe in ghosts or not doesn't matter. I have a thing with haunted houses," he said. He downed the rest of his beer in one large gulp. "I had a bad experience as a kid."

"Halloween?" Paige guessed.

"Yeah. A group of us were going through one of those haunted houses they set up at Halloween every year. We got locked in a room with a guy and a chain saw," he said with a shaky laugh. "The door jammed. The guy playing the murderer had us all peeing in our pants before they got the door opened again."

Billy laughed. "Really?"

"Yeah, really. And the dude thought it was funny as hell too. It took months before I was able to sleep with the lights off," he admitted.

"How old were you?" Paige asked.

"Ten."

"I guess that ruined Halloween for you."

"To say the least."

As they normally did, empty beer bottles got shoved to the center of the table. CJ raised her arm for another round.

"Anybody want nachos? I'm starving," she said.

"If you get beans only and leave off the cheese, I'll split an order with you," Paige offered.

"Are you still on that vegetarian kick?" Billy asked.

"It's not a kick and it's vegan," Paige said. "I've never felt better."

"I'll just stick with a burger."

"I'm going to have wings," Ice said.

"Thanks, guys," CJ said dryly. "Leave me with the vegan nachos then." She turned to April, their waiter. "Another round please. And I'll have black bean nachos. Cut the cheese."

"No cheese? What's wrong with you?" April asked as she scribbled her order.

"Paige is what's wrong with me," CJ said as she pointed across the table.

Ice and Billy placed their orders too and waited only a minute before she returned with another round of beer.

"We're taking two cars, right?" Billy asked.

"Yes," Paige said. "I'll drive." She looked at the others. "Who else?"

"I guess I can take my truck," Billy offered.

"Yeah, you and Ice take your truck. I'll ride in the Mercedes," CJ said.

"A black man should not be seen riding in a redneck truck," Ice said. "It's just wrong."

"Oh, hell, Ice, I bet my redneck truck will fit in a lot better in Pecan Grove than Paige's Mercedes will."

"I didn't think of that," Paige said, almost apologetically. She turned to CJ. "Maybe we should take yours."

CHAPTER FOUR

CJ stood at the bottom of the stairs, looking up toward Paige's apartment. An involuntary smile lit her face, something that had been occurring more and more frequently. She'd changed so much since Hoganville; they both had. She knew the guys—especially Ice—had noticed. She no longer had to drag her ass in to work, smelling of tequila and wearing yesterday's clothes. There had been no trips to the bar, looking for a quick hookup. So yeah, surely they noticed. But neither had said a word about it.

She and Paige spent nearly every night together, mostly here, at Paige's. It was much nicer than her place and closer to work. In fact, the only time she went to her own apartment was to do laundry, pick up her mail and get fresh clothes. Of course, on those nights, she took the opportunity to grab a greasy burger or a pizza to take home with her, two things Paige had eliminated from her diet. She didn't really miss them—Paige was an excellent cook—but it was just habit.

She jogged up the stairs two at a time, pausing to catch her breath before knocking on the door. She heard Paige inside and again a smile formed as she waited.

When the door opened, she found herself pulled inside and pinned against the door, Paige's hands tugging her shirt from her jeans.

"What took you so long?" Paige murmured against her lips.

"Stopped to get gas," she said, her hands sneaking inside Paige's robe, finding her completely naked. She groaned in anticipation as their kisses turned fiery hot. They pulled apart long enough for Paige to slip CJ's shirt and bra off, then Paige's mouth was there again, letting CJ know who was in control.

Paige had CJ's hands clasped to her sides as she ducked her head, her hot mouth closing over one of her nipples, her tongue teasing it as CJ leaned her head back against the door, her breathing coming in quick bursts. She knew not to protest. Paige would take her sweet time, making her squirm, making her want to *beg* her to finish. And sometimes she couldn't wait that long, sometimes she would pull Paige's thigh between her legs, the contact making her come instantly.

Paige's mouth moved back to her lips, kissing her slowly now, drawing it out. She pulled away from her, and CJ rested against the door, her chest rising and falling as she drew deep breaths. Paige slowly untied her robe, letting it hang open. CJ's eyes took in her nakedness, the robe covering just enough of her breasts to leave her wanting more. She brought her gaze back to Paige's face, meeting her eyes, seeing desire and, God, so much more. Sometimes that frightened her—the look in Paige's eyes. And sometimes it made her heart melt, like it was doing now.

She reached for Paige, pulling her close again, the robe opening, their breasts touching as their mouths found each other once more. CJ's tongue drew Paige's inside. She moaned as Paige's hands seemed to be everywhere at once. They both paused in mid-kiss when Paige's phone rang out.

"God, I swear if that's my mother, I'm going to kill her," Paige said as she finished the kiss.

"You know most people just set ringtones, don't you?" CJ countered as she pulled Paige closer, only to feel Paige move away. She opened her eyes fully. "You're going to *answer* it? *Now*?"

Paige pointed at her. "Don't move."

CJ leaned her head back against the door, still breathing hard. "She's trying to kill me," she murmured. She glanced down her naked torso, finding her jeans unbuttoned and the zipper halfway down. *When did she do that?* She wasn't listening to Paige's conversation although by her demeanor, she knew it wasn't her mother.

Paige turned to her and mouthed "Howley."

CJ banged her head slowly against the door. "This can't be good," she whispered. She glanced back at Paige, now listening to her one-sided conversation. Paige was nodding, and then she heard the words she dreaded.

"Okay, I'll be right there." Paige tossed her phone down, walking slowly back toward her, her robe still open.

"You've got to be kidding me."

"Sorry, tiger."

CJ groaned. "His timing sucks."

Paige grinned. "Got you in a little heated state, do I?"

"You think?"

Paige moved closer, nearly touching her again. "Well, we can't just leave you like this, can we?"

CJ nearly trembled. "No," she whispered. "Not unless you want me to finish it myself."

Paige's mouth was on hers again. "Not unless I can watch."

Before CJ could take another breath, Paige's hand slid inside her jeans and panties, her fingers finding her clit in one stroke.

"So wet," Paige murmured dreamily. "I love that I can do this to you."

CJ couldn't speak as she spread her legs helplessly, letting Paige pin her to the door as her fingers moved with lightning quickness, knowing exactly how to touch her. CJ was moaning into Paige's mouth as their tongues battled. She tried to prolong it—God, she wanted it to last forever—but when Paige pulled her mouth away, going to her breasts instead, CJ's orgasm hit the instant Paige sucked her nipple into her mouth.

She clamped her thighs together, holding Paige's fingers hard against her as she tried to catch her breath. Paige finally moved, her lips brushing against CJ's neck, her cheek, finally her mouth, kissing her softly, gently.

"Get some sleep," Paige whispered. "I don't know when I'll be back."

CJ opened her eyes, watching as Paige headed to the bedroom. "What's up, anyway?"

"Howley wants me and Billy to visit with Ronnie Duran. He's the one who worked the cold case," Paige said as she ducked into the bathroom.

CJ took a deep breath, still reeling from Paige's lovemaking. She reached down and zipped her jeans up again, walking on shaky legs toward the bedroom.

"Why now?" she asked.

"He's flying to El Paso in the morning," Paige explained as she pulled on jeans. "Howley wants us to pick his brain before we head to Pecan Grove."

CJ plopped down on the bed, her energy level drained. She rolled her head to the side, watching as Paige slipped a blouse on. "You're so beautiful," she said without thinking.

Paige paused, a slight smile on her face. "Tired?"

"Uh-huh."

"Why don't you get undressed and go to bed?"

"If I do, will you wake me when you come home?"

Paige nodded. "Get some rest."

CJ watched her go, feeling her eyelids getting heavy. When she heard the door close, she made herself get up. She should shower, she knew, but she simply didn't have the energy. She stripped out of her jeans and crawled under the covers.

CHAPTER FIVE

Paige woke to the smell of delicious coffee. She opened her eyes to find CJ standing beside the bed, a cup of the steaming liquid in her hands. She pushed up on her elbows, taking in CJ's appearance. She was already showered and dressed.

"What time is it?"

"Six."

"What time are we meeting the guys?"

"Seven."

Paige groaned and lay back down. "Why again so early?"

"Traffic." CJ put the coffee on the bedside table. "Come on. I made your favorite."

"Guatemala Antigua?"

"Yes."

Paige sat up again. "I didn't get back until midnight."

"You were supposed to wake me," CJ reminded her.

"You were sleeping like a baby," she said with a smile. "I couldn't bring myself to wake you."

CJ nodded, then pointed at the coffee. "Up," she said. "I'll take your bags down while you shower."

Paige pointed across the room. "Those."

CJ's eyebrows shot up. "Three? Really?"

"What?"

"We're there two days. One night."

Paige got out of bed, smiling as CJ's glance took in her nakedness. "I like to be prepared for any occasion," she said. She held her hand up when CJ took a step toward her. "We don't have time. Don't even think about it," she said as she grabbed her coffee and hurried into the bathroom.

"Tease," CJ called after her.

Forty minutes later, they were racing toward the office, the morning's rush hour traffic already getting thick. Ice and Billy were waiting for them in the parking lot and waved them over. There was only a slight moment of awkwardness when Ice stood between Billy's truck and CJ's. He stared at Paige with raised eyebrows, but she made no attempt to move.

"I guess I'll ride with Billy then," he said.

Paige nodded. "Get him to fill you in on our visit with Duran last night," she said.

"You guys worked last night?"

"Yes, while you and CJ were no doubt sleeping like little babies," she said.

"I'll follow you," Billy said out the open window.

CJ nodded but left her window down as she pulled away. "It feels kinda fallish this morning," she said.

"It does feel nice," Paige agreed. "I love October. It feels different. The air is not as humid, the sky is bluer. Leaves are starting to turn."

CJ pushed her window up when she pulled back into traffic. She glanced in the mirror, no doubt looking for Billy's truck.

"So what did you learn from Duran?" CJ asked.

"Not much," Paige said. "He had to read over the file just to jog his memory. He said the chalk had them convinced it was a teacher, and they thoroughly investigated every single one at the school. He said there wasn't even a hint of a suspect among them."

"There are other schools in the area. Not just the elementary," CJ said.

"Yes. He said they ran checks on them too."

"What about the house?"

"Just like the notes said. It was locked up. No evidence of a breach. He said they took a walk through the whole thing. Nothing was disturbed. No sign of activity."

"So pretty much, you just had a wasted night," CJ said.

"Yes. I would have much rather been in bed with you."

"Would you now?"

Paige reached over and touched CJ's hair, brushing it away from her eyes. "Have I told you how sexy you look?"

"Oh yeah?"

"You look good in black. The holster just adds to it."

"You do know the guys are behind us, right?"

Paige withdrew her hand quickly. "Sorry. I forgot."

CJ blew out a breath. "This is going to be hard. They're going to find out."

"We'll be fine," she said. "We've made it this far."

"Yeah, but we're going to practically be around them twenty-four-seven. And you can't keep your hands to yourself," CJ said with a grin.

Paige reached over and touched CJ's thigh, running her fingers up and down her leg. "You weren't complaining last night," Paige reminded her.

"No, I wasn't. I happen to love your naughty side."

Paige laughed. "Naughty?"

"Yes. You're so…perfect. Refined. A girly-girl," CJ said, covering Paige's hand with her own. "But you have a naughty side that I love. The guys would be shocked."

"Wait a minute. Girly-girl? I'm not a girly-girl." She held up her hands. "If I were, I would have long, painted nails. Which I don't."

CJ gave a pointed glance to her feet. "And your toenails?"

"Well, I'm not totally uncivilized," she said. "I don't think a twice-a-month pedicure makes me a girly-girl. And just because I have a fondness for red nail polish still doesn't make me a girly-girl."

CJ laughed. "Whatever you say, baby."

Highway 59 morning traffic was at a near standstill heading into the city, but they had fairly clear lanes heading out. Paige figured it would take them less than an hour to reach Cleveland.

"How do you want to work this?" CJ asked.

"Small town sheriff's office, I think we should let the guys talk to them," she said.

"Might be a cute lady sheriff," CJ suggested.

"Are you volunteering your services?"

"No…just saying."

"Well, I think we should interview some of the residents of Shady Pines, the neighbors of the original missing boys. Maybe take a look at the house too." Paige shrugged. "I don't feel very hopeful that we'll find anything. Do you?"

CJ shook her head. "You ever worked a cold case before?"

"No. Have you?"

CJ nodded. "Just once. I was still with Houston PD. We recovered a gun at a homicide. It matched ballistics from a convenience store robbery where the clerk was abducted. His body was found two days later, shot in the head, execution style. Those two cases were six years apart."

"And how did it turn out?"

"Gangbangers. They can disappear into the bowels of the city and never be seen again. Never solved either case."

"So you're not optimistic about this one either then?"

"Oh, we might stumble upon something. But fourteen years is a long time."

Paige relaxed back against the seat and they fell into a comfortable silence. It didn't take long for them to be out of the city and into more rural surroundings. While it wasn't the deep, dark forest of Hoganville, the tall pines and oaks did remind her of their adventure earlier that year. She made a mental note to check on Don Hogan—the lone survivor from Hoganville—when they got back. She found him to be quite intelligent and engaging, although being around him did conjure up memories of that awful night in the cave with Mother Hogan and Fiona. She stared out the window, remembering the last words Fiona whispered to her before she died.

"Don't run from CJ. Trust her. She wants to love you. Let her."

She glanced slowly at CJ, questioning again if that was true. CJ turned then and caught her eyes, holding them for a second before looking back to the road. Paige reached across the console once again, letting her hand rest lightly on CJ's thigh, just wanting the contact. Without a word spoken, CJ covered her hand, her fingers linking tightly with Paige's. They both squeezed and Paige wondered just what it was they were saying to each other.

CHAPTER SIX

CJ slowed to a crawl as they drove past the elementary school. It was a few minutes before eight and parents were still dropping off their children.

"So where's this trailer park?"

"Mobile home park," Paige corrected her.

CJ rolled her eyes. "What? We're being politically correct here?"

"Shady Pines Mobile Home Park," Paige read from her notes.

"Look, you don't have to be sensitive for my benefit," she said. "I grew up in a trashy trailer park. Everybody called it a trailer park. Only outsiders called it a mobile home park."

"I just think we should be respectful of where people live. This is all some can afford."

"I know. I've been there," she said. She was also resentful of that fact, but it didn't change anything. The trailer park life was all she knew until that fateful day when her sister spilled all the family secrets about their father's sexual abuse. But she didn't want to go there. Didn't want to revisit that again. Paige now knew all her secrets too, and whenever they talked about it, Paige's eyes would fill with tears. Tears for her, tears for her childhood, but tears nonetheless. And that was one thing she never wanted to see in Paige's eyes.

"You'll turn on the next street to the left," Paige said, using her iPhone for navigation. "Oak Lane."

"I guess we need to talk this out with the guys, don't you think?" she said as she turned onto Oak Lane.

"Yes. But I think they'll jump at the chance to interview someone from the sheriff's office rather than go door-to-door here," Paige said. "Okay, there's Morgan Cemetery Road," she pointed. "Turn right."

"And where's this house?"

"It's on Morgan Cemetery Road too. About a half-mile from Shady Pines."

"Okay, now who owns the house? It's not a local, right?"

"No. Alex Underwood and Betsy Erwin. Siblings. One lives in Seattle, the other in Portland. They inherited it from their parents more than twenty years ago."

CJ nodded. "I didn't read the section on the house," she admitted. "Howley said it wasn't significant."

"No. But interesting," Paige said. "Their grandparents were the last ones to actually live in it. It's been up for sale on and off for the past forty years. The file didn't give any other specifics, but I'm sure some of the locals might know the history of it."

"Okay, so it's got a perimeter fence that was breached, right? And both bodies were found out in the open? The killer wasn't trying to hide them?"

"The first body was found in the rose garden in the back of the house. The current victim was found in the front of the house, easily seen from the road."

"So the victim fourteen years ago wasn't necessarily put there to be found. The current one was?"

"Duran said the body in the rose garden was laid out very carefully, and a rose had been cut and placed on his chest. They determined the body had been there for at least two weeks. So it was almost as if the killer was indifferent as to whether the body was found or not."

"And with this new body put close to the road, this has the feel of coincidence and not a link to the cold case."

"I agree."

CJ slowed when she saw the sign to Shady Pines. "I hate cases like this."

"I'm interested to see the haunted house, though," Paige said with a quick laugh. "Or to see Ice's reaction."

She stopped in front of a tiny wooden building, the once white paint peeling away in most places. The sign announcing they were at the office was missing the "e." CJ glanced at Paige as they got out.

"Let me do the talking."

Paige raised her eyebrows questioningly.

CJ shrugged. "These are my people."

This time Paige rolled her eyes, and CJ winked at her just before Ice and Billy joined them.

"What's the plan?" Ice asked as he tugged at the collar of his shirt.

"Well, someone's got to go to the sheriff's office and interview them. We thought maybe you guys would take that." CJ motioned to the rows of trailers behind them. "Probably going to be mostly women here, mostly older. They'd probably feel a little more comfortable talking to us than you two."

Billy frowned. "So me and Ice would partner on this one?"

"I think this assignment is more of a team effort," Paige said, "and not so much partners."

Ice said, "I'm cool with that. You two are going to check out that house while you're out here, right?"

CJ laughed. "No way, baldy. That's a group effort right there. When you get what you need from the sheriff's office, meet us back here."

"And check into our hotel this afternoon?"

"Yeah. And we'll grab lunch somewhere too."

Ice stared at her for a long moment, and she wondered what questions were floating around in his mind. He finally nodded and held up his phone. "Stay in touch."

As soon as they were back in Billy's truck, CJ turned to Paige. "Ice suspects something," she said quietly.

"You mean with us?"

"Yeah."

"Maybe so. Billy doesn't have a clue, and I don't think Ice would just come right out and ask us. Do you?"

"I hope not," she said as she held the office door open for her. She smiled at the woman sitting behind an ancient desk.

The woman, who appeared to be in her forties and at least fifty pounds overweight, tossed the fashion magazine she'd been reading to the side, a cigarette still hanging from her fingers.

"Help ya?"

CJ and Paige simultaneously held up their FBI credentials. "I'm Special Agent Johnston."

"Special Agent Riley," Paige said.

"Well, I'll be," the startled woman said. "Female agents. I thought that was only on TV."

CJ gave her a humorless smile. "Yeah, they finally let us in." She squared her shoulders just a bit. "How long have you worked here?"

"Oh, my family owns the place. I've been office manager since I got out of high school," she said.

"So you were here back when those four boys went missing?"

"Oh, yeah," she said, shaking her head. "That was back in 2000. Horrible time. My boy was eleven when all that happened."

"Any of those four families still living here?"

"No. But little Markie Poole's grandfather still lives here." She narrowed her eyes a bit. "Why are you asking?"

"I'm sure you heard about the boy who was found last week," Paige said.

The woman leaned back, the old chair creaking with her weight. "At the old Wicker house," she said quietly. "Kids around here grow up calling it the Wicked house." She lowered her voice even more. "Some have seen ghosts out there."

"Really?"

The woman nodded, her face solemn. "Screaming and crying too."

"You ever heard or seen anything?"

The woman shook her head quickly. "I don't go near the place. Not since high school. We would go there on a dare. Kids still do."

"Inside the house?" Paige asked.

"Oh, no. It's locked up. Windows are boarded up on the first floor. Even if it wasn't, I wouldn't go in the place," she said.

"So…what? The kids just go *to* the house?" CJ asked.

"Inside the fence," she said. "To win the dare, you had to go up on the front porch." She waved her hands dismissively. "The older kids go there now to drink beer and hang out."

"I see." CJ glanced at Paige. "We're really not here for the house, though. Besides Markie Poole's grandfather, are there others still around from 2000?"

"Quite a few. There's not a lot of turnover here." She smiled quickly. "Just when people die."

"Okay," Paige said brightly, plastering a smile on her face. "Then do you mind if we walk around? We wanted to interview some of the ones who were around back then."

"Start with Lizzie Willis. She's in Lot Twenty-eight. Not much goes on that she doesn't know about." She lowered her voice again. "A bit of a busybody, if you know what I mean. She'll talk your ear off."

"Great. We'll start there then," CJ said. "I'm sorry, what was your name?"

"Brenda Cooper. My daddy owns the place now. It was my grandfather's, but he passed on. Six years ago. Of course, my daddy had been running it for years anyway," she continued.

Paige smiled politely. "We appreciate your cooperation, Brenda. We won't be long." Paige handed her a business card and CJ did the same. "If you need to be in touch with either of us…for any reason."

"Oh, I will." Brenda folded her hand around the cards. "Does this mean the FBI is investigating the disappearances again? Do you have some new evidence?"

"No new evidence, no," CJ said quickly. "But we really can't discuss it with you. I hope you understand."

"Oh, sure. I watch TV. I know how it is."

CJ nodded. "We'll let you get back to work then. Thanks for your time."

She turned to go, feeling Paige right behind her. Once back out in the sunshine, she took an exaggerated breath.

"I know," Paige said. "We both probably smell like cigarettes now."

"But she was chatty," CJ said.

"How about we drive to Lot Twenty-eight instead of walking?" Paige asked as a dog—chained to a tree—started barking at them.

"Gets my vote," she said as they got in her truck.

CJ drove slowly down the narrow lane as mobile homes of varying sizes and shapes lined both sides. Some were spaced very close together, others had small yards. Most were unkempt and shabby—showing their age. Clutter surrounded nearly every one.

"God, this brings back memories," she said quietly.

"Is this similar to where you grew up?" Paige asked gently.

CJ nodded. "Yeah, a lot of trailer parks look like this. Back then, ours wasn't quite this run-down."

Paige reached across the console and squeezed her thigh affectionately.

"I'm okay," CJ said.

"Yes. I know you are."

CJ met her eyes quickly, smiling slightly. Paige never judged her—for that she was thankful. She never had to explain anything. Paige simply accepted her past as it was.

"Here it is," Paige said, pointing to an old but tidy trailer. Absent was junk around the outside and there was even a patch of green grass and two flowerpots filled with red flowers.

"What's her name again? Lizzie?"

"Lizzie Willis." Paige got out and looked at her across the hood of the truck. "You want me to take this one?"

"Sure."

CJ watched with amusement as Paige walked up the rickety wooden steps and stared at the door, obviously trying to decide where to knock. A screen—torn in several places—shielded the thin aluminum door.

"Knock on the frame of the screen door," she finally said.

Paige knocked three times in quick succession. "Mrs. Willis?" she called.

They could both hear the sounds of footsteps inside.

"What is it? What is it?"

A small woman with snow-white hair and slightly humped shoulders opened the door to them. CJ couldn't guess her age despite her hair. Her face was nearly void of wrinkles.

"Mrs. Willis, we're with the FBI," Paige said as she held out her credentials. "I'm Special Agent Riley. This is Special Agent Johnston."

Lizzie Willis's face broke out into a grin, revealing clean, white dentures. "Well, I'll be. This brings back memories. Of course back then, the ones who came around were men." She looked pointedly at CJ. "They wore suits and ties."

CJ looked down at her running shoes, jeans and FBI T-shirt. She supposed she could have brought a suit jacket, but hell, it was still too warm for that. Paige, of course, was dressed as Paige always was. Professional yet practical. She looked back to the woman and smiled.

"If I have to chase down a bad guy, I bet I could run faster than your guys with suits and ties."

Lizzie Willis pursed her lips. "You young people, so casual these days."

"Mrs. Willis, we just have a few questions, if you don't mind," Paige said.

"Call me Lizzie. I've been a widow over forty years." She stepped back and held the door open. "Come inside. I have the fans on."

CJ hid her smile as Paige bravely crossed the threshold. CJ imagined this was her first time to be inside a trailer. Everything was tidy and neat. While warm, it wasn't unbearably hot inside. Lizzie had no less than three fans blowing air around. She imagined in the heart of summer, it would be sweltering inside.

"Sit," she said, pointing at the sofa. It was torn and the floral pattern faded but a sheet had been placed across the seat cushion. It appeared clean, and she and Paige exchanged glances before they sat.

"I'm sure you heard about the young boy they found down the street," Paige started.

"Oh, yes. At the Wicker house. A little Mexican boy, they say."

"He appears to be Hispanic, yes, but he has yet to be identified," Paige said.

"Why do you call it the Wicker house?" CJ asked. "That's also what Brenda called it."

"Well, that's its name," Lizzie said simply.

"Spencer was the original builder and owner. The last owners are Underwood," Paige said. "They've owned it for fifty-six years."

Lizzie waved away her explanation. "The Underwoods only lived there for a short time. It's been vacant since. The Wickers owned it before that." She folded her hands together, her thin fingers showing arthritic swelling at each knuckle. "Mr. Wicker went crazy one night. They think he had lead poisoning or something. He made moonshine whiskey," she said matter-of-factly. "Must have poisoned himself."

"Okay," Paige said. "But this boy, he was found—"

"He killed three that night," Lizzie said, her eyes wide. "Chopped them up."

CJ frowned. "Mr. Wicker?"

"Yep." Her voice lowered. "With an ax. On the stairs. They said there was blood all over the walls, just dripping down."

"And this would have been when?"

"It was in 1948. The Underwoods bought it ten years later after it had been standing vacant. Now who in their right mind would buy a house like that? Probably still had blood on the walls," she said with a shake of her head.

"I hope you don't mind me asking," Paige said, "but how old are you?"

Lizzie let out a surprisingly loud laugh. "Young lady, I'll be eighty-nine this December." She tapped her forehead. "But my memory is still strong."

"You've lived in this area then for most of your life?" CJ asked.

"Not most...*all*. Of course, not here at Shady Pines. No, when Earl was alive we lived closer to town. Had us a nice house. The cancer got him, though. We never got around to having kids so I was on my own," she said. "Little by little, the money ran out." She waved her hands out to her side. "I could have moved down to where my younger sister lives, down in Conroe. But no. I moved back out to Pecan Grove. This is home. Been here twenty-eight years now. It's all I can afford, what with only my Social Security checks."

"You've been here in Shady Pines all that time?"

"Oh, yes. Right here. Bought this trailer new. My sister and her husband helped me get settled." She smiled brightly. "We have the same birthday. She comes up to see me every April. Brings a pie or a cake or something. Oh, how she can bake. Got that from our mother."

"That's great," Paige said politely. "So you were living here when the four boys went missing then."

"Oh, yes, dear. It was a horrible time for everyone. Folks were afraid to send their children off to school for fear they wouldn't come home." She shook her head. "Some people even moved away. Of course, some wanted to close the elementary school, but they never did. They bus kids over to it now."

"Did you know any of the families personally?" CJ asked.

Lizzie let out another laugh. "Of course. Back then there were forty or fifty families living here. Now, not everybody was friends with each other, but everybody knew everybody," she said.

CJ glanced at Paige, not sure what they were gaining by questioning this woman, other than a history lesson. She was trying to think of a polite way to wrap it up and move on when Paige asked a question that surprised her.

"What do *you* think happened to the four boys?"

Lizzie folded her hands together tightly. "Something most awful, I imagine," she said. "Paulie Canton was the only one they found," she said, her voice trailing off. "Terrible thing for the families."

"Why do you think he was left at the Wicker house?" Paige asked.

"The Wicker house is evil," she said. "Whoever did this was probably drawn to it." She leaned closer, her voice low. "I won't even drive past it. I take the long way into Cleveland when I have shopping to do."

"So you still drive?" CJ asked.

"Oh, yes. Now don't you worry. I'm perfectly capable."

"Do you think the house is haunted?" Paige asked, and CJ noted the serious expression on her face.

"Of course it is. Those foolish enough to go near it have seen shadows in the upper windows. Some hear screaming, others hear crying." Again her hands clutched together. "Horrible, horrible place. So many terrible things have happened there. It was before my time, but it started with Mr. Spencer. They say he killed two kids stealing eggs from his chickens. After that, the Wickers bought it. They had eleven children." She shook her head slowly. "Not a one of them lived to adulthood."

CJ raised her eyebrows.

"All died right there at the house in one way or another. Two fell from the top of the third-floor stairs. One of the little girls fell off of the second-floor railing. Another drowned after he fell in the well." She shook her head again. "They *say* fell. Pushed, more like it."

"By Mr. Wicker?" Paige asked.

"Evil man," Lizzie said with certainty.

"Did you know the children?"

"Oh, yes. Back then there was only the one school." Her glance went past them and there was a wistful look on her face. "Things were simpler back then." She was quiet for a moment, then a smile lit her face. "I was sweet on Tommy Wicker," she said. "Earl picked a fight with him one day after school."

CJ doubted that this would shed any light on the case and they were most likely just wasting time, but she let Lizzie reminisce. Any interviews they did today were more formality than anything else. Fourteen years was a long time to go looking for new evidence.

"That was the last time I saw Tommy," she said sadly. "He never came back to school."

"What happened to him?" Paige asked.

Lizzie looked at them, her eyes serious. "He was helping his father remove a pine tree that had fallen near the house." Her eyes closed for a second. "He was such a pretty boy," she said, her voice barely a whisper. "He took an ax to the head. Mr. Wicker said he was swinging at the tree and Tommy just got in the way."

"So an accident?"

"Everything was always an accident. Until that fateful night when he killed his wife and his two remaining daughters. Then they finally stopped thinking it was an accident. Of course, the whole family was gone by then. Mr. Wicker hung himself from the third-floor railing."

"Wow," CJ murmured.

"They say Mr. Spencer hung himself from that very railing right before he was to be arrested. After he killed those two kids he thought were stealing from him, you know. The house sat vacant for ten years before the Underwoods bought it. Their children were grown so it was just the two of them." She shook her head slowly. "I heard the stories Mrs. Underwood would tell. Hearing children running along the stairs. Screaming in the hallways. Feeling hands touching her." Lizzie shook herself, as if warding off those very hands. "Swore her husband never heard any of it. Nearly drove her mad. Toward the end, she refused to even go upstairs at all."

"And the house has been vacant again for years now, right?"

"Yes, ever since old man Underwood died. Hung himself from the same railing, same as old man Wicker, same as old man Spencer. They say he tied the rope to the corner post and just jumped." Her lips pursed. "That's what they say, but who really knows? Maybe he was pushed."

"By his wife?"

"Oh, no. She wouldn't go up the stairs, remember? No, she found him hanging there when she got home from the grocery store. She was so spooked, she wouldn't even go up to check on him. Turned right around and drove away." Lizzie shook her head. "After all that, she left here. I imagine she went to live with family somewhere. This would have been in the late seventies, I believe. It's been vacant ever since," she said. "They used to have someone go by to tend to the yard and such, when that big For Sale sign was out. But that stopped years and years ago."

"The little boy found last week—do you know anything about him? Or have you heard anything?" CJ asked, wanting to steer the conversation back to the present.

She shook her head. "Not from here, no. I haven't heard of anyone who knew him. Now rumor is he's from one of the families who live over at the nursery," she said.

"Nursery?" Paige asked.

"There's a big nursery—trees and plants and flowers—north of town, near the National Forest boundary. Thompson's Plants. He's got a lot of 'illegals,'" she said, making quotation marks in the air, "working for him. He's probably got ten or twelve trailers out there where they live."

"Did anyone from the sheriff's office come around here?" CJ asked.

"No. Why would they? The boy wasn't from here."

CJ nodded, again glancing at Paige. "Well, I guess we've taken up enough of your time then. We should probably get going."

"Oh, young lady, I love having visitors. People don't come around and visit like they used to. Everyone's always in a hurry these days."

"Us included, I'm afraid," Paige said and smiled as she stood up. "It was nice meeting you, Lizzie. If you hear anything, give us a call," she said, handing her a card.

Lizzie stared at the card. "Paige," she read. "Why, you're too pretty to be working for the FBI, dear. How in the world did you get dragged into this work?"

CJ stood too, wondering what line Paige would offer her and was surprised to hear the truth.

"I wanted to help people."

Lizzie took CJ's card, and CJ waited for a perusal of her as well. Lizzie's smile faltered. "You seem to fit in okay. Except for your clothes."

CJ smiled good-naturedly. "Thanks."

She watched as Lizzie pulled herself from her chair, struggling to straighten her shoulders.

"Let me walk you out," Lizzie said. "You come by and visit anytime. I miss having company."

"We may have more questions," Paige said.

"Well, you come back then." She held open the screen door for them, then followed them outside. "I see my flowers need a drink of water," she commented. "It was nice and cool this morning, but the afternoons still get hot, don't they?"

"Yes, ma'am, I'm ready for cooler weather myself," CJ said as she watched Lizzie's neighbor come outside with a bag of trash. The woman looked at them suspiciously as she shoved the bag into a trash bin, then hurried back inside without bothering to close the lid.

"Oh, don't mind Edie," Lizzie said. "Edith Krause." She held on to the wobbly railing beside the steps. "Edie hasn't been the same since she lost her little boy."

CJ glanced at her sharply. "Her son was one of the four boys?"

"Oh, no, no. He died at least a year before all that happened." She pursed her lips and shook her head slowly. "He was a small, frail thing. The bigger kids picked on him constantly. Edward Krause. They called him Eddie."

"What happened?" Paige asked.

Lizzie tilted her head. "Actually, it was one of the four who did it."

"Did what?"

"They got into a scuffle at school one day, Butch Renkie and him. Butch was a big boy for his age. Oh, we never did learn all the details, but most say Eddie was on the ground and Butch stomped on him." Lizzie glanced at her neighbor's trailer. "Little Eddie's throat was crushed." Lizzie looked at CJ. "They said he died so fast."

"And Little Eddie lived next door?" Paige asked.

"Yes. He was their only child. Edie sheltered him so much, wouldn't let him play like normal kids. She was always afraid he would get hurt or get sick." Lizzie brushed at her snow-white hair, moving it away from her face. "Edie was never the same after that."

CJ followed her gaze to the old trailer next door. Not even one screen remained on the windows, and cinder blocks had replaced the wooden steps that were shoved to the side, forgotten, the wood long rotted.

CJ had a ton of questions, but she thought it best that she and Paige discuss all this before bombarding Lizzie Willis with them.

"Well, again, thank you for your time," she said. "We're going to drive around, see if we can talk to anyone else. Maybe some of the neighbors of the four boys." She paused. "We were told Mark Poole's grandfather was still here," she said.

"Yes, he lives down the way a bit," Lizzie said, pointing down the narrow street. "Lot Thirty-five, I want to say." Again her thin lips pursed. "I don't envy where he lives," she said with a shake of her head. "Got him some dreadful neighbors." She lowered her voice to nearly a whisper. "Moved in a couple of months ago. Drug dealers, they say."

CJ's eyebrows shot up. "Drug dealers? Has he not called the sheriff's office?"

Lizzie waved her question away. "Like they would do anything. He's called them out here many times. They keep saying they don't have…" She closed her eyes, her head tilted a bit. "What's that they say on TV?"

"Probable cause?" Paige supplied.

"Yes, that's it. Why, he was telling Mrs. Baker that Deputy Brady basically told him not to bother them anymore." She shook her head disapprovingly. "Can you believe that? Drug dealers right under their noses."

"Well, we'll go see him. Mr. Poole? What's his first name?"

"Allen. Nice enough fella. Gettin' on in years, though."

CJ smiled. "Thank you, Lizzie. You've been very helpful."

The old woman nearly beamed, and she tried to straighten her humped shoulders.

"You come back anytime," she said.

CJ and Paige waved as they drove away and Lizzie watched them round the corner.

"What a delightful woman," Paige said.

"Yeah. Full of stories."

"There's nothing in the original file about Eddie Krause. I guess that didn't come into play for them."

"A little bit of a coincidence, yeah."

Paige smiled quickly. "But we don't believe in coincidence, do we?"

"No." CJ picked up her phone and called Ice. "Let's see if the boys hit on anything." It only rang once before Ice answered.

"Please say it's lunchtime."

"It's not even eleven, baldy. Did you find anything?"

"What were you expecting us to find? Just like the report said, unidentified Hispanic male, approximate age six to eight."

"Who all did you talk to?"

"We spoke with the deputies who were the first on the scene. We then talked to the team investigating the death. They got nothing."

"Howley said the medical examiner would have the final report in this week. Did you ask?"

"Yeah, they don't have it yet. They're putting a call in. Maybe we'll get something later today."

"So where are you now?"

"About to head back your way. You get anything?"

"Yeah, we got a little history lesson. Listen, before you leave there, see if they have anything on file regarding the death of Edward Krause. It would have been a year or so before the four boys disappeared."

"Who's he?"

"He was six. He was killed at school. Deemed an accident. One of the four boys was involved."

"Okay. We'll check on it."

"We're going to interview the grandfather of one of the four boys, then we'll wrap it up here. Let's just meet at the hotel instead of you coming out here, then we'll head out for lunch."

"Deal."

CJ put her phone down and glanced over at Paige. "They got nothing."

Paige nodded. "This is Lot Thirty-five," she said.

An old Ford truck sat in the driveway. CJ pulled off to the side of the road. The trailer was much like the others, years past its prime. Five tires leaned against the side of it, the weeds grown almost tall enough to cover them.

As soon as they got out of the truck, they heard ferocious barking. CJ turned quickly. Across the street, a vicious-looking dog was chained to a tree. The pit bull strained against its collar, barking loudly at them, slobber dropping from its mouth as he bared his teeth.

"I hope that chain holds," Paige said.

"You and me both, baby," CJ murmured, aware that her hand had automatically landed on her gun.

Before they could knock, the front door ripped open and a man bellowed out in a loud voice, "Shut that damn dog up!"

CJ automatically took a step back. "Mr. Poole?"

His eyes narrowed. "Could be. Who are you?"

She and Paige simultaneously held up their credentials. "FBI. I'm Special Agent Johnston, this is Special Agent Riley," she said. "May we have a word?"

"Well, I see my complaints have finally reached the top," he said. "These local yahoos around here didn't do one damn thing about it." His gaze drifted across the yard to where the dog continued to bark. "I want them out."

"Oh." CJ smiled and shook her head. "No, actually, we're not here about your neighbors," she said.

"Then why the hell are you here?"

"It's about your grandson," Paige said. "Mark Poole."

"Markie? What? You got a lead finally?"

"May we come inside?" CJ asked. "It'll be a little quieter."

"That damn dog," he muttered as he went back inside, leaving them standing there. CJ shrugged and followed him inside.

Whereas Lizzie's trailer was spotless and tidy, this one was in desperate need of a cleaning. She looked around for a place to sit, but newspapers littered the sofa. She eyed the table instead where remnants of both last evening's dinner and this morning's breakfast still sat. He seemed to read her thoughts.

"Yeah, since the wife passed, I haven't gotten into the swing of keeping the place clean," he explained.

"I'm sorry," Paige said. "Was it recent?"

He nodded. "Yep. It'll be two years next month."

CJ pulled out a chair away from the table, and Paige did the same. Mr. Poole took his well-used recliner.

"Now what's this about Markie?"

"Well, we're just following up," CJ said. "The young boy who was found last week at the Wicker Place—there were similarities to Paul Canton, the only one of the four boys who was found."

"Heard about him, of course. Little Mexican boy."

"His parents haven't come forward," Paige said.

"Illegals," he said bluntly. "Can't blame them."

"This boy was never seen around here?"

He shook his head. "I wouldn't think so. They all live over by the nursery, if it's one of them," he said. "Not a whole lot of kids here in the park anyway. Not like back in the old days. Markie and his friends would play baseball in the street. You could hear those kids laughing and screaming all over the damn place," he said with a smile which faded quickly. "After that, some of the families moved away. Mostly just us older folks now. Except for those bastards living next door," he said.

"Mr. Poole, I know you were interviewed back when Mark went missing. You indicated there was never anything suspicious, no strangers hanging around, nothing out of the ordinary," Paige said.

"That's right."

"With this boy found last week, do you think we could have the same situation as before?"

"I'll admit, when I heard the news, I thought of Markie," he said. "But that was what? Fourteen years ago now?" He shook his head. "Can't imagine someone would kidnap that little Mexican boy and bring him all the way over here to the Wicker house, just to mimic how they found Paulie Canton."

CJ ran her fingers through her hair. She'd known ahead of time they probably wouldn't glean any new information. He, like everyone else in the trailer park, had been interviewed several times fourteen years ago. She was about to suggest to Paige that they leave when a truck with loud music blaring stopped across the street. The dog started barking loudly again.

"It never stops," he said. "Got people coming and going at all hours of the night. Then this, hoodlums showing up during the day."

CJ stood and went to the window, watching as a young man got out of the passenger's side and ran up to the door of the trailer across the street. He went inside for only a few seconds. He came back out, hands shoved in his pockets as he jogged to the truck. The truck pulled away, taking its loud music with it. She turned to Mr. Poole.

"Do you know who lives there?"

"Don't know their names, no," he said. "It's an odd mix, best I can tell. It's only a two-bedroom trailer, but there's at least seven or eight people living there. Got one black man, two white men, and an oriental," he said. "Got two black women and I've seen two white women coming and going."

"What have you told the sheriff's department?" she asked.

"I told them I got drug dealers living across the street. Hell, I watch TV. I'm not stupid. They probably got a meth lab going over there too."

"And have they come out and talked to them?"

"Hell, no. Said just because I *think* there's drug sales going on didn't make it so."

CJ grinned and glanced at Paige. "Let's go talk to them."

Paige shook her head. "CJ, no. We're here only to—"

"I just witnessed what looked like a drug buy," she said. "I think it's our duty to investigate."

"Yeah," Mr. Poole said. "That's what I've been trying to tell those yahoos in the sheriff's department. Just come out and take a look. Hell, they wouldn't even do that."

"Come on," CJ said. "It'll be fun."

CHAPTER SEVEN

"So we leave you two alone for a couple of hours and you manage a drug bust." Ice shook his head. "How does that happen?"

"Just trying to add a little fun to our day," CJ said.

Paige glanced at Billy and gave him an exaggerated eye roll as they followed Ice and CJ down the hallway to their hotel rooms. He had been nice enough to carry one of her bags for her.

"I'm glad we got adjoining rooms," Billy said.

CJ looked over her shoulder. "Oh, yeah. Me too," she said dryly, and Paige hid her smile as they stopped at the guys' room.

Ice used the key card and pushed the door open. "Not bad," he said. "At least they're queen beds."

CJ walked on to the room next door, and Paige took her bag from Billy. CJ stood in the doorway, staring inside.

"What's wrong?"

CJ pointed at the beds. "Can you believe that?"

Paige let the door close behind them and quietly laughed at the expression on CJ's face. "Gonna put a cramp on things for you, tiger?"

CJ pointed again at the beds. "Our beds share a common wall with their beds." She tossed her bag on one of them. "So, yeah, we'll be behaving like choir girls."

Paige opened up her smallest bag and took out the bottle of wine she brought. CJ took it from her.

"You brought wine?"

"Of course," she said. She carefully unwrapped two wineglasses and set them on the table.

"Oh, no, you didn't," CJ said as she stared at the glasses. "*Really*? Glasses too?"

Paige handed the bag to CJ. "I brought something else," she said. She waited only a moment before CJ's eyes widened.

"Oh my God," CJ whispered. "You brought...*it*?" She quickly closed the bag. "Our bed is *right there*," she pointed. "On the wall where their bed is."

Paige walked closer, unable to wipe the smile from her face. She kissed CJ slowly. "Then we'll have to be very, very quiet."

CJ finally smiled. "God, you're evil. I love it."

"Thought you would."

Loud knocking on their door caused CJ to quickly zip the bag and hand it to Paige. "Hide that."

Paige laughed. "I doubt they're going to search our bags and look for sex toys."

Ice and Billy stood at the door, looking inside. Neither she nor CJ had made one attempt to unpack and all of their bags sat on one bed. As nonchalantly as possible, Paige took her small bag—and their toy—into the bathroom.

"Lunch?" Ice asked.

"Not fast food," Paige called from the bathroom.

"Mexican?"

Paige knew that would be their second choice. She also knew it would have been CJ's first choice. She smiled at her when she went back into the bedroom. "Mexican okay with you?"

"If I must," CJ said with a grin. "But not some chain. Let's find a local place."

After a quick check at the front desk, they were all four in CJ's truck heading to "the best" place in Cleveland. Even though the name—Judy's—did not exactly conjure up images of someone's beloved grandmother cooking up delicious authentic dishes, the parking lot was at near capacity. CJ took one of two remaining spots.

"I smell fajitas sizzling on the grill from way out here," Ice said as he rubbed his hands together.

"I want enchiladas smothered in so much cheese I can't even find them," CJ said with a grin. "Rich, creamy cheese," she added.

"They're your arteries," Paige said. "Feel free to clog them at will."

"I'm thinking fajitas sound good too," Billy said as he held the door open for them.

The inside was crowded and noisy, and they waited in line to be seated. Even though it was almost one, the lunch crowd was still thick. Waitresses hurried between tables, dropping off fresh baskets of chips and topping off glasses with tea and water. The background noise of mariachi music was not really needed as the hum of voices and laughter filled the restaurant.

Before long they were seated at a booth table and Paige slid in beside Billy. "It's a shame we're not here for dinner instead," she said, eyeing a waitress passing by with a tray. "That margarita looks good."

"We can always come back," Ice said. "But you'd probably get tired of black bean nachos," he teased.

"Oh, I don't know," she said as she looked over the menu. "They have spinach and mushroom enchiladas." She glanced at CJ and smiled. "Of course they appear to be smothered in your rich, creamy cheese."

"Yeah, but you know, we're sharing a room." CJ wiggled her eyebrows. "Maybe you should lay off the beans during this trip."

Ice and Billy nearly howled with laughter, and Paige couldn't prevent the blush that lit her face. She summoned up as much dignity as she could. "Gas is a perfectly normal bodily function," she said. "And let's please not discuss this at lunch."

CJ's smile faded and Paige guessed she was feeling chastised. So as the waitress dropped off two baskets of warm chips and four bowls of salsa, Paige gave CJ a subtle wink.

CJ shrugged and whispered "sorry," but Paige waved off her apology. "So, flatulence aside, did you guys learn anything?" she asked, bringing the discussion back to the case.

"No, not on the unidentified boy. There was nothing at the scene. ME's cause of death is pending still."

"Oh? You got it?" CJ asked.

"Finally," he said. "Not much more than what Howley already told us. There were contusions to the pelvis and lower limbs. And he had a broken neck, probably from the force of the strangulation. They're doing more tests. Said they'd have the final post in three days at the latest."

"What's inconclusive about it?" Paige asked.

"Whether blunt force trauma killed him or the broken neck," he said as he scooped up salsa on a chip. "Both of his femurs were fractured. Broken ribs. Punctured lung."

"Was he beaten?" CJ asked.

"No defensive injuries," Billy said.

"Then it sounds like he was hit by a car," CJ said before shoving a chip in her mouth.

"Yeah, could be. But why strangle him hard enough to break his neck?"

"Maybe our guy panicked," CJ said. "Maybe—"

But she paused as their waitress appeared with a bright smile. "Ready to order?"

"The lunch special. Beef fajitas," Ice said. "And tea."

"Me too," Billy said.

The waitress glanced at Paige. "Black bean nachos," she said. "With no cheese, please. And a side of guacamole. Tea also."

"Chicken enchiladas," CJ said. "With extra cheese all over it. In fact, whatever cheese you're taking off of hers, put on mine. And tea."

"Sounds good," the waitress said. "I'll have your drinks right out."

"Careful, tiger. Those killer abs that chicks love so much might take a hit after this meal," she teased.

"Baby, I'll show you those killer abs later and you can decide if they took a hit or not."

Billy and Ice laughed. "You know, ever since you got back from Hoganville, you two have really lightened up," Billy said.

"Are you saying that before, we were *uptight*?" CJ asked. She grinned as she flicked her gaze toward Paige. "Well, one of us, maybe."

"I was not uptight," Paige insisted. "You were simply obnoxious." She grabbed a chip. "*That* hasn't changed."

"That will *never* change," Ice said with a laugh. He looked at CJ. "So what's your theory?"

CJ shook her head. "No. It makes no sense. If our guy hit the kid—an accident—why panic? Why snap his neck?"

"Why dump his body?"

CJ raised her eyebrows. "Drunk driver?"

Billy nodded. "Yeah. He panics. The kid's not dead."

"So he strangles him, finishing him off?" Ice shook his head. "That's reaching. I mean, who's going to think to do that? You hit someone, the kid's still alive, even if you're drunk on your ass, you're still going to try to help."

"Maybe. Or maybe you're only concerned with your own ass," Billy countered.

"Even if our guy panicked and killed the kid, why go to the trouble of dumping his body at the Wicker house. According to everyone we've talked to, the kid didn't live around there, so he wouldn't have been hit there," CJ said.

"Two of the people we interviewed today said that the boy probably belonged to one of the families who live at the nursery," Paige said. "Thompson's Plants. Apparently he hires and houses noncitizens," she said, still not comfortable calling them "illegals" as Lizzie and Mr. Poole had.

"Noncitizens?" Ice asked skeptically. "You mean illegals?"

"Yes. I was trying to be—"

"Politically correct," CJ finished for her. She eyed Ice and Billy. "Any mention in their report that they sought out those families?"

"None," Billy said. "In fact, I kinda got the impression they didn't do a whole lot on this one."

"Me too," Ice said. "Deputy Brady was the lead on this. He was accommodating and his report was professional and by the book, but there wasn't much meat in it. Benefit of the doubt, I guess they assumed the parents of the boy would come forward."

"And when none did, they let it go cold?"

"We all know that when you have no victim's family badgering you, it's easy to let things slip through the cracks," Ice said. "No forensic evidence, no witnesses, nobody asking questions." He shrugged. "Easy cold case."

"Speaking of cold case," Paige said, "did you find anything on Edward Krause?"

"There was an accident report, nothing more," Billy said. "The boys got into a fight at school. Butch Renkie apparently fell on Edward, his knee landed on his throat, crushing it. He essentially suffocated. Called it an accident."

"Lizzie said Butch picked on Eddie all the time. Said Eddie was frail," Paige said. "She also indicated that Butch stomped on Eddie intentionally. Not fell. I don't have a description of Butch Renkie, but just his name implies he was a big kid. Lizzie said as much."

"Who's Lizzie?" Ice asked.

"Lizzie Willis. Deemed the community busybody," CJ said. "Very talkative. Nice grandmotherly type."

"Don't you think the original cold case would have a description of all four missing boys?" Billy suggested.

"Yes. I guess we need to read through it more thoroughly," she said. "Not that it matters, really. Even if Butch was a big kid picking on a weaker classmate, it won't mean anything at this point."

"So when Butch Renkie was one of the four who disappeared, did the investigators talk to Edward Krause's parents?" CJ asked.

"Edie Krause is the mother. She seemed a bit…well, paranoid," she said. She looked at Paige. "Wouldn't you say that?"

"Yes. But as Lizzie said, she hadn't been the same since that accident." She paused. "Lizzie made no mention of her husband."

"Maybe we should read through the file tonight, see what questions we come up with." Ice rubbed his hands together. "I see fajitas on the way. Must be our order."

He was right. Four plates filled with steaming food were placed in front of them. Paige's nachos seemed almost meager compared to CJ's enchilada plate with rice and beans. Ice and Billy's fajitas were still sizzling and covered in onions and peppers. For a moment, she wished she hadn't decided to change her diet to vegan, but that faded when she saw the meat soaked in grease. She picked up a crisp chip laden only with black beans and tried to ignore the sounds of pleasure coming from the others.

"Okay, so I say you guys go back to your buddies at the sheriff's department," CJ said as she took a big swallow of tea. "Ask them about the families who live at this Thompson's Plants. Maybe take a drive out there."

"And you two?"

"I think we need to interview Edie Krause."

"She didn't seem very likely to be forthcoming," Paige reminded her.

"Then I bet Lizzie Willis would be." CJ grinned at Ice. "And don't forget, we need to take a look at that house."

"I don't know what's with you and that damn house," Ice said. "They've already been there. Nothing was disturbed. No evidence that anyone was inside."

"But we still need to take a look around. Find out how we get a key."

CHAPTER EIGHT

Ice slammed the truck door, still wondering how he and Billy managed to get stuck together as partners. While they got along fine, he was used to CJ. He knew what questions she would ask and knew how to play off of her. With Billy, they hadn't yet seemed to be on the same page.

"How is it again that you and I got stuck together?"

Billy shrugged. "We rode together. We're in the same room."

"Yeah. And that's too much togetherness," he said. "And now we've got to get a key to the damn haunted house."

"What about this Thompson's Plants? You think we can get someone to go out there?"

"I guess if they won't, we will."

They walked into the offices, nodding at familiar faces. They'd spent damn near three hours there already.

"Brady still in?" he asked.

"Yep, go on back."

The door was open, but he paused to knock. Chuck Brady was staring at his monitor, a frown on his face, and he motioned them to enter without looking.

"Deputy Brady, we have a few more questions for you."

He looked up then. "And the FBI returns." He motioned for them to sit. "What's on your minds now? You plan to do some more drug busts while you're in town? Those women were kinda ballsy, weren't they? We had that house on our radar. It was just a matter of time before we moved in."

"Well, seeing a drug deal in broad daylight is kinda hard to ignore," he said. "But yeah, they can hold their own. Saved you some time, I guess."

His smile was forced. "So what's up now, Agent Freeman?"

"Two things, really," Ice said. "We're going to need a key to the Wicker house."

"The Wicker house? You mean the Underwood place?"

"I think the local residents in Pecan Grove call it the Wicker house," Billy said. "Or at least the ones at Shady Pines do."

He nodded. "Yeah, we got a key. But like I said, we already checked it out. There wasn't anything disturbed. Place is covered in dust and cobwebs."

Ice smiled politely. "We'll still need the key."

Brady tapped the desktop with his fingers. "Okay. No problem. And two?"

Ice glanced at Billy, and he took the cue. "Thompson's Plants," Billy said.

"What about them?"

"We understand they have undocumented workers, that they house them," he said.

Brady smiled. "Yeah? Now you want to be an immigration officer? Maybe border patrol? Want to go round up some illegals? Doing a drug bust wasn't enough?"

"Actually, we were wondering if anyone has gone out there to question them," Ice said. "Maybe one of them is the parent of our unidentified boy."

"That's not how it works," Brady said. "We go out there, they'll scatter like fleas on a dog's back. Ain't none of them going to talk to us."

"Have you approached the Thompsons, then?"

"Look. We have a young Mexican boy here. Do you think we're going to go around Cleveland and ask every Mexican family if they're missing one? Hell, it's been all over the news. Don't you think someone would have already come forward?"

"Do you?"

Brady leaned back. "If they come forward and they're undocumented, well, we gotta do what we gotta do. You know how it is."

Ice leaned back too. "Then we'd like to take a trip out there. If you'll point us in the right direction."

"If you think they'll talk to the FBI, you're wasting your time."

"He was someone's son."

Brady raised his hands up. "Your choice, man. Thompson's is about eight or ten miles north of town. But I'm telling you now, they're not going to talk to you."

Billy stood first. "If we could just get the key to the house then, we'll be on our way."

"Sure. Let me hunt it down. I'll be right back."

As soon as he was gone, Ice rubbed his hands over his bald head, noting that he'd not shaved that morning. "He's a prick," he murmured.

"These are his people," Billy said. "He probably knows what he's talking about."

"Come on, man. They're not working this case."

"Yeah, I know. But the chances of this one and the cold case being linked are nil," Billy said. "Once we leave here, that poor kid will probably never be identified."

Ice rubbed his head again. "You think the girls are wasting their time talking to this Edie Krause woman?"

"I don't know. Could be a link there," Billy said. "Kinda a coincidence that the kid who killed her son was one of the four boys to go missing. Seems like that should have been a red flag way back when."

* * *

"Déjà vu," CJ murmured as they drove slowly through the run-down trailer park where they'd been only a few hours earlier.

"Do you want to talk to Lizzie first or go directly to Edie Krause?"

"Let's talk to Lizzie again. I'm not really sure what questions to ask Edie. Are you?"

"No. I'd like to get a little background on her first." Paige reached over and touched her thigh. "I forgot to tell you. When I spoke to my mother the other morning, she again asked about you."

CJ raised her eyebrows. "Oh yeah?"

Paige smiled. "I may have...well, I got tired of her asking me the same question."

"The half-naked woman question?"

"Yes. That one." Paige squeezed her thigh. "So I told her you weren't half-naked. You were totally naked."

CJ laughed. "You didn't?"

"I also told her it was none of her business."

"Wow. Sneaking out of the closet?" she teased. "Good for you."

"Yes, but she hasn't called me back. That means she's either still in shock, or she's planning a surprise visit and interrogation."

"Well, maybe she called Seth. Maybe he explained it all."

Paige shook her head. "I would have heard from him if he'd had to endure the inquisition alone. Besides, knowing Seth, he would play the victim and beg as much sympathy out of her as he could."

CJ turned into Lizzie's driveway and stopped. She took Paige's hand, holding it tightly in her own. "Whatever you need me to do, I will," she said. "If your mother comes down here and wants answers, then I'll be there for you, if you're ready to have that talk with her."

"Thank you. But I would never subject you to my mother. You may run away screaming and I'll never see you again."

CJ wasn't entirely sure if Paige was teasing or not. "Your mother could never make me run away from you." She gave a quick smile. "I kinda like hanging out with you, you know."

There was a look on Paige's face that she couldn't quite decipher. Paige's eyes were questioning.

"Is that what we're doing? Hanging out?"

There was suddenly a tension between them that CJ had no clue how to dissolve. For that matter, she didn't know what answer Paige expected from her. But now wasn't the time to delve into their relationship. She decided to take the safe approach.

"I guess we're doing more than just hanging out, seeing as how we're together almost every night." She released Paige's hand. "Come on. Let's go talk to Lizzie."

Paige held her eyes for a few seconds longer before nodding.

They walked up to the door in silence, finding only the torn screen blocking their view inside. CJ knocked twice on the frame.

"Lizzie? Can we speak with you again?" CJ heard the squeaking of the chair Lizzie had been sitting in as she got out.

"Well, my, my," Lizzie said, smiling broadly at them. "How lovely it is that you returned."

"We have a few more questions, if you don't mind," Paige said.

"Oh, not at all, dear." She pushed open the screen door. "Come in, come in. I was just watching TV. I so miss Bob Barker. That other fellow just isn't the same."

She and Paige exchanged a quick smile as they followed her back inside, again sitting where they had earlier.

"We came to talk to you about Edith Krause," CJ said.

"Oh? About Little Eddie?"

"That too," she said. "But we just wanted to know the whole story, not just what we got from the police report."

Her eyes crinkled nearly shut as she grinned. "Oh, you mean gossip."

Paige leaned forward, resting her elbows on her thighs. "You said that Butch picked on him," she prompted.

"Constantly," Lizzie said. "Now he wasn't the only one. Other boys picked on him too. In fact, Markie Poole was another one who did. He was tall for his age. Poor Eddie didn't stand a chance. He was such a small boy." Lizzie pursed her lips. "She never fed him enough when he was little. Waited too long to start him on solid foods, I say."

"And Butch was a much bigger boy?"

"Oh, yes. Not only that, Eddie was only six. Butch was already close to eight then." She shook her head. "Butch was mean. Not only to Little Eddie. He picked on anyone littler than him. He threw rocks at birds. One time he took a baseball and hit Mary Beth Crowley's poor little poodle."

"So after the accident at school, were there ever any altercations between Edith and Butch's parents?"

"Oh yes. Before the accident too. Edie was down there all the time. The Renkies lived four trailers down from us," she said. "Now Herbert, not so much."

"Herbert?"

"Edie's husband. He was, well, not to sound cruel, but a bit of a sissy. Thin man. Wore glasses. Little Eddie took after him. Now Edie, she wore the pants in that family."

"So where is Herbert?" CJ asked.

Lizzie shrugged her thin shoulders. "When Edie came back, Herbert wasn't with her. Said he'd left her."

"Came back from where?" Paige asked.

"And when?" CJ added.

"Oh, they just up and left one day. Practically in the middle of the night. I got up one morning just in time to see them driving away. A few days later, her cousin was moving in." She frowned. "This would have been…oh my, I can't say for certain, but maybe 2001 or 2002."

"Were they still here when the four boys went missing?"

Lizzie nodded. "Yes, they left after that." Her eyes brightened. "Yes, now I remember. After Bradley Simon went missing—he was the last one—Edie said it was such a painful reminder of her Little Eddie, having to watch those parents go through what she went through. I guess it was a few months after that."

"And when did she come back?"

"Let's see…I guess it's over a year now." She nodded. "Yes, late last summer. Her cousin stayed with her for a few more months, then she moved out. It's just Edie now."

"But her husband didn't come back with her?"

"No. Just her."

"Where had she moved to?" Paige asked.

"They went to live with her mother, Norma. That was in Midland, out in West Texas," she said. "Now her mother was from here originally. Her husband—Edie's father—died in a horrible train accident." She shook her head slowly. "Tried to beat a train across the tracks, over near Highway 59. She had to get a job then," Lizzie said, shaking her head. "Most awful job, if you ask me. She went to work at the Wicker house, for the Underwoods. Edie was still a young girl then, I suppose in high school or close to. Norma didn't last long there, though. Who could blame her? After that, she worked in the cafeteria at school. It was there she met some man. A delivery man. Moved off with him. Edie had just married, if I recall. Norma was younger than me, but we got along." She smiled and showed off her dentures again. "I got off topic, didn't I? Well, as I was saying, Edie and Herbert went to Midland. Her mother took ill, so they ended up staying. As I hear it, Herbert ran off with a younger woman." Her lips pursed again. "I just don't see it. I mean, Herbert was nothing to look at, if you know what I mean. I can't imagine some young thing wanting to be with him."

CJ nearly laughed at the expression on Lizzie's face but managed to keep it in. "Do you and Edie talk much?"

She shook her head. "Not so much. Like I said, she's been different ever since she lost Eddie. Keeps to herself. Goes into town for groceries once a week, that's about it. And church on Sunday, of course."

"Do you think she'd speak with us?" Paige asked.

"Oh, I doubt it. She never has visitors, except maybe her cousin. And she won't say much more to me than 'hello' or a comment about the weather." Lizzie clasped her thin, arthritic hands together. "Terrible way to live life, I say."

CJ nodded. "You've been a big help, Lizzie. Thank you for seeing us."

Lizzie smiled broadly. "I feel honored that the FBI is seeking my help."

"You don't happen to know her mother's last name, do you?" Paige asked.

"Oh, I couldn't say. But I do know Edie's maiden name was Gilbert."

CJ stood and Paige did the same. "No need to get up," she said as Lizzie was about to pull herself out of the chair. "We can show ourselves out."

"Well, that's bad manners on my part, but okay," Lizzie said as she settled back down. "You come back anytime."

"Thank you," Paige said with what CJ knew was a genuine smile.

They walked back to the truck in silence and she glanced at Edie's trailer but saw no movement. The blinds were all shut tight.

"So what do you think?" she asked as they got back inside the truck.

"Interesting, that's for sure," Paige said. "I suppose we should try to locate Edie's mother and verify her story."

"Yeah, maybe Edie snapped after her son died. Maybe she and her husband took out their revenge on the neighborhood boys who used to pick on Eddie."

"Or maybe the husband did and that's why he's missing. He's in hiding."

CJ laughed as she drove away. "You don't think he ran off with some sweet young thing?"

Paige smiled. "I like Lizzie. She would be a perfect grandmother."

"Yeah? Are your grandparents still alive?"

Paige nodded. "Both on my mother's side. My father's mother died when I was young, but my grandfather is still alive."

Her statement was said without much emotion and CJ wondered if she had a relationship with any of them. Paige must have sensed her question.

"We're not close. My mother's parents certainly didn't approve of my career choice and my other grandfather, well, I was never fond of him. He's not what you would call warm," she said. "He was very gruff, very regimented. Honestly, I was afraid of him when I was young." Paige tilted her head as she looked at her. "You never mention yours."

CJ stiffened. "No. I don't." She stared out the windshield, not looking at Paige. "Why don't you give Howley a call? See if he can find something on Edie's mother."

Paige's answer was to pull out her phone. CJ was aware that she had a firm grip on the steering wheel and she made herself relax. She hadn't thought of her grandmother in a number of years, and she didn't know if she was still alive or not. She didn't really care one way or the other. All she remembered was her grandmother's accusations and the blame and guilt she tried to lay on both her and Cathy. Of course after Cathy's suicide, the blame and guilt was solely for CJ. For some reason, her grandmother never blamed their father for his actions.

She jumped when Paige squeezed her thigh.

"Okay?"

CJ saw her white knuckles, and she again relaxed her hands. "Sorry." She glanced at her. "I'm sorry. I wasn't paying attention. Howley?"

"Yes. He'll let us know what he finds." Paige's hand rubbed lightly against her leg. "Want to talk?"

CJ shook her head. "Maybe later."

CHAPTER NINE

Ice slammed the truck door, looking at rows upon rows of greenhouses, their doors opened for ventilation against the afternoon heat. The directions Brady had given them were true, and they found Thompson's Plants without incident. The drive up to the main house was through fields of shrubs and trees in black rubber tubs, all various sizes, linked together by irrigation hoses. It was a massive operation and he could only imagine how many workers would be required to make it all run. They headed toward a white building where a car and three trucks were parked.

"You think anyone will talk to us?" Billy asked for the third time.

Ice just looked at him and let out a frustrated sigh. His answer hadn't changed so he saw no reason to reply.

"What? I'm just asking," Billy said.

"Look, man. I know you'd rather be partnered with Paige. And I'd rather be with CJ. But now they want to be buddy-buddy on this one—for whatever reason—so I guess we're stuck with each other."

"Yeah. Why is that?"

Ice shook his head. "I'm trying not to think about it."

Of course, who was he kidding? He thought about it all the time. He watched them, looking for signs, even a tiny hint that they were having an affair, but only if he let his imagination run could he find anything. Sure, they were friendlier than ever, but he still doubted there was anything going on between them. Because, well, Paige was Paige and...CJ was CJ. They were as different as night and day. But was that really still the case? They bickered and teased and made light of their differences, but really, were they that far apart? Paige had changed a little, but CJ the most. As far as he knew, she wasn't cruising the bars anymore and he couldn't remember the last time she'd shown up to work wearing the same clothes as the day before, smelling like tequila. In fact, it had to have been before the whole Hoganville mess. She never mentioned women or sex, never mentioned *anything*. He stopped walking, his eyes widening. She hadn't been going to the bar. She hadn't been going out. Then what the hell was she doing? And with whom?

"What?"

Ice slowly turned to Billy, but he closed his mouth before sharing what he'd been thinking.

"Nothing," he said with a quick shake of his head. *Damn. Paige and CJ? Sleeping together?* He shook his head again. *Damn.*

The sign on the outside of the door read "Thompson's Plants. Wholesale only." He assumed it was an office and opened the door without knocking. The inside was cool and air conditioned, making him take note of the warm afternoon. Two desks were on opposite sides of the room, facing each other and a long countertop blocked traffic from the rest of the building.

"May I help you?"

Ice pulled out his credentials and held them up to the young lady sitting behind one of the desks. He saw instant fear in her eyes.

"Special Agents Freeman, Calhoun," he said. He smiled, trying to put her at ease. "First of all, we're not here to do a bust. This isn't an immigration issue."

She relaxed but only slightly. "What...what can I help you with?"

"We'd like to speak to the owner. Mr. Thompson? We're just needing some information," he said.

She nodded, already reaching for the phone. He noticed that her hand was shaking.

"Dad? There are two FBI agents here." She shook her head. "No, I don't think so." She looked up at Ice skeptically, then hung up without another word. "He's in the back."

"Down the hallway?" Billy asked.

"Yes. He'll meet you."

"Thank you."

They walked around the counter and into the hallway. A door at the far end opened and a tall man wearing a baseball cap came in. He took his cap off and brushed at his hair as he came closer.

"I'm Shane Thompson," he said.

Ice held out his hand. "DeMarcus Freeman."

"Billy Calhoun," Billy said as he also shook his hand. "Is there a place we can talk?"

"My office," he said.

They followed him into a cluttered room, where he immediately began straightening papers on his desk.

Ice sat down in one of the chairs and Billy did the same. Shane Thompson watched them, then put the papers he'd been sorting down on his desk.

"How can I help you?" he asked, finally sitting.

"You can start by relaxing," Ice said with a quick smile. "We're looking for information only. We're not here to go through your employment records."

"Look, they come to me with papers, that's all I need. I know some of them are forged, but hell, I'd go out of business without them. There's nobody in this town that'll do the work they do."

"We're not here for that, Mr. Thompson," Billy said. "It's about the little boy who was found last week, over in Pecan Grove."

"Hispanic. No one's come forward to claim the body. We believe he's undocumented. And his family too," Ice said.

"Is that why the FBI's involved? Because he's undocumented?"

"No," Ice said but did not elaborate.

"You think he's from here? My place?"

"Is he?"

"I house twenty-four families," he said. "Most have kids. I don't know them all, of course."

"Have you heard anything?"

He studied them for a long moment, then shook his head. "No."

Ice had been in the business long enough to know when someone was lying to him. So he tried again. "Look, I promise you, I don't care about their papers or whether they're real or not. I only care about identifying the boy and finding out what happened to him."

Thompson's eyes narrowed. "The last time the Feds were here, they took sixteen of my guys away. I damn near lost everything. Why should I trust you?"

"We're not immigration officers," Billy said. "We're working a possible homicide."

Thompson's eyebrows shot up. "Homicide?"

"We just need your help," Ice said.

"You know who the boy was?" Billy asked.

Thompson seemed to contemplate the question but gave a noncommittal answer. "Maybe."

Ice let out a frustrated sigh. "Will the parents talk to us?"

Thompson shook his head. "No way. I employ them, I protect them. They trust me. You guys step back there and I won't see them for a week."

Ice leaned forward. "Look, I'm telling you this in the strictest confidence," he said. "This hasn't been released to the media. The boy was most likely hit by a car. But then someone choked him, strangled him, hard enough to break his neck," he said "The body was left at an abandoned house in Pecan Grove, but we don't believe he was killed there."

Thompson stared at him but said nothing.

"We want to identify the boy," Billy said. "And hopefully find out who did this. Maybe somebody saw something." He paused. "I'm sure the parents want him, want to give him a proper funeral."

Shane Thompson finally leaned back, his facial expression changing. "You know, when it was first on the news, I didn't even consider it was someone from here. I mean, all the way over in Pecan Grove, you know." He slowly shook his head. "Then I started hearing things." He sat up again and squared his shoulders. "I'll talk to them. I'll see what I can find out."

"Thank you," Ice said. He pulled out his card and handed it to Thompson. "We'll be in town at least through tomorrow."

"Okay. I'll call you tomorrow."

He and Billy stood and Ice reached out his hand, firmly shaking Thompson's. "You've got quite an impressive operation here. It must be successful."

"Thank you. Yeah, it's grown, that's for sure. I'm third generation. My father is still alive and he has a hand in it still. Now my son is on board so we're going on four generations here," he said proudly. "But I can't get anyone in town to work out here. My guys here, I pay them well, I take care of them. I can trust them to do the job."

"I understand. We'll let you get back to it. Look forward to hearing from you."

Once back outside, the afternoon humidity made it feel more like August than October. Ice pulled at the collar of his shirt, thinking he'd follow CJ's dress code and opt for an FBI T-shirt tomorrow.

"That was more productive than I thought," Billy said. "Makes you wonder why the sheriff's department didn't come out here."

"Yeah, I know. They did a half-ass job all the way around."

Back in Billy's truck, Ice pushed the window up and turned the AC vent toward his face.

"I'm feeling like a steak for dinner," Billy said. "You think we could talk Paige into a steakhouse?"

"Only if CJ agrees."

"What do you mean?"

"Three against one. But have you noticed how CJ has been accommodating to Paige lately? I mean, hell, at the bar the other night, they shared bean nachos with no cheese. And you know how much CJ likes cheese."

Billy's voice lowered as if afraid they'd be overheard. "You think something's going on with them?"

"Why do you keep asking me that question? You know as much as I do."

CHAPTER TEN

"Steak? You want steak?" Paige turned to CJ. "You too?"

CJ nodded. "The guy downstairs said there's a place up Highway 59 that has chicken fried steaks that are this big," she said, holding her hands apart.

"And a rib eye that is two inches thick," Billy added.

Paige shook her head. "Sure. Take me to carnivore hell. I guess I can get a baked potato."

"They have fish and shrimp too," CJ said. "You know, in case you want to cheat a little, but not go all the way to the dark side."

Paige wondered if CJ knew that shrimp was her number one weakness. She already felt her resolve slipping as she imagined biting into a juicy, succulent shrimp. Damn, but it was hard being vegan.

They found the restaurant without incident—all four of them riding in CJ's truck. Paige took pity on Ice and sat in the back seat with Billy. It was nearing seven, but the parking lot was only half full. They were seated immediately and again they opted for a booth.

"You want to get a pitcher of beer and split it?" Billy asked.

"I'm in," CJ said as she looked over the menu.

Ice flagged down a waitress and ordered the beer. A bowl of roasted peanuts was placed on their table, and Ice and Billy each grabbed a handful.

"Looks like our kind of place," Ice said as he cracked open a shell.

Paige had to agree, but it still startled her sometimes when she thought about what was normal for her now compared to her early life. Not that she went out much. The bar they all hung out at in Houston was as familiar to her as anything. And since she and CJ had become lovers, nights out for dinner had been replaced with cooking in and just spending time together. Of course, since she'd changed her diet and started eating healthier, cooking in was so much simpler than trying to wade through menus looking for something she could eat.

Like now.

She let her gaze slide over to the seafood section, landing on *fried shrimp*, then *grilled shrimp*. She closed the menu quickly.

Four frosted mugs and a pitcher of beer were placed on the table, and CJ carefully filled each mug. They all took their glasses, meeting in the middle of the table with a silent toast.

"Oh, yeah. Nice and cold," CJ said.

Their waitress was back with pad and pen, looking at them expectantly. "Ready to order?"

"Chicken fried steak," CJ said. "Mashed potatoes instead of fries."

"Mixed vegetables or corn?"

"I'll have the mixed veggies." She winked at Paige. "Gotta get something healthy in me."

"I want a rib eye, medium rare," Billy said. "Baked potato and corn."

"Same," Ice said. "Although more medium than rare."

"And you?"

Paige bit her lower lip, trying to chase images of shrimp from her mind. "Baked potato. Mixed veggies." She closed her eyes. *Damn.* "And grilled shrimp," she said as she handed her menu to the waitress.

CJ laughed. "Oh, yeah…come to the dark side," she teased.

Paige leaned forward. "It's your fault. You had to mention shrimp. Nice, juicy…succulent shrimp," she said slowly, her eyes never leaving CJ's.

CJ's mouth turned up in a smile. "If you want something juicy and succulent, I can help you out there."

Even though she knew it was coming, she blushed anyway. "Easy, tiger. Don't embarrass the boys."

CJ laughed. "You're the one blushing, not them."

The guys laughed too. "I think I may have blushed a little on that one," Billy confessed.

Paige took a swallow of her beer. "Let's talk business," she said. "What's on the agenda tomorrow?"

"Hopefully Shane Thompson will call and we can go out and interview the parents," Ice said. "I'm debating whether we should include Deputy Brady and his team."

"They dropped the ball," CJ said. "Howley said it's technically our case if we want to work it."

"He also said if the cases weren't linked to let the locals have it," Billy reminded her.

"So we tell him we think they *are* linked. Simple."

"I swear, do you ever follow the rules?" Billy asked.

CJ smirked. "Baldy, tell him."

"Rules are subjective and ever-changing," Ice said.

"What the hell does that mean?"

"Oh, Billy boy, it means that CJ's interpretation of Howley's directive might be different than yours…or Howley's." Ice grinned. "Or mine."

"It means rules are made to be broken," CJ said with a mischievous grin.

Billy shook his head. "I'm surprised you haven't been suspended yet."

"What? Me?" CJ added more beer to her mug. "If I recall correctly, the last verbal directive we were given was 'don't shoot anyone' when we were in Hoganville. And I do believe I did not fire my weapon." She glanced over at Paige. "But our dear, sweet Paige Riley turned into Annie Oakley."

The guys laughed along with CJ, but then CJ surprised her by reaching across the table and squeezing her hand.

"I'm just kidding. I know Ester Hogan had her bony fingers wrapped around your neck."

Paige nodded. "Figuratively, at least."

She could still remember the vise-like grip around her throat, shutting off her air, even though Ester Hogan was a good twenty feet away. She tried not to picture Fiona as she lay in a pool of her own blood...of her own making. She shook those thoughts away, meeting CJ's gaze. CJ squeezed her hand once more before releasing her. The guys were unusually quiet, and Paige looked at them now, both of them staring at her hand. The one CJ had just been holding.

"So, what about this haunted house? You get a key?"

"Yeah, we got a damn key," Ice said. "I don't know why you're insisting we go in there. The sheriff's department has already checked it out."

"This same sheriff's department that didn't even bother going to Thompson's Plants?" CJ asked with an arch of one eyebrow.

Ice let out a sigh. "Yeah. Okay."

"Did you two learn anything today?" Billy asked.

"Got some background on Edith Krause. Howley is running it," CJ said.

"She and her husband left here shortly after the last boy went missing," Paige explained. "She returned last year. Alone."

"Were they questioned in the original investigation?"

"I would assume no more or no less than the other families in the trailer park," CJ said. "And like we've said all day, we need to go back and read the file thoroughly. I just skimmed through it, as I guess we all did."

Ice didn't answer, his gaze locked on a large tray of food heading their way.

"Oh, man. Look at that steak," he said.

Paige skipped over the steaks, instead feeling her mouth water as she stared at the pile of large grilled shrimp calling her name. *Damn.*

CHAPTER ELEVEN

CJ tossed the key card on the small desk beside the door, then found Paige's hand and pulled her close. "I've wanted to do this all day," she murmured as she leaned closer for a kiss. Paige slid her hands up CJ's chest, lightly brushing her nipples before slipping them around her neck.

Their kiss was slow and unhurried, lips moving with familiarity against one another. She moaned quietly when she felt the tip of Paige's tongue trace her lower lip. But Paige took it no further, even though CJ recognized the subtle change in her breathing.

"I brought wine," Paige reminded her.

"We could have it later," she suggested.

Paige met her gaze, a smile playing on her lips. "We could, I suppose." She moved closer again, this time letting her hand linger.

CJ felt her nipple harden as Paige's fingers traced it. Her own breathing shifted.

"Can you be quiet?" Paige whispered before kissing her.

CJ smiled against her lips. "Shouldn't we be worried about you?" Her hips jerked as Paige's hand found its way between her legs.

"Take your clothes off," Paige said as she pulled away. "I'll be right back."

Paige headed to the bathroom and CJ quickly ripped her shirt off and tossed it aside, along with her bra. She knew where Paige was going. She knew what she'd bring back. She nearly trembled at the thought. She turned the light off, leaving on the lone lamp in the room. Her shoes, she kicked off, letting them land where they may. Her jeans, socks and panties followed, leaving her naked. She turned the sheets back on the bed, trying not to think about Ice and Billy in the next room, their beds up against the same wall.

Paige came out of the bathroom wearing a robe. CJ knew she was naked beneath it. She found it sexy as hell when Paige did that, but her eyes were drawn to what Paige held in her hand.

The strap-on dildo—a gag gift from Ice and Billy when they'd been in Hoganville—wasn't something they used often. But when they did…God, it was incredible being inside Paige, making love to her that way.

She stood there as Paige's eyes roved over her. She felt her nipples harden in response. Paige slowly untied her robe, letting it hang open.

"Are you trying to kill me?" CJ whispered.

Paige had a lazy smile on her face. "Can you be quiet?" she asked again.

CJ walked closer, taking the dildo from her. "I'll be as quiet as you are." She pushed the robe off of Paige's shoulders, letting it fall to the floor. No matter how many times she'd seen Paige naked, she was still stunned by her beauty. Sometimes, she was still stunned that they were lovers.

"Put it on," Paige commanded quietly.

* * *

Paige lay still, watching…waiting. CJ had yet to touch her, but her pulse was already racing. She let her gaze travel down CJ's body, and her lips parted, short, quick breaths matching the pace of her pulse.

"Roll over."

Paige swallowed, then did as CJ asked. She felt CJ move behind her, and she closed her eyes as CJ's hands explored the back of her thighs.

"Up on your knees," CJ whispered.

Paige let out a tiny moan when CJ's hands drew her up. She trembled as CJ moved the hair from her neck and soft, warm lips nibbled her skin. Trying to remain quiet, she bit down on her lip when CJ's hands reached around her, her fingers squeezing her nipples with just enough pressure to take her arousal to another level. She pressed back against CJ, feeling the dildo graze her clit.

"*God...*CJ, don't tease me," she pleaded. She could feel the slickness of her arousal coat her thighs.

CJ's mouth moved to her ear, her tongue snaking inside. "You have to be quiet," CJ reminded her.

"Maybe this wasn't a good idea," Paige murmured, doubtful she would be able to control herself.

"Try."

It took all of her willpower not to cry out in pleasure when CJ entered her from behind. CJ's hands left her breasts and grabbed her hips, pulling her back into her, the dildo sliding easily through her wetness, filling her. CJ pulled out slowly, then back in, this time a little deeper, a little harder. Paige concentrated on CJ's rhythm, feeling CJ's hips slap against her backside with each stroke, moving faster and harder. But quiet, they were. The only sounds were that of their near panting for breath and the skin-on-skin contact as CJ slammed into her from behind.

It was so good, so thrilling, she wanted it to go on forever. But CJ reached around her, two fingers finding her clit, rubbing against it as she continued to move inside her—in and out—long strokes filling her. It was all too much and Paige let her orgasm claim her, let it wash over her as she gave herself to CJ. The intensity of it seemed to magnify as she struggled to remain silent, keeping her sounds of pleasure inside. She squeezed her eyes shut, swearing she saw fireworks as CJ's fingers squeezed hard around her clit.

Then CJ pulled out of her and Paige collapsed onto the bed. She heard CJ fumbling with the dildo, knew CJ needed her own release. She managed to roll over and pull CJ to her, her hand moving between their bodies, finding CJ. With fingers on her clit, she let CJ move against her. She was so wet, Paige had a hard time finding purchase but it didn't matter. CJ came quick and hard, her moan muffled as she buried her face against Paige's neck.

CJ rested her full weight on top of her, and Paige's arms wrapped around her, holding her close as they relaxed, their breathing slowing, trying to get back to normal. She kissed CJ's forehead, her lips lingering on her damp skin.

With eyes still closed, she accepted what she'd been warring with. She was in love with CJ. That declaration would have frightened her a month ago, two weeks ago even. But now, right here, with CJ in her arms, it didn't scare her in the least.

CJ pulled up, shifting slightly as she rested her weight on her elbows. Their eyes met in the soft light around them and there was nothing that CJ tried to hide. Paige felt tears dampen her eyes, and she was surprised to see the same in CJ's. Could CJ read her too? She swallowed, wondering if she should say the words, wondering if it mattered.

CJ's hand touched her cheek, fingers grazing lightly across her skin, moving over her nose and to her lips, then back up to her ear, a lazy finger tracing it. Their eyes held for a long moment and she felt trembling, not knowing if it was her or CJ. Then CJ kissed her, her lips moving so slowly and tenderly against her own, Paige thought she was going to burst with the love she felt in that moment.

But they said nothing. CJ pulled the covers around them and Paige snuggled against her, feeling safe and secure in her arms... feeling loved.

CHAPTER TWELVE

CJ pulled to a stop in front of the Wicker house, and all four of them stared out through the windows at the imposing structure. The skeletons of long-dead oaks and pines stood guard in front of the house, their bare limbs spreading like fingers, protecting it.

"Man, I don't know why we have to do this," Ice said again. "I got a bad feeling about this place."

"It's broad daylight," CJ said, as if that mattered. "You really don't want to go in?"

"Oh, hell no," he said. "First you had me in the woods being chased by a goddamn monster and now this?" He pointed to the house. "Hell no."

"You don't really believe in ghosts, do you, baldy?" she asked.

"No, I don't believe in ghosts. I also didn't believe in monsters out in the woods, but that proved to be wrong, didn't it?"

From the backseat, Billy held his hand out. "Here's the key to the gate."

CJ drove on to the side of the house where the driveway was. Ice got out and opened the gate.

"I've never seen him like this," Billy said.

"Me either," CJ said. "But it's his phobia so we have to respect that. If he doesn't want to go inside, that's his choice."

She pulled through and waited for Ice to close the gate again and get back inside. She drove slowly toward the house, coming to a stop where tall weeds had overtaken most of the driveway. She turned to Ice.

"You want to stay inside the truck or wait for us outside?"

He hesitated and CJ knew he was fighting with himself over his decision. Even though she was sure his choice would be to stay inside the truck, he chose the opposite.

"I'll walk the perimeter of the fence, see if anything is disturbed," he said.

"Okay. We're just going to take a quick run-through, see if anything jumps out at us." As soon as the words were out of her mouth, she realized the double meaning. She laughed. "Not literally jump," she clarified.

The windows were boarded up on the bottom floor, the wood discolored and faded, held in place by rusted nails. The boards had been pried away in places, offering a view of the inside. She bent down at one corner, cupping her face as she tried to see inside. It was dark and shadowy and she was surprised to find furniture.

"Looks like it's still furnished," she said.

"It is kinda creepy," Billy said quietly. "A lot of the windows are busted out."

"It's just a house," CJ said. "Let's open her up."

Billy produced the key Deputy Brady had given them. The house was old, but the deadbolt on the door was modern, probably added when the Underwoods lived there.

The hinges screeched in protest as Billy pushed the door open. Nearly simultaneously, all three of them clicked their flashlights on, chasing some of the shadows away. The air was dank and musty. A thick layer of dust covered nearly every surface and cobwebs stretched from ceiling to floor.

"Why must there always be spiders?" Paige asked in a near whisper.

CJ smiled at Paige's reference to the tunnels in Hoganville, which had been littered with spiderwebs.

"It doesn't look disturbed," Billy said.

"You can tell that from right here at the door?" CJ glanced at him. "Ice's paranoia rubbing off on you?"

"I'm just saying."

CJ reached out and moved a web out of the way. "I'll take the stairs. You two take a look down here."

"Yeah, okay, you take the stairs," Billy said quickly, as if afraid she'd change her mind. "I'll take this way." He headed down a side hallway to what CJ assumed was the kitchen.

"This looks like a living room or a den," Paige said, pointing her light toward the large room opening off of the entryway. Her feet crunched on broken glass as she passed a boarded-up window.

"I'm just going up to the second-floor landing," CJ said. "But Billy is right. It doesn't look like anyone's been in here in years."

The stairs creaked under her weight, and she paused at the fourth step, sensing eyes on her. She glanced down, thinking she'd find Paige watching her, but Paige was nowhere in sight. She shook her head slightly, then moved up another three steps. She immediately felt cold air surround her, as if she'd stepped into an air-conditioned room.

"Okay, this is weird," she whispered out loud. It lasted only a few seconds, then was gone.

She moved up another few steps but quickly leaned against the wall as running footsteps sounded along the stairs. She felt a whoosh of air as the sound faded.

"I did *not* just hear that," she murmured. "Paige?" she called. She saw Paige's flashlight turn her way.

"Yes?"

"Everything okay down there?"

Paige walked to the bottom of the stairs. "Nothing looks disturbed," she said.

"You...you hear anything?"

Paige tilted her head questioningly. "Like what?"

Billy came up behind Paige. "Spiderwebs, dust. No footprints," he said. "No one's been in here."

CJ stood frozen in place, almost afraid to look up to the second-floor landing. Four steps remained. She swallowed nervously, then shined her light up the stairs. Nothing. She let out a nervous breath, then shook her head. *Damn*. Maybe Ice's fear was rubbing off on her.

"Okay. Nothing up here."

She was just about to turn and go back down when she felt a hand brush her neck. She whipped her head around, seeing nothing. But in an instant, ice-cold air literally made her shiver. Just as quickly, it was gone, replaced again by warm, muggy air. She turned and nearly ran down the stairs, not stopping until she was outside.

Ice stared at her as she put a hand to her chest, feeling her hammering heartbeat. She opened her mouth, taking in big breaths of fresh air.

"What the hell's wrong with you?"

She shook her head. "Nothing."

Paige came up behind her and touched her arm. "What's wrong?"

"Yeah. You ran out of there like a ghost was chasing you," Billy said with a laugh.

She turned to him, her face serious. "Maybe it was."

Ice backed up a few steps. "Whoa now. What the hell? Are you jacking with me?"

CJ turned to Paige, meeting her gaze. "You didn't hear anything? Running footsteps on the stairs? Cold air?" She swallowed. "A hand touching you?"

"Oh, fuck," Ice muttered as he jumped off the porch and headed to the truck. He turned, pointing at CJ. "If you're fucking with me, I'll be so pissed."

She shook her head. "I'm not fucking with you." She looked at Paige. "Anything?"

She slowly shook her head. "No. I didn't hear anything. I didn't feel anything."

"Me, either." Then Billy grinned. "Are you serious?"

"Shit. Maybe I...maybe I imagined it." She shrugged her shoulders. "Maybe I let Ice's haunted house story get to me."

"Tell me what happened," Paige said.

CJ ran her hands through her hair and blew out a breath. "I was about, I don't know, five or six steps up when I felt this cold air surround me. It only lasted a few seconds. Like it was a draft or something. Then I was almost at the top when I heard running footsteps on the stairs. Like two or three people—kids—were running up behind me. I felt a whoosh of air as if they'd run past me."

Billy's eyes opened wide. "Seriously?"

She nodded. "Then when I turned to go back down, I felt a hand, fingers, brush the back of my neck and then another blast of cold." She laughed nervously. "That's when I bolted."

"Okay, can we get the hell out of here now?" Ice said. "I told you, I had a bad feeling."

Paige held up her hands. "Wait. Let's just wait a minute," she said. "If you really felt—heard—all this, and it wasn't your imagination, then…"

"Then what?" she asked.

"I don't know." Paige pointed to the still-open door. "Let me go in, retrace your steps."

"Oh, hell, you're crazy," Ice said as he backed up even further. "Let's just get the hell out of here."

"Ain't nothing going to get you, baldy," CJ said, hoping that was true.

"You want me to go with you?" Billy asked.

Paige nodded. "Yeah. At least come inside with me." Paige looked at CJ. "You?"

CJ looked past her to the open door. "I'll…"

"I'll wait out here" is what she wanted to say. But instead she said, "I'll watch from the door."

CJ stood just inside the threshold, expecting to feel cold hands on her at any moment. Paige walked confidently to the edge of the stairs, pausing to look back at her. CJ nodded. Billy stood at the bottom, one hand on the railing as Paige started up. She went slowly, deliberately, stopping a few times, cocking her head as if listening. At the top of the stairs, she flashed her light around, then shrugged.

"Nothing."

CJ bit her lip. Hell, maybe she had imagined it all.

"You want to go up again?" Billy asked.

CJ shook her head. "No, no. I'm good."

Ice came toward them as they went back outside. He held up his phone.

"Shane Thompson called. He's got some info for us."

"That's great," Paige said. "Maybe we can catch a break."

"Did you call Deputy Brady?" Billy asked.

"No. And I don't plan to."

CHAPTER THIRTEEN

Ice held his hand out, shaking Shane Thompson's. "Thanks for calling." He pointed to CJ and Paige. "Special Agents Johnston and Riley."

"I don't have a whole lot for you, but I was able to persuade some of the parents to ask their children," he said. "As much as they trust me, they were fearful."

"I gave you my word," he said. "We're not here to bust anyone."

Thompson nodded. "I hope your word is worth something." He motioned to the door. "Come inside. I'm sure we're being watched."

"Do you know who the parents are?" Paige asked.

"Yes. They're willing to come forward." He turned to Billy. "Like you said, they want a funeral."

He didn't take them down the hallway and into his private office. Instead, he stopped in the main office. The same young woman was behind the same desk—his daughter. He glanced at her and she immediately got up and left them.

"The young kids, they play along the forest road that runs along the edge of our property," he said. "The boy's name was Juan. He had just turned six. They didn't have him in school yet."

"What road?" CJ asked. "National Forest Road?"

"Yes. A dirt road that goes into the Sam Houston National Forest."

"Did the other kids see what happened?" Ice asked.

"Yes. A car came speeding down the road from up in the forest. They tried to get out of the way. Juan didn't make it."

"When was this?" Paige asked.

"A week ago. Last Wednesday."

"His body was found on Thursday," Billy said.

"He was obviously moved," Ice said. "What happened after the car hit him?"

"There were two men in the car. They put Juan in the trunk and drove off."

"Can anyone describe them? The car?"

Thompson shook his head. "It was dusk. It gets dark early in the forest. The best I could get was that it was some kind of sports car. It only had two doors."

Ice turned to the others. "It's almost dark. You hit a kid on the road." He shrugged. "It's an accident. Why take the body and run?"

"Someone who couldn't afford an accident," CJ said.

"It's all I have," Thompson said. He took his cap off and twisted it in his hands. "Look, Juan was born here. His parents, not. They don't speak any English. I don't know what protocol is here when they want to claim his body. There's a small Catholic church used by the Latino community. My people go there. They want to have a funeral and bury him there."

Ice nodded. "I understand. We can see about granting immunity to the parents. That's not really my call. I'm just giving you my word that immigration is not involved."

"We can ask the sheriff's department to release the body," CJ said. "Providing the ME is finished."

"Not yet," Ice said. "He hasn't issued his final report." He turned to Thompson. "I'll call the ME, get him to release the body as soon as he can. I'm assuming you'll take the parents there?"

He nodded. "Yes. Thank you. I appreciate it."

Ice shook his hand again. "Thank you for the information. If you hear anything else…"

"Of course. I'll call."

Back outside, they got into CJ's truck. She pulled out of the driveway and headed in the direction of their hotel. They had checked out earlier, but Billy's truck was still there.

"What do you think?" Ice asked.

"About what we had assumed," CJ said. "Except we have two guys and not one."

"Why take the body to the Wicker house, though?" Paige asked. "That just doesn't make sense."

"Yeah, we can speculate all day long, but until we have some concrete evidence, we got shit," Ice said.

"Howley will want to meet in the morning. I guess we can speculate then," CJ said. "Let's go home."

CHAPTER FOURTEEN

Paige studied CJ from behind, noting her light grip on the remote, noting the eyes that stared at the TV, eyes that rarely blinked. She had no doubt that CJ hadn't a clue as to what she was watching. She walked around the sofa, holding out a glass of wine. "You want to talk?"

CJ looked up, acknowledging her finally. She smiled quickly. "Sorry. What?"

Paige sat down beside her and took the remote, turning the TV off. "Talk? You want to talk?"

CJ blew out her breath, then leaned back, holding her wineglass but not drinking. She turned slowly, her gaze thoughtful.

"I keep telling myself that I imagined all that in the house." She swallowed. "But I know I didn't. I felt the cold. I *heard* running on the stairs."

"I'm not doubting you," she said.

"But why didn't you feel it too?"

Paige sipped her wine, trying to find the words that she assumed CJ needed to hear. "Do you remember the first time we went into Hoganville? To the café?"

"Yes, of course."

"We were at the table and Ester Hogan came in. I didn't feel anything. Yet you felt as if someone was choking you. You said you felt a weight on your chest."

CJ nodded. "Yes. But you felt it too, later, in the chamber, in the cave. When she was—"

"Yes, I felt her hands around my throat, felt her choking me, yet she wasn't close to me, wasn't touching me. But at the café, we both were there. Yet only you felt something."

"What are you trying to say?"

"She targeted you in the café, not me. If there is something...a presence...in the house, it targeted you today, not me."

"Like a ghost?" CJ laughed nervously. "Seriously?"

"Look, I don't really believe in ghosts." Paige smiled. "At least I don't think I do. But we know there are people who do. There are documented cases. There are haunted buildings—hotels, houses— all over the world. But I don't mean ghosts, like I see a shadowy shape in the corner and," she laughed, "if I do, that's where I run screaming from the room."

CJ smiled slightly. "An apparition then?"

"An apparition is still a visible sighting of something, isn't it?" Her voice softened. "Did you see anything?"

CJ shook her head. "No. But I *felt* something."

Paige nodded. "And that's what I mean. If there's something in the house, whether we call it a presence or a spirit...or a ghost, it reached out to you. I don't doubt that you felt something, CJ. Just because I didn't doesn't make it true."

"If we hadn't been in Hoganville, if we hadn't witnessed what Ester Hogan could do, if we hadn't had that damn creature chasing us through the woods, would you still believe me?"

Paige let her hand run through CJ's hair, caressing it. "If Hoganville hadn't happened, if we weren't lovers...I don't know. Even then, why would I doubt you?"

"Okay, say we all three went into the house and Billy was the one who said he *felt* something. Then what? I'd probably say he was crazy."

"And maybe that's why you were the one targeted today."

CJ leaned back against the cushions, her eyes closed. "Was it trying to tell me something? Was it trying to scare us away? Was it playing games?" She shook her head. "Hell, maybe it was all my imagination. Maybe there was nothing there."

"So maybe we should go back," Paige suggested as her hand fell from CJ's hair.

CJ turned her head, meeting her gaze, her expression serious. Then it changed, back to the playfulness that CJ normally sported. "Yeah, maybe I'll have a new career. Ghost hunter." She took Paige's hand and pulled it to her lap. "You want to be my assistant?"

Paige put her wineglass down, moving closer to CJ to snuggle. "I don't know. What are the qualifications?" She tucked her head against CJ's shoulder, snaking her arm across her waist. She sighed contentedly when she felt CJ's lips brush her forehead.

"This will definitely be on the job description," CJ murmured as her lips nuzzled her again.

Paige raised her head, smiling as their mouths met, the kiss light and playful. Then it deepened, the playfulness gone as she felt the fire between them come to life. She pulled back just enough to meet CJ's eyes.

"I accept."

"It doesn't pay well," CJ warned.

"No?" Paige's hand moved between them, cupping CJ's small breast. Her thumb raked across the nipple, noting the change in CJ's breathing. "Then I suppose we'll have to agree on compensation." She moved closer, kissing CJ again, letting her tongue tease CJ's. "I can think of a couple of things."

CJ shifted, pulling Paige on top of her as she lay down fully on the sofa. Paige slipped between her legs, their hips pressing into one another.

"Wouldn't the bed be more comfortable?"

"Yes, but I don't want to take the time to go there," CJ said, her mouth cutting off any other protest Paige may have had.

Their kisses turned heated as they battled for control. Paige gave up the fight when she felt CJ's hand slip past her waistband. She lifted her hips a little, giving CJ more room. It apparently wasn't enough as CJ's other hand fumbled with the zipper.

She pulled her mouth away, gasping for air, then jerked hard into CJ when her fingers brushed against her clit.

"Do you want me inside you?"

"No," Paige said, moving against CJ's fingers. "Like this." She kissed CJ, drawing it out. "Just like this," she whispered as her eyes slipped closed.

CHAPTER FIFTEEN

CJ found Ice exactly as she imagined—kicked back at his desk reading the morning newspaper. It was quiet at this early hour, none of the other teams were in yet. He glanced at her as she headed to the coffeepot.

"Kinda early for you, isn't it?" He lowered his feet to the ground. "You don't look like you've been to the bar, though."

She grimaced as she took a sip of coffee. She had to admit, Paige's gourmet blends had grown on her. "Why would you think I've come from the bar?"

"Because it's not even seven. The only time you're early is when you didn't go home the night before."

Yeah, that seemed like a lifetime ago. God, how did she survive those nights? But she shook her head. "I already got in a five-mile run. What about you?"

"Took the stairs instead of the elevator," he said.

"Sure you did, baldy."

He folded up the newspaper and put it aside. "So what's up?"

She shrugged, then pulled out her chair and plopped down. She couldn't sleep and had finally given up, leaving Paige's bed at three thirty. At her own apartment, she found piles of dirty laundry and took the time to wash two loads, but she couldn't shake her restlessness. The five-mile run hadn't helped either.

"It's that damn house," she finally said. "I can't stop thinking about it."

He leaned forward. "You really...*felt* something in there?" he asked quietly.

She nodded. "I'd rather say it was my imagination and be done with it, but I can't make myself believe that." He studied her, and she wondered if he thought she was just jacking with him.

"Look, we've seen a lot of shit in our job. But I never thought I'd see anything like what happened in Hoganville," he said. "After that, well, the idea of a ghost or a spirit or something, hell, why not?"

"Does that mean you'll go back inside with me?" She nearly laughed as the color drained from his face.

"If it came down to it, if I had to, I'd go in. Do I want to? Hell, no."

"Well, maybe Howley won't send us back. We got shit. Maybe he'll just hand it back to the locals and we'll be out of it."

"Yeah, except Howley's in the doghouse. What better way to get out than to solve an old cold case? I think he has us work it."

"He's in the doghouse because of us," CJ reminded him. "He might only send us back as some sort of punishment." She shoved her coffee cup aside. "This tastes like shit."

"Yeah? Well, maybe Paige will be a sweetheart and pick up Starbucks this morning."

As if speaking the words made it so, the elevator doors opened and Paige and Billy came in, Paige holding a tray with three cups. Billy already was sipping from his.

CJ and Ice exchanged grins as they each reached for a cup.

"Thanks," Ice said.

"Yeah, thanks, Paige."

"You're here early," Paige said. Her statement had a bit of a question in it. CJ had left without as much as a note.

"Took my run earlier than usual," she said. "Figured Howley would want to meet with us first thing."

"And he does," Howley said as he came up the hallway, a cup of coffee in one hand and a thick file in the other. "Conference room. Now."

When they were all seated, he opened the file he carried and slid papers across the table to all of them. It appeared to be a report on Edith and Herbert Krause.

"Before we go over this, tell me what you found out about the boy," Howley said. "I looked over your report briefly."

"ME's report is not final," Ice said. "Inconclusive."

"Why is it still inconclusive?"

"Whether blunt force trauma killed him or he died as a result of strangulation," Ice explained.

"We now know he was hit by a car. That was the assumption to begin with," CJ said.

"Okay. So what's your theory?" Howley asked.

They all looked at CJ. "Well, the only theory we have is a drunk driver," she said. "Thompson got some of the kids to talk to him. They said after Juan was hit, the guys got out of the car, picked him up and put him in the trunk. Drove away. So maybe he was drunk and he panicked. Thompson said there were two guys in the car."

"Why take him to the Wicker house?" Paige asked.

"It would have to be someone who remembered the earlier case," Billy said.

CJ shook her head. "It doesn't make sense, though. You're drunk. You hit a kid. Who in their right mind is going to have the presence of mind to think, oh yeah, remember that kid who was found strangled fourteen years ago? Yeah, I'll mimic that." She shook her head again. "Come on, that doesn't happen. Even if the guy wasn't drunk, he's not going to think of that."

"What if they took the kid to one of their homes?" Ice asked. "He's injured but still alive. They have time to think. Do they take the kid to the hospital? Do they drop him off somewhere and hope he lives? If he lives, can he identify them?"

"So they panic," Billy said. "Maybe they argue. Decide to kill him and dump the body. Maybe it's a coincidence that it matches Paul Canton."

"Dropping him at the Wicker house? I don't think so," CJ said.

"Maybe they live in Pecan Grove," Paige offered. "Everyone there thinks the Wicker house is haunted," she said with a quick glance at CJ. "Why *not* put the body there? Maybe Billy is right. Maybe it has nothing to do with Paul Canton."

Howley looked at them all and sighed. "So you got nothing, basically."

"We only had two days," CJ reminded him.

"Yes, I know." He motioned to the papers in front of them. "Take a look at the report there. We didn't find much. Herbert Krause was laid off from his job seven months after his son died. We were only able to find that because his company's human resources department doesn't purge old employment records. Anyway, that would have been about three months before the disappearances. There were no divorce records. There were no hits on his Social Security number since. No job, no credit card, no banking info."

"Disappeared?"

"From what Paige told me," Howley said, "he and his wife, Edith Krause, moved to Midland. Paper trail is a dead end." He pointed at Billy and Paige. "You two fly out to Midland. See if you can interview her mother. Norma Manning. She's in a nursing home. Talk to her old neighbors too." He slid two packets to each of them. "Flight is already booked. You leave at two. What little we could find on the mother is in there."

CJ dared not look at Paige. She'd left in a funk that morning, and they'd not had a chance to talk. It looked like they wouldn't get one.

"What about us?" Ice asked.

"You get to stay and do paperwork. Try to come up with something more plausible than a drunk driver."

"So you want us to work the case?"

"If you can even call it a case," Howley said. "Any chance you can get out there to question the witnesses who saw the car?"

Ice shook his head. "To quote Deputy Brady, 'they'll scatter like fleas on a dog's back.'"

"Thompson told us they wouldn't talk to us," Billy said. "They think we're immigration officers."

"And did it occur to you to report Thompson's Plants to immigration?"

"The only way we got Thompson to help us was to promise no raid," Ice said. "Besides, the man's just trying to make a living. The people working for him, they're just trying to get by."

"Come on, Ice. Don't tell me you're one of these damn bleeding hearts wanting to grant immunity to them?"

"I'm just saying—"

Howley held his hand up. "I know what you're saying." He turned to CJ. "What about this house? Any evidence someone was there?"

"It didn't appear breached," she said. She glanced at Paige, wondering if she should tell him about…well, about what she felt. Paige gave her a subtle shake of her head. "We didn't get a chance to check the exterior, though. Thompson called, said he had something, so we left."

"Maybe you and Ice should head back there. Check out the house thoroughly," Howley said.

"Me…me and CJ? You want us to check out the house?" Ice asked. "Alone?"

"I just want to cover all our bases. You need to share what we learned about the car with the locals. Call Deputy Brady and make sure he's in the loop." He turned to Paige. "Your return flight is tomorrow afternoon. That should give you enough time in Midland. When you get back, give me your report, then head to Cleveland. Hopefully, CJ and Ice will have something." He looked back at CJ. "If it comes down to it, fleas on a dog's back or not, see if you can at least talk to some of the kids who saw the car." He stood. "I know we don't have much and we're grasping at straws here, but let's try to find something." He paused. "I want this one."

"Fourteen-year-old cold case," CJ said. "All we have is Edith Krause and her husband. And an eighty-nine-year-old woman who mentioned that the boys picked on their son."

"Yes, I know. But Larry Figures was originally assigned to the case. He dumped it off after a week."

"Whoa," Ice said. "Figures? As in your new boss?"

Howley nodded. "My boss. Your boss. Yes. So I want this one."

"Bad blood?" CJ guessed.

Howley's smile was humorless. "We came up together. Went to Quantico together. He's an ass-kisser, always has been. Therefore, his promotions happened more frequently than mine. He was a field supervisor then."

"And now he's your boss," Paige said. "So this case got away from him?"

"I think he knew it was a dead-end and dropped it in Duran's lap. Anyway, as you all know, since the Hoganville debacle, we've been—"

"Wait a minute," CJ said. "*Debacle*? We cannot be held responsible for the mass suicide," she said. "I told you—"

"I know what you told me. I know what's in your report. *They* know what's in your report. However, someone had to answer. That fell on me." His smile this time was genuine. "Shit rolls downhill." He turned to leave, then stopped again. "We close up the cold case. We clean up the new one. Maybe we get back in good graces. Probably not with Figures, though. Not when I make it known that my bunch of misfits closed out a case he gave up on fourteen years ago."

"Misfits?"

"Yeah. What was that again, CJ? 'Yellow rock in the clock'?"

"Look, I didn't know it was a goddamn suicide trigger."

"Yeah, yeah. And some big fella named Belden was choking you. Was that before or after the big scary monster was chasing you?" Howley shook his head. "I know the damn file by heart, I've read it so many times."

He left them then, closing the door rather loudly behind him. CJ leaned back in her chair. "I'd say he's still pretty bitter about the whole thing." She tossed her pen down. "Why does he still call it a monster? In my report, I said 'unidentified creature,'" she said.

"Me too," Paige said.

"I put 'monster,'" Ice said. "Big, scary monster."

"Yeah. And now you get to go into a big, scary haunted house," Billy teased.

"Oh, man," Ice groaned. "I'll give you a hundred bucks if you'll switch places with me," he offered.

Billy laughed. "Make it a thousand and we'll talk."

CHAPTER SIXTEEN

CJ tried to be as inconspicuous as possible as she followed Paige into the ladies' room. She raised her eyebrows as she walked in and Paige smiled.

"We're alone."

CJ walked closer, hesitating only a moment before pulling her into a tight, albeit quick hug.

"Are you okay?" Paige asked. "You left kinda early this morning."

"Yeah. Just couldn't sleep. I went to my place and did some laundry." She made a show of washing her hands when she heard the outer door open. "So Midland, huh?"

"Yes. Just what I want to do—interview someone in a nursing home." Paige nodded a greeting at Teresa Beckett, a woman from one of the other teams.

"Ladies," Teresa said. "How goes it?"

"Still pulling the dead-end cases," CJ replied dryly.

"Yeah. That's what happens when you kill fifty people," she said as she disappeared into a stall.

CJ rolled her eyes. "Will that *ever* go away?" she asked quietly.

Paige grasped her arm lightly and squeezed. "Doesn't matter. They weren't there. They don't know what all when down."

"I know. But—"

"It's over with," Paige said. "We've got to move on." She headed out and CJ followed. "I need to go pack. Billy's going to pick me up at my apartment."

CJ nodded. "Okay." She looked around, seeing no one watching. "I'm gonna miss you," she murmured.

"Me too. I'll call you tonight." Paige locked eyes with her. "I mean, if you want me to."

There was suddenly awkwardness between them that hadn't been there before. CJ wasn't certain when—or why—it had sprung up. Right now, what she really wanted to do was find an empty office and drag Paige in there. She wanted to hold her and kiss her and tell her she loved her and...*whoa*. Her eyes widened. *Jesus. Love?*

"Okay. Well...call *me*, then, if you want," Paige said as she turned on her heels.

CJ sprang into action, realizing Paige had taken her hesitation the wrong way. She grabbed Paige's arm, turning her around. She searched her eyes, seeing doubt and uncertainty there.

"I do want you to call me," she said. She swallowed. "And if it's okay with you, I'd kinda like to sleep at your place tonight. In your bed."

Paige's eyes softened and she nodded. "I'd like that." Paige took a step away, then paused. "Do we need to talk?"

CJ tilted her head. "I don't know. Do we?"

Paige was about to say more when Billy called out to her.

"I'm leaving. Pick you up in an hour?"

Paige nodded. "Yes. I'm heading out too." She turned to CJ. "I'll...I'll be in touch."

CJ watched her leave, not turning away until the elevator doors closed on her. *Damn.* What was happening with them all of a sudden?

"Hey."

She met Ice's questioning stare with raised eyebrows. "Yeah?"

"Let's whip through this report and head out of here early. Go grab a beer or something," he said.

"Sounds good. It's been awhile since just you and I hung out," she said.

"Yeah. That's what I was thinking."

CHAPTER SEVENTEEN

It was a quick and uneventful flight into Midland. Paige had taken a cue from CJ's packing and only brought a carry-on, as did Billy. They were in their rental car and on their way to Edith Krause's old neighbor by four.

"Man, the weather is nice here, isn't it? I could get used to no humidity."

"Yes, cool and dry," Paige agreed.

"I'd miss the trees, though. It's kinda barren here."

"Uh-huh."

Billy glanced at her. "You've been really quiet," he said. "Everything okay?"

She forced a quick smile to her face. "I'm fine. Tired," she said, which was the truth. She'd gotten so used to CJ being in her bed that she'd woken up before four that morning. The coolness of the sheets indicated CJ had been gone a while. She'd tried, but she couldn't fall back to sleep, the bed glaringly empty.

Paige knew CJ was a little freaked out about what had happened in the Wicker house, but she wondered if that was all that was bothering her. She had seemed a little distant and the fact that they hadn't had a chance to talk, a chance for a real goodbye, left her questioning things.

Maybe…well, maybe CJ was tiring of their relationship. Maybe she missed going out to the bar, missed her one-night hookups. Paige felt a tightening in her chest as she imagined CJ in another woman's arms, imagined CJ making love to someone else. If CJ wanted to end things, God, what was she going to do? She'd fallen too hard, too fast.

She mentally shook herself. She was jumping to conclusions and she knew it. Instead of the doubt that was creeping in, she recalled the look in CJ's eyes instead, that dreamy, almost wistful look after they made love. That look was not the look of someone who had tired of their relationship. That look was…the look of someone in love.

She bit the corner of her lower lip. Was that the problem? Had it caught up with CJ too? Had love caught CJ in its net as well? She closed her eyes briefly, hoping that was the case. She'd hate to be the only one feeling this way.

But they were working now. She pushed thoughts of CJ away, needing to focus on the case instead. She'd already programed the neighborhood into the GPS on her phone and had directed Billy to head east on Interstate 20. The international airport was located between Odessa and Midland, and it was larger than she expected. The two cities, while small, had prospered with the latest oil boom. Midland appeared to be the more metropolitan of the two.

"Take the next exit," she said. "We'll take the loop—250—to the north."

"There's a lot of traffic," he commented.

She smiled. "After driving in Houston, can you really say that with a straight face?"

He laughed. "Yeah, I guess you're right. Five o'clock traffic is relative."

Traffic on the loop was lighter than the interstate, and he kept a steady speed as they headed north.

"Exit to the right," she said. "Andrews Highway. We'll come upon the hospital. You'll take a left there on Midland Drive."

"What's the neighborhood we're looking for?"

"Wedgewood Park," she said.

Once past the hospital and surrounding clinics, they entered into a more residential neighborhood.

"Take a right on Neeley," she said.

Traffic was nonexistent as they entered the neighborhood. Older homes and mature oak trees were the norm. It appeared to be a mix of homeowners and renters, judging by the contrast of the houses and yards. Some were neat and well-kept, while others were in various stages of neglect.

"There's McDonald," she said. "Take a left." A few blocks later they found Suncrest, their destination.

"The neighborhood is kinda shabby," Billy noted.

"Yes. I was thinking the same thing."

Billy parked on the street in front of the house where Edith Krause's mother lived up until last year. Their hope was that the neighbors were the same and would remember if Edie and her husband were here and for how long. She only hoped they found people at home. They were prepared to hang out until after five for those working normal jobs.

Luck was with them as the first house they tried, the door was answered quickly.

"Yes?" The woman appeared to be in her mid- to late-sixties and she opened the door cautiously.

Paige and Billy immediately held up their FBI credentials. "Special Agents Riley and Calhoun," Paige said.

"Oh, my." The woman tried to tidy her hair as she opened the door wider. "Is there something wrong?"

Paige smiled. "No, ma'am. We just have some questions, if you have a moment."

"Questions for me? From the FBI? Do I need an attorney?"

Billy laughed quickly. "No, no. You're not in any trouble. We're needing some information," he said.

"From me? Well, I can't imagine what information I would have."

Paige was going to ask if they could go inside, but the woman seemed nervous enough without that intimidation.

"What's your name?" Paige asked.

"Maggie Helms. Margaret," she clarified, "but I've been called Maggie my whole life."

"Maggie it is, then," she said. "It's about a former neighbor of yours. Mrs. Manning. I believe she lived here until last year," Paige prompted.

"Norma Manning, yes. Her daughter put her in a nursing home finally. Poor thing couldn't remember her own name anymore."

"Do you know Edith Krause?" Billy asked.

"Edie? Oh, yes. She came to live with her mother years ago. I thought she would stay, but she left after she moved her mother. She said she was going back to East Texas." Maggie glanced to the house in question. "The new neighbors are kinda standoffish," she said. "Younger folks. They both work. No kids. I've tried to be neighborly and take them pies and such, but they're not very friendly." She lowered her voice. "They're not from around here. Oil business brought them to town."

"What about Edie's husband," Paige said. "Did he live here too?"

Maggie frowned. "Her husband?" She shook her head. "No, no, I never met him. From what I hear, they divorced before she moved here."

"So he was never here? Did Edith mention him?" Billy asked.

Maggie shook her head. "Never once talked about him. Norma is the one who said they divorced. They lost their only child. I think it must have taken a toll on their marriage."

Paige thought back to what Lizzie Willis had told them. That Edie and Herbert had driven away from the trailer park early one morning. That Herbert had allegedly run off with a young woman he'd met here in Midland. Maybe they should try another neighbor. Surely someone would have seen Herbert, even if he was only here a short time.

She smiled politely at Maggie. "Thank you for your time. Do you know if there were other neighbors who were here back then? Back when Edith first came to live with her mother?"

"Mrs. Axel, across the street," she said, pointing to a well-kept home. "She's lived here thirty years, at least. She and Norma were good friends."

"We'll pay her a visit too," Billy said. "Thank you again."

"Is Edie in some kind of trouble?"

Paige shook her head. "No. Actually, we're trying to locate her husband."

"Oh. Well, like I said, he was never here. Edie never once mentioned him to me."

They headed across the street, toward Mrs. Axel's house. Billy leaned closer.

"Old Herbert is a mysterious guy."

"Yes he is. Maybe Mrs. Axel will remember him."

CHAPTER EIGHTEEN

After CJ and Ice had finished their report on their two-day stay in Cleveland and after they'd given Deputy Brady a call, they stayed to brainstorm with Howley again on more plausible theories for dumping the boy. Unfortunately, they couldn't come up with any. For some reason, CJ couldn't get the drunk driver scenario out of her head.

"Let's get out of here," Ice said as the clock ticked close to five. "I've had about as much speculation as I can take."

"Beer?"

"Or three," he said with a grin.

They drove separately to the only bar they ever visited. They recognized the faces of local cops and CJ nodded as they lifted a hand in greeting.

"We know practically everyone in here by face, but we don't really know any names," she said. "Why don't we ever go introduce ourselves? We've been coming here for years."

"Because everyone is doing the same thing we are. Letting off steam and talking about cases. There's not a lot of mingling between tables," Ice said.

They had barely sat down before April brought over two cold longnecks. Ice slipped her a five-dollar bill, knowing that would keep her coming around. They touched bottles in a silent toast before drinking. The beer was as cold as it looked.

"Man, this is what I'm talking about," he said. "We come to this bar all the time. They know what we drink. April brings it over without asking. There's no small talk." He shrugged. "Doesn't get any better than this."

CJ smiled but couldn't help but look at the two empty seats at their table. She'd done a good job of putting Paige from her mind all afternoon, but here, right now, she missed her. Ice would be baiting them, and they would tease and flirt with each other. She could almost hear Paige's laughter, reacting to something outrageous CJ said.

"Is now a good time to bring it up?"

CJ looked at him. "Bring what up, baldy?"

Ice leaned a little closer, meeting her stare. "You and Paige."

CJ had a moment of panic. She knew Ice was suspicious, but she didn't really think he'd come right out and ask. "What about us?"

"Come on, CJ. I'm not blind." He picked at the label on his bottle. "What's going on?"

She took a long swallow from her beer, stalling for time. Hell, they knew they couldn't keep it a secret forever. She slid the empty bottle to the middle of the table.

"What is it you're asking, Ice?"

Ice shook his head. "Are we going to keep answering questions with other questions? Because it's annoying." He turned, getting April's attention. He held up two fingers.

She shrugged with a nonchalance she wasn't feeling. "What do you want to know?"

"Are you guys…you know…more than friends?"

"Is that what you think?"

He leaned back. "Hell, CJ, I don't know anymore. I see the way you look at each other. But hell, I don't know. It's the same…yet it's different."

She nodded her thanks as April brought them fresh beers. "The whole Hoganville thing, we got to know each other a little better," she said. "We're…we're better friends now."

"And that's all?"

She met his steady gaze, wondering why she wasn't coming clean with him. He was her partner. She trusted him with her life. She should be able to trust him with this.

"No. No, that's not all." She paused, looking away, then back at him. "We're lovers."

He looked shocked. Maybe because he hadn't expected her to admit it. He took a swallow of beer before commenting.

"So…you're having an affair?"

She arched an eyebrow. "An affair? Yeah, I guess that word applies here."

"What the hell happened? You two could barely stand each other."

She shook her head. "That is so not true. We avoided each other. Because we were attracted to each other. It was safer." She took a swallow of beer, trying to decide how much to tell him. "We had a…we had a one-night stand. Last, I don't know, January, I think it was."

"Are you serious? Paige doesn't do one-night stands."

"No. She doesn't. But I do." CJ twirled the bottle between her hands. "Or at least I did."

"So does this mean, like, you two are dating?"

CJ smiled. "Dating? I think we're past dating. We lived together in Hoganville. Since we've been back, we spend nearly every night together."

"Man…I mean, I suspected, but…*man*." He rubbed his bald head. "So what happened? I mean in Hoganville?"

"Hell, we shared a bed, Ice. It was a one-bedroom cabin. We were pretending to be lovers, pretending to be a couple. And the line got blurred between play and reality." She let out a sigh. "Honestly, I thought that once we got back here, I thought it would end." She met his gaze. "For her, anyway. I'm so out of her league, you know. But I'm in over my head," she admitted.

"Are you in love with her?"

CJ's heart was beating nervously, nearly choking her. Admitting it to herself was one thing. Admitting it to Ice…well, she felt exposed. And vulnerable. And—

"Yes. I'm in love with her."

He laughed quietly. "Damn, CJ. I didn't think I'd ever hear those words come out of your mouth." He shook his head. "You normally don't even remember their names."

"That seems like a lifetime ago. I'd go to the bar, I just wanted to forget. Forget everything. Forget our case, forget my past. Forget everything." She leaned back, trying to relax, trying to get past the nervousness. "I didn't like that person I'd become. But I couldn't seem to shake her. But at Hoganville, I talked and Paige listened. My past...you know some of it. Not all," she said vaguely. "I told Paige all of it. And she didn't judge me. Not once." She took a deep breath. "We became friends...and lovers. I don't have any friends, Ice. You, that's it. And the women from the bar, I wouldn't call them lovers. There wasn't any lovemaking involved," she admitted. "It was just down and dirty sex with a healthy dose of tequila tossed in."

He watched her but didn't say anything.

"I don't know when I fell in love with her, but the game we were playing in Hoganville became real. And now, I'm so scared she's going to break my heart."

"You haven't told her?" he guessed.

She shook her head. "No. I'm afraid to. What if she doesn't feel the same? What if this is just an affair to her?"

"There's only one way to find out, CJ."

She blew out her breath. "I know. And when I work up the nerve to say something, I will." She slid her empty bottle to the middle, joining the others. "You can't say anything, Ice. If Howley finds out, who knows what he'll do."

"I don't think Howley suspects anything," he said.

"Billy?"

"Oh, yeah." He laughed. "So what about the...the gift we sent you guys? I expected you to bust my balls for sending it. You never even mentioned it."

She leaned closer. "The dildo? Oh, yeah, I need to thank you for that, baldy. Paige has a little bit of a naughty side to her."

Ice's ebony skin turned a lovely dark red as he blushed.

CHAPTER NINETEEN

"So what did Howley say?" Billy asked as soon as Paige put her phone down.

"He'll try to find his last whereabouts," she said. "Fourteen years ago—I'd say that's going to be virtually impossible." She glanced at his empty plate. "Good steak?"

"Oh, yeah." He stared at her plate, the remnants of her baked potato and steamed veggies pushed around. "Sorry they didn't have shrimp on the menu."

"I'm not supposed to eat shrimp, remember." She sipped from her glass of water, wishing they'd had a decent bottle of wine on the menu.

"So do we still have to go to the nursing home tomorrow?"

"No. I told him that by everyone's account, Norma Manning hasn't been coherent in over a year. We can try to get an earlier flight out," she said. And she hoped they could. She was ready to get back. One day away and she was already missing CJ. She looked up, feeling Billy watching her. She could tell by the look on his face that he was struggling to say something.

"Can I...can I ask you a personal question?"

Paige raised her eyebrows. Over the years, she'd kept her personal life private, even from Billy. She never told him she was gay. She just assumed he knew, especially when she and CJ played the games they did, flirting with each other incessantly when the guys were around. And they still did that. Now she wondered just what it was he wanted to ask. So she nodded.

"Okay."

He stared at her for the longest time, opening his mouth to speak but closing it before words spilled out. He finally shook his head. "Never mind."

She planted her elbows on the table, resting her chin on her closed fists. She sensed what he wanted to ask. Maybe she was inviting trouble. Or maybe she just wanted to tell someone, so she pushed him a bit.

"What do you want to ask me, Billy?"

It wasn't a question that came from his mouth. "You've been different," he stated.

"What do you mean?"

"Ever since Hoganville. CJ's been different too."

She leaned back slightly, her hands folding together, fingers crossing and uncrossing as she tried to think of an explanation other than they were lovers.

"It was quite an experience, seeing everything we saw. There was so much—"

"That's not what I mean," he said, interrupting her.

She took a deep breath, pausing to sip from her water. She met his gaze head on. "What is it you want to know?"

She saw him visibly swallow and thought she saw a slight blush on his face. Again, he struggled with the words, and she wondered if he was too embarrassed to ask. She could let it go. She could change the subject. He wouldn't push it. But she decided she didn't want to let it go.

"Do you want to know if we took our roles in Hoganville... our undercover assignment...do you want to know if we took that assignment literally?"

"Did you?" he asked quietly.

"Would it matter if we did?" She gave him a quick smile. "You and me, we're the same. We're partners."

He shrugged. "I thought we were. But on this one—"

"That's just kinda how it worked out on this one, Billy. But you and me, we're partners. CJ and Ice, they're partners."

He stared at her, blinking quickly several times. "So does that mean...yes?"

She nodded. "Yes."

He leaned back, his eyes wide. "Wow."

"It doesn't change anything with us, Billy. Just because I'm... I'm having a relationship with CJ outside of work, it doesn't change anything. You and me, we're still the same." She laughed lightly. "There is such a thing as too much togetherness, you know."

Billy smiled too, but it left his face quickly. "Why didn't you tell us?"

"Because we were afraid they'd break up the team. We thought it was safer this way. We were already under a microscope because of what happened at Hoganville. We didn't want to take a chance of anything else coming out and breaking up the team."

Billy nodded and let out a heavy sigh. He rubbed his forehead back and forth. "I think I'm going to need a beer. You?"

She shook her head. "No thanks."

He flagged down their waiter, who took the time to remove their plates.

"So how did it happen? I mean, you know, you two sometimes acted like you didn't even like each other."

"We did pretend that was the case, didn't we?" She looked down at the tablecloth, wondering how much to tell him. "About six months before we left for Hoganville...you remember this case we had? A family was held hostage. The guy set them on fire. He—"

"Oh, God, yeah. With the two kids?"

"Yes. That one. Well, with cases like that, we all know CJ's MO."

Billy laughed as the waiter brought his beer to the table and topped off Paige's water glass. "Yeah. Hit the bar and show up the next day wearing the same clothes. Sex and tequila." He frowned. "That hasn't happened in a while."

"I would hope not." She took a sip from her water. "Anyway, that night, after that case, I...I didn't want to be alone. That night, I needed someone. And I knew CJ did too. So I went to the bar."

His eyes widened. "You slept together then?"

She nodded. "I went to her apartment." She took the napkin that was still in her lap and twisted it in her hand, remembering that night. "I left before dawn. We both got to work that morning and we didn't say a word. In fact, we avoided each other for several weeks. We never said a word about that night."

He nodded. "Yeah, I remember there was a time there when you two didn't talk at all."

"I know. And things eventually got back to normal with us. But we never once mentioned that night. So when we were thrown together in Hoganville, there was a history between us. And there was always an attraction," she admitted. "The teasing, the flirting… it was a game but there was still an underlying truth to it. There in Hoganville, the attraction was impossible to ignore. Everything just sort of blended together—the roles we were supposed to play and what was really happening between us—and we no longer were just pretending to be lovers."

He nodded slowly as he drank from his beer. "So…so what about this guy that your mother introduced as your fiancé? Seth, I believe she said his name was."

Paige nearly blushed. "I'm not exactly out to my mother. Seth and I, well, it was convenient for us to pretend to date. It kept both of our families out of our personal lives."

"So you're not really engaged then?"

Paige laughed lightly. "No. Only in my mother's eyes was there ever the possibility of a wedding."

"So then with CJ, is it serious?"

"We haven't really talked about that."

"What about you? Are you in love with her?"

She held his gaze. "I sometimes think that would be a very dangerous thing…to be in love with CJ Johnston. Don't you?"

He shrugged. "The old CJ, sure. The one who got her relief with one-night stands at the bar, the one who coped that way." He shook his head. "But I don't think that CJ is still around, is she? I haven't seen her."

Paige realized her smile was one of relief. "No, you're right. That CJ hasn't been around in a while now."

"So? Are you in love with her?"

Paige nodded. "Madly."

And later, she realized just how madly when a sleepy-voiced CJ answered her phone.

"I'm sorry. I didn't think you'd be in bed already," she said, double-checking the time.

"No, it's okay. Ice and I went out for beers," CJ said. "I crashed when I got here."

"Where are you?"

"On your side of the bed, smothering your pillow," she said around a yawn.

Paige smiled, picturing CJ doing just that. "Okay. Go back to sleep, sweetheart."

"I love it when you call me sweetheart," CJ murmured.

Paige smiled again, feeling a pleasant tightness in her chest. "Goodnight," she whispered.

"Goodnight, baby."

CHAPTER TWENTY

"I say we talk to Deputy Brady first, then go to the house," Ice said.

CJ nodded. "Yeah, okay. I'm not looking forward to going to the house either, you know."

"But you're going to check the inside and I'm going to check the outside, right? I mean, you're not going to want me inside with you, are you?"

"Oh, sure, baldy. Leave me inside with the ghost all by myself. That sounds fair," she said sarcastically.

"I'm just saying."

"Look, whatever *thing* I felt in that house…well, I don't know what the hell it was but come on…*ghosts*?" She shook her head. "I know I said that it felt real, whatever *it* was. But I can't—not if I want to keep my sanity—say it was a ghost." She wasn't sure if she was trying to convince herself or Ice. "Maybe my imagination got the best of me. So I want to go back there with a clean slate. And an open mind." She glanced at him quickly, then looked back to the highway. "If you don't want to go inside with me, that's okay."

"I don't know why we need to worry about the house anyway," he said. "They found nothing in there fourteen years ago. And the boy, he was left outside on the grounds. The house wasn't disturbed."

"How do we know the house wasn't disturbed? We weren't in it long enough to find out."

"The lock was intact," he reminded her.

"It's a big-ass house. Did we check every window on the ground floor? The windows aren't boarded on the second floor. Is there a tree close by where someone could have climbed up and gotten inside?"

"CJ, if the dudes hit the boy with a car and dumped his body, why the hell would they break into the house?"

"I don't think the house is significant in this case. But it could possibly have been fourteen years ago."

"Why? The case file says the house was undisturbed."

"It said it *appeared* undisturbed." She slowed as they approached their exit in Cleveland. "Think about it. At first, you just have your local LEOs working it. They would all have heard the rumors that it's haunted. You think they're going to go over it in detail? Then they hand it over to the FBI. They've read the original report: haunted house. They talk to the locals in Shady Pines: haunted house. So what do you think they're going to do?"

"Take a quick look inside and call it good," he said.

"Exactly." She turned right, then stopped as the light turned red. "And I still haven't read the entire file. Have you?"

"No."

"Maybe we should start at the beginning." She went through the intersection when the light turned green. "The Sheriff's Department had the case until the third boy went missing, right?"

"Yeah. I think they found Paul Canton's body the next day. That's when the FBI took over the case."

"And one more boy disappeared. What was his name?"

"Simon something, wasn't it?"

"Bradley Simon," she said, remembering. She pulled to a stop in front of the Sheriff's Department. "Why don't we pull their file on it?"

"Couldn't hurt," Ice said as he got out. "By the way, Brady didn't sound too thrilled that we wanted to check on his progress."

"That's assuming there is progress," she said. "We gave him next to nothing, Ice."

"I know. I just don't like the dude."

He walked over to the reception desk and held up his credentials. CJ did the same.

"FBI," he said.

"Yes. I remember you from the other day. You looking for Brady?"

"Yes. Is he in?"

The man motioned with his head. "Down the hall."

CJ followed Ice as he seemed to know where he was going. He stopped at the third office down and knocked on the open door.

"Well, well, the FBI returns. You got a different partner, Freeman?"

Ice glanced at CJ. "Special Agent CJ Johnston."

The smile left Brady's face. "Oh yeah. The drug bust," he said dryly.

"You're welcome," CJ said with a smirk. "Always glad to help."

"We were this close," he said, holding his thumb and index fingers together, "to raiding the place."

"Sorry I beat you to it."

He leaned back with a sweeping motion at his two visitor's chairs. "What can I do for the FBI today?"

CJ and Ice both took a seat. CJ decided to let Ice take the lead. He had a history with Brady, she didn't.

"Any luck finding a car?"

Brady laughed. "Oh, yeah. Thanks for the tip. Dark, two-door car, possibly a sports car of some type. Sure, we've got about a thousand possibilities." He leaned toward his desk and picked up a pen, twirling it around in his fingers. "Besides, you really believe all that? Somebody hit the kid on the forest road and hauled off the body?"

"Why wouldn't we?" CJ asked.

"Because you're hearing it...what? Thirdhand? Besides, most of those kids don't even speak English. The fact that they fed Thompson some bullshit and you're running with it is crazy," he said. "Say we find a dented-up car? Then what? We got no witnesses."

Ice nodded. "I know, man. It was all we got. At least it was something."

"Look, I'll go out and talk to Thompson. Maybe, just maybe, he can get some of those kids to talk to us. If we get something firsthand, something more concrete than a dark car, then maybe we can do something."

"Did you go out to the forest road?" CJ asked.

"Sure. Took a drive out there this morning. I drove four miles up. Thompson's property borders the road for maybe a mile, probably less. Nothing out of the ordinary. No skid marks in the dirt." He shook his head. "Besides, we had rain three days after we found the body. Any marks would have been washed away."

"Well, if you could find out more from Thompson, that would be great," CJ said. "Exact location, perhaps."

"Yeah, sure. I'll go talk to him." Brady sat up closer to his desk and grabbed a stack of papers, straightening them. "You drove all the way up here just to have this chat?"

"No. We're working on something else," Ice said.

"The cold case still?"

"We need the file," CJ said. "The original one, before the FBI took over. You know the one?"

Brady nodded. "Sure do. I remember it well. I was out there."

"You worked the case?" Ice asked.

Brady laughed. "I was green behind the ears back then. They didn't let me do a whole lot. Had the whole town freaked out, I'll tell you that, even if it was at some trailer park." He looked at Ice. "You find anything in that house?"

"No. We're going back today."

He shook his head. "Man, I used to be scared of it. When I was a kid, we lived down on Morgan Cemetery Road, about ten miles or so west of Pecan Grove. Rode the school bus past that house every morning." He glanced at Ice. "They say some people hear voices. Screaming and such. Some of the high school kids go out there at night, wait for a full moon, dare each other to go up to the porch." He lowered his voice. "Some say they saw shadows of people in the windows." He grinned. "Hell, I wouldn't set foot in there."

"We don't expect to find anything," CJ said. "Our boss just wants us to take a peek. Cold case, fourteen years old, doubt anything new will pop up. We'll be out of your hair soon enough."

"Oh, I always enjoy working with the FBI. Learn something new every time." He stood up. "Let me see about fetching that file for you."

* * *

"So you're right. He's a prick," CJ said as she headed toward the Wicker house. "But we got the file."

"Yeah, he's a prick," Ice said. "He's a little too arrogant for my liking."

CJ was quiet for a moment, then spoke what was foremost on her mind. "A lot of people have comments about that damn house, don't they?"

"Yep."

"Notice how it's all secondhand, though? Even Lizzie. 'They say,' or 'some say.' Even the lady we met at the trailer park office. What was her name? Brenda? She said the same thing." CJ glanced at him. "Not a one of them have firsthand knowledge of anything."

"What are you saying?"

"I'm saying, rumors can be rumors, handed down over the years. But if no one—not ever—actually *saw* or *heard* something, then the haunted house thing is going to be more of a joke. Like stories told to little kids to scare them. And then they tell the next group of kids and so on."

"I don't get your point," Ice said. "You said *you* heard something," he reminded her.

"I know. What I'm saying is, for this thing to have been kept alive all these years, then someone had to have seen or heard something at the Wicker house. Someone had to have been in the house and witnessed it."

"What about the Underwoods?"

"Well, Lizzie said that the wife was so spooked living there that she refused to go upstairs. But again, Lizzie heard that from someone."

"Okay, CJ. But what's your point?"

"Hell, baldy, I don't know. Maybe I'm just trying to justify what I heard, what I felt, you know. If there was someone else who had the same experience as me, someone firsthand, not just some story that was passed down, then maybe I could reconcile this as the truth." She smiled, but it was forced. "Because right now, the more I think about it, the more I'm convinced I'm losing my mind."

"So maybe today, you go in there, you don't hear anything, you don't feel anything. It's just a house. An old house that nobody's been in, and we can say it's undisturbed and go on. And we won't have to ever go back again."

She turned onto Morgan Cemetery Road and soon passed Shady Pines Trailer Park. She could feel her apprehension growing as they got closer to the Wicker house. Her pulse was pounding in her ears by the time she pulled up to the gate. Ice got out and opened it, and she pulled inside, her hands tight on the steering wheel.

"Look, no offense, baldy, but I sure wish Paige was here."

He laughed. "Oh, I'm sure you do."

"She would at least come inside with me."

His smile vanished. "I told you, if you need me to go inside with you, I will." He took a deep breath. "I mean, I'll at least stand by the open door."

"There's not a guy with a chain saw in there, you know." Then she grinned. "Lizzie said he used an ax."

The color faded from Ice's face. "Very funny."

She got out. "Just trying to lighten the mood."

"Well, it's not working."

She stood near the truck, her gaze traveling over the windows, hoping—praying—she didn't see any shadows moving about.

"It's so quiet here," Ice said.

"Yeah. Like…like nothing's here. No birds, no squirrels, nothing."

"And the trees around the house," he said. "All dead."

"It's like a dead zone," she said.

"Damn creepy," he said. "They're like guards or something."

"I know what you mean," she said as she moved closer to the house.

He followed her up to the porch. "So what's the plan?"

"Billy checked the kitchen area and Paige took the den. I made it to the second-floor landing," she said, trying not to think about her first trip inside. "If someone broke in, used the house as a holding place for the boys, it stands to reason it would be on the first floor."

"I still think if they went through the house fourteen years ago they would have found something," he said.

"You'd think, right?"

"But we're going in?"

She didn't know what good it would do to have him standing guard at the door. "Why don't you check all the windows on the first floor? See if there's anyplace where someone could have gotten in." She looked around. "I'd say from the back where they couldn't be seen, but it's so grown up around here, you can barely see the house from road."

"Yeah, okay. I can do that."

She smiled at the relief she heard in his voice, but her smile faded as she turned to the door. She paused. Paige and Billy's flight would be landing soon. After they briefed Howley, they would be on their way out here. Maybe she should wait. There was safety in numbers, after all. But no. That would be late afternoon. The shadows would be long. The days were getting shorter and shorter. Dark came earlier here in the deep woods. So she walked up the few remaining steps to the door. She realized her hand was shaking as she tried to fit the key into the lock.

She heard Ice's footsteps fading as he walked away from her, the old porch boards creaking under his weight. She turned, almost calling for him to come back, but he rounded the corner out of sight.

"You're being ridiculous," she muttered as she pushed the door open.

The dank smell of the house was almost familiar. Her eyes immediately flew up the staircase, halfway expecting to see... *something*...there waiting for her. Instead of taking the stairs, she took the short hallway to the left. It was the direction Billy had gone. The beam of her flashlight bounced around the walls, the floor, looking for anything that was disturbed. There were smudges in the dust where she assumed Billy had walked. She rolled her eyes as she realized he had only taken a few steps inside before retracing his route. She went farther in, finding herself in the kitchen. It had obviously been remodeled over the years with somewhat modern fixtures in the sink. The stove, however, appeared ancient.

She paused. Listening. Waiting. She was a bit surprised that she felt nothing in there, *heard* nothing. Perhaps it had been her imagination after all.

Past the kitchen was a closed door. She went to it and turned the handle. It was locked. She tilted her head, studying the doorknob. It was obviously locked from the other side.

"Odd. So what's on the other side?" she asked in a whisper.

She turned, glancing at the outside-facing wall, seeing streams of light sneaking inside from breaks and cracks in the boards that covered the windows. Nothing big enough to allow entry from the outside.

She went back to the entryway, stopping up short. She'd left the front door open. It was now closed. She immediately opened it again, letting in more light. She glanced into the den where Paige had looked but decided to skip that for now. She walked along the edge of the staircase, refusing to look up. Instead, she walked along the base of it. There was a small door under the staircase—a storage closet. Her hand was trembling as she opened it.

The inside was empty. She closed the door quietly and continued on. She came to another closed door. This one was not locked. It opened into a large room. It appeared to be a formal dining room as a massive table took up nearly half of the space. It was an interior room with no windows, making it pitch-black inside. Her flashlight did little to push at the shadows. At the far end was another door. It too was closed. She headed toward it even as the hair on the back of her neck stood up. She touched the doorknob but couldn't bring herself to open it. She feared that…what? That something was waiting for her on the other side?

Suddenly she was surrounded by cold air.

"Open it."

She whipped her head around, not knowing if the words were echoing in the room…or in her mind.

Just as quickly, the cold air vanished, replaced again by the stale, warm air of the closed-up house. She stared at the knob, still afraid to open it. Her palm was sweating and the flashlight felt slippery in her hand. She paused to wipe her palm on her jeans, then took a deep breath before pushing the door open.

It was simply an empty room. Another interior room, but much smaller than the dining room. With the flashlight, she scanned the walls. They were bare, as was the floor. She guessed the room to be no bigger than eight feet wide, maybe ten feet deep. A large closet, perhaps. Nothing looked disturbed, although there were scrape marks gouged in the wooden floor. She bent down, running her fingers over them. They were smooth and worn, evidence of something repeatedly being scraped across the area.

She heard a noise behind her and she turned her head, just in time to see the door swinging shut. She jumped up, stopping it before it closed. Her hand was shaking—her whole body was shaking—and she went back into the dining room, thankful that door was still open. As she was about to leave, the door to the small room slammed shut. She swore her heart stopped beating as she stared at it in disbelief. Her fear got the best of her and she nearly ran from the room.

"Up here."

Her eyes followed the length of the staircase, but she didn't move. The front door was closed again.

"Come play."

"Jesus…God," she murmured, again not knowing if the words were spoken out loud or only in her mind. She was shocked to find herself heading up the darkened staircase. On the sixth step, she heard it. Running. She looked behind her, then hugged the wall as running footsteps pounded on the stairs. As before, she felt a breeze as they passed. She took two more steps up, expecting to feel cold air at any moment. Instead, it was screaming she heard. A high-pitched child's voice.

"Daddy, no. Daddy, no. Daddy, no."

She heard a slap, and her face stung as if she'd been the recipient. Another scream and she stared at the top of the landing as she saw the railings bend against the weight of something.

"No, Daddy!"

CJ heard the crash and breaking of bones, and she leaned over the railing, expecting to find a body lying on the floor. Lizzie's words came back to her. "One of the little girls fell from the second-floor landing."

She shook her head, trying to convince herself she'd not just heard that, trying to convince herself it was only her imagination. The cold air that surrounded her told her otherwise.

"Come play with us."

The light was bouncing along the stairs, her hand was shaking so. Even then, she managed to take another two steps up. She felt hands on her back, urging her on. She tried to swallow, but her mouth was dry. She was having a hard time breathing.

"Up here."

Her lips trembled as she tried to speak. "Who...who are you?"

Child's laughter was the only reply. Suddenly the laughter stopped, replaced with crying. That too stopped as quickly as it had begun. She felt like she was in a trance as she took the final two steps to the landing. It was brighter up there, the windows on the second floor not being boarded up like those below. It was almost with a sense of relief that she went to a window, looking out on the unkempt grounds, the weeds having overtaken what shrubs remained, the woods encroaching ever closer to the house. She looked at the floor, seeing smudge marks in the dust, as if someone else had been standing at the window before her.

She turned quickly, feeling eyes on her. She knew without a doubt she was not alone.

"Who's there?" she asked, staring down the dark hallway, trying to see through the shadows.

She felt a wisp of cold air and a soft hand brush her cheek. She pulled away from it.

"Goodbye for now."

CJ blinked several times, shaking her head, trying to chase the words from her mind.

"Come back soon."

CJ looked around, convinced the words were spoken out loud, not just in her mind. Her heart was hammering in her chest, and she nearly screamed when the front door opened. But it was only Ice standing in the threshold.

"CJ?"

"Up...up here," she said, finding her voice. She took several deep breaths, no longer feeling like she was being watched. No longer feeling like she wasn't alone up on the second floor. She was. How she knew that, she couldn't be certain. But whatever had been there…*if* anything had really been there…it was gone. She relaxed. It was just a house again.

"You okay?"

She nodded. She turned her flashlight off, then retraced her steps, albeit much faster than her trip up. The first time she'd been in the house, she'd been terrified. Now? Someone…*something*… was trying to talk to her. Terrified didn't *begin* to cover it.

"Billy called. They're on their way. Should be here within the hour."

"Okay. Good." She took a deep breath. "You find anything?"

"Some missing boards on a few windows. Not big enough for entry. A lot of the windows are broken," he said. "I did find one oddity. There's a window in the back that was broken from the inside."

She raised her eyebrows. "You sure?"

He nodded. "Glass is on the porch." Ice tilted his head as he studied her. "You okay?"

"I'm not really sure."

"What happened? You see the ghost?" he teased.

She followed him out onto the porch, the sun hiding behind the tall pines in the back, casting shadows in the front. She leaned against one of the wooden pillars and closed her eyes for a moment. "CJ?"

When she opened them, Ice was watching her intently, his smile long gone. She nodded.

"There's something in the house."

He took a step away from her. "What…what are you talking about?"

She started to tell him what had happened, what she'd *heard*, but stopped. She decided to wait for Paige and Billy. It was a story she didn't want to have to tell more than once.

"Let's wait."

"Wait?"

"I want a drink," she said, heading for her truck. "Where are they meeting us?"

"At the hotel."

"Good. Then let's find a bar. I could use a shot of tequila," she said.

Ice hurried after her. "What do you mean, something's in the house?"

"Either that or I'm losing my goddamn mind," she muttered as she got into the truck.

CHAPTER TWENTY-ONE

After Ice's cryptic phone call urging them to hurry—CJ was apparently "freaked out" after being inside the house again—Paige bravely drove five miles over the speed limit, something she rarely did. When they exited the highway, they bypassed the hotel, instead heading to the local bar Ice had given them directions to, three blocks away.

"Wonder what happened," Billy said.

"I imagine it was similar to the first time," Paige said.

She parked beside CJ's truck. It was late afternoon, too early for the after-work crowd. There were only three other vehicles in the parking lot. She really didn't know what state of mind she'd find CJ in, but the calm, lazy smile she was greeted with wasn't it. The four empty beer bottles and two shot glasses could have something to do with it.

"Better go easy on the tequila, tiger," she said.

"Oh, man, am I glad to see you." CJ glanced at Billy. "You too, Billy Boy," she added.

"Sure."

They pulled out chairs and joined them at the table. Ice was strangely quiet, just picking at the label on his beer bottle. Paige met CJ's gaze across the table, realizing just how much she'd missed her. The look in CJ's eyes said the same.

"So I understand you went to the house," she said. CJ's expression changed immediately.

"Yeah. I went inside the damn house again," CJ said. "Baldy here checked the outside. He found a broken window."

"A lot of the windows were broken," Billy reminded them.

"Not from the inside out," Ice said.

"Did you see where someone could have gotten inside?"

"Nope."

Paige looked at CJ. "What happened?"

CJ swallowed nervously. "Something's…something is in there," she said quietly. "It—she—talked to me."

Ice sat up straighter. "Come on, man. Don't do this to me."

"Sorry, baldy. I wish to hell I hadn't heard anything," CJ said. She met Paige's eyes. "Doors closing on their own. I heard a child begging her daddy not to hit her. Then he pushed her—or she fell—over the railing, second floor." CJ took a drink of her beer. "Felt the cold again. Felt hands touching me. And it talked to me. 'Come play with us.'"

"Seriously?" Billy asked.

"You think I'm making this shit up?" CJ snapped at him. She then took a deep breath. "I started in the kitchen. There was a locked door at the far end. I don't know if it was a closet or another room or what. Locked tight. So I went back to the entryway. The front door was closed. I opened it again. Past the stairs, there's a large dining room. The door was closed, but it wasn't locked. An interior room. Pitch-black. Against the far wall was a door. It was closed too." She paused, taking another sip of beer. "That's when I felt…well, felt like I wasn't alone. I touched the doorknob but was afraid to turn it. That's when I felt cold air and a voice said 'open it.'"

"Jesus," Ice whispered.

"No shit," CJ said as she tried to smile. "Anyway, I opened it. It was another interior room. A large closet, maybe," she said. "It was empty. Some odd marks on the floor caught my attention. While

I was squatting down looking at them, the door started closing. I caught it before it shut. I got the hell out of there. When I was leaving the dining room, I heard the door slam shut behind me."

"Okay, I'm going to need a beer," Billy said. He looked at Paige. "You?"

"Yes, please."

"Make it another round," Ice said.

They were silent while Billy went to the bar. CJ met her gaze and gave her a weak smile. Paige returned it but said nothing.

"Nice and cold," Billy said, setting a beer in front of each of them.

"Thank you," Paige said. She looked again at CJ. "What happened next?"

"I went back to the entryway. The front door was closed again. I went upstairs."

"Why the hell would you go upstairs again?" Billy asked.

"Because it told me to," CJ said.

"Jesus," Ice muttered again.

"It was like before. I heard running on the stairs. That's when I heard the child crying, begging her daddy not to hit her. I heard the screams, I heard the slaps. It was like it was happening right in front of me," CJ said, her voice quiet and calm. "I could see the boards at the top of the railing bend, heard the scream as she fell. Heard her hit the ground below."

Paige noticed Billy's hand was shaking as he took a drink. Ice had a death grip on his beer bottle. CJ had yet to take a drink.

"I was going to turn around and get the hell out, but that voice," CJ said. "I don't know if I heard it or if it was just in my mind. She kept saying 'up here' and 'come play with us.'"

"A child's voice?"

"Not so much a child. A young girl," CJ said. "I went up to the second-floor landing. Up there, the windows aren't boarded up. At the first window, there were prints—smudge marks—on the floor where someone had been standing, looking out."

"Jesus...*man*," Ice murmured.

"Then it was like...like she knew Ice was about to open the door. I felt a touch on my face and she said 'goodbye for now.' Then before Ice opened the door, she said 'come back soon.'" CJ finally picked up her beer bottle and took a long drink. "When Ice opened the door, I nearly screamed like a girl," CJ said with a shaky laugh.

"Okay, let's talk this out logically," Paige said.

"Logically? I'm hearing goddamn ghosts," CJ said loudly. "How can we talk *logically*?"

Paige smiled, trying not to take offense to CJ's outburst. "Well, everyone said the house was haunted. Why *wouldn't* we hear—see—things out of the ordinary?"

"You really believe it's haunted?" Billy asked.

"What does haunted mean?" Paige asked. "Are we talking about what we read in stories or scary movies? Or are we talking about real life? There are people who devote their lives to filming and recording apparitions and images," she said.

"Ghost hunters," CJ supplied.

"Yes. Some people have the gift of seeing—feeling—the presence of...well, spirits, if you will," she said. Then she smiled. "Although I don't know that I would exactly call it a gift."

"You got that right, baby," CJ said, some of her normal swagger returning.

"That's all well and good, but what the hell does it have to do with our cold case?" Ice said. "I mean, the house wasn't even supposed to be a player in this."

"Maybe the boys are in the house," CJ said.

"Fourteen years ago, they checked the house," he said. "There were no breaches, nothing disturbed. No evidence that anyone had been in the house in years."

"And I go back to a point I made earlier," CJ said. "How well did they check the house? It's supposed to be haunted. You think they went through every nook and cranny?" She shook her head. "I think they just did a drive-by."

"You don't know that," Ice said.

"Yeah? Then why is there a locked door in the kitchen? Fourteen years ago, you're looking for missing boys, wouldn't a locked door demand that someone open it?"

"She has a point," Billy said.

CJ turned to Billy. "Like you. You checked the kitchen, right? Did you find the locked door?"

He shook his head. "I just kinda looked around. Nothing looked disturbed."

"Exactly. And my guess is they did the same thing fourteen years ago. It's locked up. It's dusty. There are spiderwebs. And nothing looked disturbed." CJ looked at her. "Did you find anything in Midland?"

"We found that Herbert Krause was never there."

"What do you mean?"

"When Edie showed up, she was alone. No one ever saw her husband. They were told they'd divorced."

"Didn't interview her mother, though," Billy added. "Nursing home with dementia. We didn't see the point."

"So now what?" CJ asked.

"Howley's running a search again, but he doesn't think anything will pop up. We already know his Social Security number hasn't had any hits on it since they allegedly left Cleveland for Midland," she said.

"So he just disappeared?" Ice asked.

"Looks that way."

"I think we need to officially talk to Edith Krause," CJ said.

"I agree," Paige said. "Based on what Lizzie said about her being pretty much a recluse, I did mention to Howley about possibly getting a warrant. If we do, we can interview her at the sheriff's office."

"Good idea." CJ slid her bottle to the middle of the table. "And now I'm starving. Are you guys hungry?"

"Please don't subject me to another steak house," Paige said. "How about Chinese?"

"I hate Chinese," Ice groaned. "How about Mexican?"

"I'm in," CJ said.

"Me too," Billy agreed.

Paige nodded. "Mexican it is."

CHAPTER TWENTY-TWO

CJ closed the door, then leaned against it, a smile playing on her face. Paige stood in the center of the room, her pressed slacks still looking as immaculate as if she'd just put them on.

"I missed you."

Paige smiled. "Did you?"

"We didn't have a proper goodbye, remember?" She shoved off the door, going toward her. "Didn't really have a proper hello."

Paige lifted her arms, circling CJ's neck and pulling her close. Her kiss was slow and very thorough, hinting at what was to come.

"I missed you too," Paige murmured as her lips trailed to CJ's ear. "Billy knows about us, by the way."

CJ laughed. "Good. Because so does Ice."

Paige pulled back slightly. "Is it a problem?"

"No. He suspected. He came right out and asked. I didn't want to lie to him."

Paige nodded. "It's almost a relief that they know. And I'm sure they're discussing it right now."

CJ pulled the blouse from Paige's waistband, touching warm skin. "I'm just thankful we don't have adjoining rooms again." She unbuttoned the blouse quickly and shoved it off, but Paige stilled her hands as she was about to unclasp her bra.

"Why is it that I'm shirtless and you're still fully clothed?"

CJ stepped away from her and ripped her T-shirt over her head. "There. Better?"

Paige's smile was wicked. "Almost."

CJ's pulse sprang to life at the look in Paige's eyes. She removed her bra, watching Paige's gaze travel over her breasts. In an instant, Paige's hands covered them, her thumbs raking across her nipples.

"I love your breasts," Paige whispered against her lips.

CJ moaned quietly, letting Paige do as she may. Her mouth opened as Paige's tongue rubbed across her lower lip before slipping inside. With her eyes closed, she slid her hands up Paige's back, expertly releasing the clasp on her bra. They separated enough to allow her to remove it, then Paige pulled her close again, both sighing into a kiss as their breasts met.

"I love the way you kiss," Paige murmured.

CJ smiled. "I thought you loved my breasts."

"I love…a lot of things about you."

Their eyes held, and CJ's chest tightened, her heart leaping into her throat. Sometimes when Paige looked at her like that, it all made sense. It wasn't an affair. It wasn't a fling. There was nothing for her to fear.

But fear she did. Fear that Paige would leave her heart bruised and broken. Fear that one day Paige was going to wake up and realize CJ wasn't good enough for her. CJ and her trailer park past and her abusive father. That just didn't mesh with Paige's privileged upbringing. God, Paige wasn't even out to her parents. When that happened—which could be soon—they'd take one look at her and know she'd grown up on the wrong side of the tracks. They'd—

"What's wrong?"

CJ blinked several times, focusing again on Paige. She shook her head. "Nothing."

Paige searched her eyes and CJ tried to look away, but Paige's light touch on her cheek kept her still. Paige's eyes softened and in that moment, CJ was convinced Paige could read her very mind.

"I'm going to make love to you," Paige said softly.

Those words left her breathless. "I'm sorry," CJ whispered.

Paige's smile was so sweet it nearly brought her to tears.

"What are you sorry for, sweetheart?"

CJ took Paige's hand and brought it up, lightly kissing her fingers. "I'm sorry I didn't grow up in a normal family, in a normal neighborhood. I wish—"

"Don't," Paige said, stopping her. "Don't you dare apologize for who your parents were, for what your father did to you. Those things were out of your control. But you grew into a beautiful... smart, caring woman. You're a *good* person, CJ. And I happen to like that person very, very much."

CJ let Paige pull her into her arms and she felt safe. Although safe from what, she wasn't really sure.

"You're so strong sometimes, CJ. And sometimes, like now, you let your vulnerabilities show," Paige said. "I love that about you."

CJ pulled out of her arms and cupped her face with both hands. She pulled her closer, realizing just how much of a hold Paige had on her heart. She kissed her slowly but deeply, savoring the simple softness of her lips. When the kiss ended, she saw a hint of tears in Paige's eyes. She didn't question it.

"Let's make love," Paige whispered. "I need that right now."

"Yes. Me too."

CHAPTER TWENTY-THREE

"Not the damn house again," Ice said. "Are you insane or what?"

CJ grinned at him over the brim of her coffee cup. "It's been suggested."

"Why don't we pick up Edith Krause first?" he asked as he used the last of his toast to wipe up the egg on his plate.

"It's supposed to rain this morning," Paige said. "Maybe we should save the house for later."

"What? You don't want to be inside a haunted house during a thunderstorm?" CJ asked.

"I know I don't," Billy said.

"Okay, fine with me. Let's go talk to Edith then." She was actually pleased to put off the house for a few hours. She wasn't thrilled about the possibility of hearing voices in her head.

"You're in a good mood this morning."

CJ raised her eyebrows. "What are you saying? That I'm not normally?"

"Well," Ice said, sliding his gaze to Paige. "Paige is back." His grin turned into a laugh. "I'm just guessing you might have had a good time last night."

CJ felt a slight blush on her face. "Really? You're brave enough to go there?"

He and Billy laughed, and she glanced over at Paige, who was sporting her own blush. CJ laughed too, hoping to give Ice a taste of his own medicine.

"Okay, yeah. We had a good time last night, baldy. A *really* good time. Be thankful you weren't in the next room. You'd have been pounding on the wall."

This time it was Ice and Billy who were blushing like schoolgirls.

"Now, are you guys ready to go talk to Edith? Or do you want some details about last night?"

"No, no. We're good," Ice said.

"Good. Then let's go." She stood, leaving a five-dollar bill for her tip.

Later, when they pulled into Edith Krause's driveway, it appeared they would have to put off talking to her too. Her car was nowhere to be seen.

"Man, this is a dump," Ice said.

"Yeah. Shady Pines Trailer Park has seen better days," CJ agreed. "I'll go see if Lizzie's seen her."

The misting rain was falling harder and she jogged up to the door, knocking quickly. With the cooler, damp air, Lizzie had the door closed as well as the screen.

"Oh, my, Agent Johnston, you'll catch your death standing out in that rain," Lizzie fussed as she opened the door. "Come in, come in."

"Sorry to bother you so early," CJ apologized.

"No bother. Not for the FBI." Lizzie gazed out to the road. "Where's your pretty blond friend?"

"She's in the car. Our partners are with us today," she said.

"Oh? I thought you two were partners," Lizzie said as she shuffled back to her chair. "Would you like some coffee?"

"No thanks. I just wanted to see if you knew where Edith might be."

"Edie? No. Her car was gone when I got up this morning," Lizzie said. "It was the strangest thing. I told you she didn't talk to me. Not really," she said as she settled into her chair. "But she came over yesterday morning, full of questions."

"Questions about what?"

"Said she'd seen you two over here a couple of times. Then someone who looked like your Paige there was all the way out in Midland asking questions about Edie and her husband."

"Someone called her?"

"I believe one of her mother's neighbors," Lizzie said. "Anyway, I told her the FBI was here asking about the boys." Lizzie smiled shyly. "I hope that was okay. You didn't say it was a secret or anything."

CJ smiled at her. "No, it's okay. We wanted to talk to her, though. Do you have any idea where she might have gone?"

Lizzie shook her head. "It's unusual for her to be gone this early in the morning."

"You mentioned before that she had family here. A cousin, at least. Do you know where she lives?"

"Donna Parks was her name. Couldn't tell you where she moved to when she left here," Lizzie said. "But why are you interested in Edie? Is she in trouble?"

CJ smiled. "No, ma'am. We just have some questions for her. It seems we're having a hard time finding Herbert," she said.

"Well, they said he ran off with that young woman." Lizzie's lips pursed as she shook her head. "Still don't know what a pretty young thing would see in him."

"Actually, we can't find any evidence that Herbert ever made it to Midland," she said. "But you saw them driving off together, right?"

"Oh, yes. Practically the middle of the night. I got up to get some water." She pointed to the kitchen window. "Saw them get in the car and drive off. Like I said, a few days later, her cousin moved in."

CJ nodded. "Okay. Now Lizzie, do you still have the cards we gave you?"

"Of course. I put them right there by the phone," she said.

"Good. When Edie comes back, would you call us?"

"Oh, I will," she said with a nod. "You're the FBI." She leaned forward in her chair, her voice low. "Are you sure she's not in any trouble?"

CJ smiled. "She's not in trouble. But I'd appreciate it if you didn't let her know we're looking for her. Can you keep that a secret?"

"You have my word."

"Thank you. I'll let you get back to your coffee now." CJ shook her head when Lizzie started to rise. "No need to get up. I'll see myself out."

"You come back anytime now."

CJ closed the door quietly behind her and ran out into the rain. Three sets of eyes looked at her expectantly when she got back inside the truck.

"She was gone this morning when Lizzie got up." She glanced at Paige. "Said Edie came by yesterday asking questions about us. Apparently one of her mother's old neighbors let her know that you guys were up there asking about her and her husband."

"I bet it was Mrs. Axel," Billy said. "She was a nosy woman. She asked us more questions than we did her."

A loud rumble of thunder nearly shook the truck.

"Storm's picking up," Ice said.

"Yeah. A great time for a stroll through the Wicker house," she said as she started the truck and drove away.

CHAPTER TWENTY-FOUR

Thunder still rumbled overhead when they pulled to a stop in front of the house. It looked even more ominous with the gray clouds and falling rain.

"Damn, but it looks spooky," Billy said in a soft voice.

Paige had to agree with him. She met CJ's eyes in the rearview mirror. Last night, after they'd made love, they'd talked. They had piled the pillows against the headboard and sat up, both still naked. CJ didn't try to hide the fact that she was disturbed about what had happened in the house. She didn't understand it. Paige had tried to ease her mind, but after CJ had told her in more detail about what had occurred, Paige had been nearly as frightened as CJ.

"We'll all stay together," Paige said. It was a plan they'd come up with last night. "We'll search the house as a team. No one goes off by themselves."

"I'm all for that," Billy said.

"I can't believe you guys are making me go in there," Ice muttered.

"Safety in numbers, baldy." CJ grinned at him. "Besides, whatever the hell is in the house is talking to me, not you."

"If anything, and I mean *anything* out of the ordinary happens, I'm right back outside," he warned.

A loud crack of thunder made them all jump.

"You'll be fine," Paige said. "We'll all be fine." She again met CJ's eyes and gave her a smile. She was surprised when CJ returned it.

They got out and ran through the rain and to the porch. Ice held the key out and Billy took it, quickly unlocking the deadbolt. He pushed the door open slowly, the hinges squeaking as it swung inward. She saw CJ take a deep breath and knew she was nervous. Paige decided she would offer to go first.

"Follow me," she said, walking inside with her flashlight turned on. They'd decided last night that they would check out the kitchen again and see if they could get the locked door opened.

"Oh, *man*, I don't want to do this," Ice whispered.

"I'll be right beside you," Billy said.

"Yeah, that's comforting," Ice replied dryly.

Paige heard CJ laugh quietly behind her. It was a nervous laugh, but a laugh nonetheless. She led the way into the kitchen and all of their flashlights were bouncing around the room. With the dark clouds outside, there was very little light sneaking in through the cracks in the boarded windows. CJ touched her arm, pointing her light at the closed door. It was on an interior wall and Paige thought perhaps it might be to a pantry. Of course, why would a pantry door be locked from the inside?

"Do we need to worry about prints?" Billy asked as Paige was about to touch the knob.

"I've already touched it," CJ said.

"Can they lift prints after fourteen years?" Billy asked.

"Depends," Ice said. "Inside a house that hasn't been disturbed? Probably."

"Yeah. We had a case once where they found prints on a leather holster that had been in an attic for twenty years," CJ said.

Paige tried to turn the knob but it was indeed locked. She tapped on the door, surprised that it was a solid door.

"It opens outward," Billy said. "We'd have a hell of a time kicking it in."

"It'd be easier to just shoot the lock off, don't you think," CJ said.

"Of course that's what *you* would do," he said.

"Okay. Let's leave it for now," Paige suggested. She leaned closer to CJ. "How are you? Do you...feel anything?"

"No. Nothing."

"That's good," Ice said. "Right?"

"Yeah. That's great," CJ said. "Maybe they don't like crowds."

"They?"

"They. It. Whatever," she said.

"I checked the den pretty thoroughly last time," Paige said. "You checked down here already."

CJ sighed. "Yeah, I know. That means we need to go upstairs."

"*Jesus*," Ice hissed. "I'm not sure I can do it."

"We stay together," CJ said. "It'll be fine."

They walked to the bottom of the stairs, all of them staring at the closed front door. The door they'd left wide open.

"So it doesn't like the door to be left open," CJ said.

They all turned and looked up the length of the staircase, their lights bouncing across the steps, the wall, the ceiling.

"You want me to go first?" Paige asked.

"No. Let me," CJ said. "Stay behind me. Single file."

Ice turned to Billy. "Please don't make me be last."

"I'll do it. You follow Paige."

CJ went up two steps, then paused as if listening. She went up two more and stopped again. Paige followed, staying two steps behind her. She could feel Ice practically on her back. She glanced back at him.

"You okay?"

"No."

She smiled and walked up another step. Suddenly CJ turned, her eyes wide. Then she pressed herself against the wall, as if moving out of the way of something. *The running feet.*

"CJ?"

CJ looked back at her. "You didn't hear it?"

Paige shook her head.

"Kids running up the stairs," CJ said.

"Oh, *man*," Ice murmured.

CJ went up another two steps. Paige could see the flashlight shaking in her hand.

"Girl crying," CJ said. "Like before. Begging her daddy not to hit her."

Paige could feel the fingers of fear crawling over her skin, though she heard nothing of what CJ was describing. Then CJ jumped slightly, her gaze traveling down the staircase railing to the floor.

"He pushed her," CJ said quietly. "He picked her up and threw her to the floor down there," she said, pointing.

"Okay, that's it. I can't do it," Ice said with a shaky voice. He nearly pushed Billy aside as he fled back down the stairs and ripped the front door open.

"Let him go," CJ said.

Paige looked at Billy. "You okay?"

"Yeah. It's freaky crazy, but yeah, I'm okay." He leaned closer. "Are you sure CJ's okay, though? I mean, this is crazy stuff."

"You can't whisper for shit, Billy," CJ said. "Yeah, I know it's crazy. How the hell do you think *I* feel?"

"Sorry."

They followed CJ again. She was walking slower now, one step at a time. Paige continued to stay two steps behind her. CJ tilted her head as if listening to someone.

"Yeah, right," CJ said.

Paige's eyebrows shot up, and she glanced at Billy who shrugged.

"Yeah right, what?" she asked.

CJ glanced down quickly, then back up. "I wasn't talking to you."

"Oh, *shit*," Billy whispered.

Paige had to agree. Then CJ nearly jogged up the final three steps, her light flashing down the dark hallway. Paige and Billy hurried after her. CJ went into the hallway, passing the stairway up to the third floor. There were three full-sized doors in the hallway. Bedrooms, she assumed. Along the wall were two half-doors. A linen closet, perhaps. She was surprised when CJ opened them and peered inside.

"What is it?" she asked.

"Come look," CJ said. "It's some kind of a chute, I think."

They all looked inside. It was indeed a shaft that veered to the left and dropped out of sight.

"For what? Like garbage or something?" Billy asked.

"Maybe laundry," Paige suggested.

"Here, hold my light," CJ said as she handed it to her. She hopped up, sitting on the edge.

"What the hell are you doing?"

But CJ looked past her, staring at the wall behind her. Or perhaps staring at *something*. Then she blinked several times, finally focusing on Paige.

"Okay, I'm going to turn around in here. I want to see where this goes. Hand me my light once I get situated."

"Why do you want to see where it goes?"

"I'm not sure."

"Oh, God. We're not alone, are we?"

"No."

Billy whipped his head around, his light flashing along the walls of the hallway. "I...I don't see anything."

"Be thankful," CJ said.

Before she even got turned around completely, she shot down the chute, her scream echoing off the walls of the shaft as she fell.

"*CJ!*" Paige yelled, looking into the shaft but seeing nothing but blackness.

CHAPTER TWENTY-FIVE

CJ covered her head with her arms when she felt herself falling out of the chute. She landed in a heap, her shoulder taking most of the brunt of it, but her head hit the ground nonetheless. She opened her eyes, seeing nothing but total darkness. She sat up slowly and rubbed the back of her head, feeling a knot forming where she'd hit it.

"I thought you said you wouldn't harm me," she muttered. She got no response. For that, she was thankful. She decided the next time someone—*something*—told her to open up a door, she was definitely going to ignore them. Or better yet…run.

She got into a sitting position but no more. It was pitch black, and she was afraid to move. She held her hand in front of her face but couldn't see it. Panic was about to set in. She held her arms out to her sides and moved them in a circle. She nearly screamed when she hit something.

"Paige?" she yelled. "Can you hear me?"

"CJ? Are you okay?" Paige yelled back.

CJ ignored her question. "Will you please toss a flashlight down the chute?"

"What?"

She heard something behind her and she turned toward the sound. But it was like she was in a vacuum, she could see nothing. She was nearly afraid to breathe. Her chest tightened with the tension and fear she was feeling.

"CJ?" Paige called again. "Can you hear me? Where are you?"

"Flashlight," she yelled back.

"What?"

"Jesus," she muttered. She fumbled in her jeans, finding her cell phone. The light was bright when she turned it on, but her hands were shaking so badly she needed three tries to put in her passcode. It rang twice before Paige answered.

"Are you okay?" Paige asked, fear in her voice.

"I don't know. I'm afraid to move. I can't see a thing."

"Where are you?"

"Hell if I know. But it's so dark I can't see my hand in front of my face. So, can you toss my flashlight down the chute?"

"Okay. Doing it now."

CJ heard the flashlight as it bounced along the chute, but she had no idea where the chute was. She finally saw the beam of light to her left and she ducked just in time. The flashlight landed with a thud beside her. She snatched it up like a lifeline, shining it around her in all directions, expecting to see demons or monsters waiting to attack.

"CJ?"

She picked up her phone again. "Thanks." She paused. "Please don't leave me here alone."

"I'm not going anywhere. Can you tell where you are?"

CJ looked around, seeing old pipes running up the wall. There were two large tubs and a couple of tables that she could see. She found the door and hurried to it. There was no doorknob. She pushed at all corners, but it didn't budge.

"I don't know. Could be an old laundry room. There's plumbing. There's a large door but no doorknob. It won't open," she said. "I'm obviously back on the first floor." She stood, then shone the light upward, finding the chute. "Can you see my light?"

"No."

CJ blew out her breath. When she was falling, she had no sense of how many curves there were. She was too busy screaming. She shook her head. *Screaming like a girl.*

"Look, we're coming back downstairs," Paige said. "Knock on the walls with the flashlight or something once we get down there."

CJ looked around the floor. It appeared to be an earthen floor, which seemed odd if this were indeed a laundry room. She went to the far wall, feeling along the surface. It felt like concrete. Cinder blocks, she assumed. It looked like there was writing on the wall. She stepped back away from it, getting a broader view. Stick figures. A man and a woman. Two kids. A dog or maybe a cat. She stared at the words below written in child-like scribble. *Help me.* She tilted her head. Chalk. It was written in chalk.

She walked over to the tables, flashing her light around. There was an overturned chair. She moved a table away from the wall, searching along the floor. She stopped when she saw what appeared to be a small white tube.

"Okay. We're in the kitchen now," Paige said.

CJ knelt down, a frown on her face as she picked it up.

"Jesus Christ," she murmured. "It *is* chalk."

"What?"

"Chalk."

"What are you talking about?"

"There's…there's a piece of chalk here. I've got writing on the wall. White chalk."

"White chalk?"

"You know, they found chalk on Paul Canton's belt."

"That's right. I forgot. But let's first find you, okay? Can you bang on the wall? The door?"

"There's nothing in here to use, but the walls appear to be cinder block. Any banging will have to be on the door." She went back to it and made a fist, knocking hard against it. "You hear?"

"No. Hang on. Billy's going to get Ice."

"Good luck getting him back inside."

"He'll do it for you," Paige insisted. Then CJ heard a quiet laugh. "We're doing this the hard way, you know."

"Meaning?"

"It'd be simpler if you gave us your GPS coordinates, wouldn't it."

CJ laughed too. "Our phones. Yeah, I never even thought of it. Okay, hang on," she said as she put Paige on speaker. "Can you still hear me?"

"Yes."

She fumbled with the GPS app, trying to remember how to use the damn thing. "My position," she murmured, tapping on it. Her GPS coordinates popped up immediately. "Okay, it's got a share mode. I'll text it to you."

That was almost too easy, she thought, as Paige got it just a few seconds later.

"Okay, we're back at the entryway," Paige said.

"Is Ice with you?"

"Yes, he's here. Now we're in the dining room. Can you knock again?"

She did. "Hear me?"

"Yes. Faintly."

CJ knocked again, using the end of her flashlight this time.

"Okay, it sounds like it's coming from behind the door."

"The door in the dining room? That opened into a huge closet, remember. I don't think there was another door in there," she said.

"Hang on," Paige said. "The door is locked."

"No way. I opened it. I went inside," she said. "Remember, it slammed shut after I left the room."

"Well, it's locked now."

CJ leaned her head against the wall, slowly shaking it. "Okay, so you're going to break it down then, right?"

"I think you're missing the point," Paige said.

"The point is, I'm locked in here."

"Well, there's that. But unless your ghost is locking doors, then the point is, someone's been in the house."

"Oh. That point." CJ swore she heard a noise behind her, and she spun around, her light moving back and forth, side to side. Nothing.

"You okay?"

"I thought I heard something," she said. "Please get me out of here."

"Okay, tiger, hang on. Ice is going to kick the door in."

CJ clung to her flashlight, noticing the light was getting dimmer. *Of course it is.* And even though she was prepared for it, she still jumped when she heard Ice slam into the outer door. It took three tries before she heard it burst open.

"We're in," Paige said. "But you were right. There's not another door."

CJ made a fist and pounded on her door. "Hear?"

"Yes. But it's just a wall on our side," Paige said.

CJ leaned her head against the door, trying to think.

"The floor."

The unexpected voice made her scream.

"What's wrong?" Paige asked frantically.

"Nothing," CJ said, her heart beating almost painfully in her chest. She took a deep breath. "Okay, look at the floor. Remember I told you about some marks. Like scraping."

"Yes. I see them."

"Something sliding across the floor repeatedly, right?"

"Yes."

"So feel along the wall. There's got to be a trigger somewhere for this door. I'll check my side too."

Tucking the phone against her shoulder and ear, CJ ran her hand along the wall next to the door, feeling for any abnormality. She jerked it back when she got it tangled in a spiderweb. She reached above the door and slid her hand along the top, still finding nothing. She then went to the left of the door, the beam of her light getting dimmer by the second.

"You know, if you want to help, now would be a good time," she murmured.

"What?" Paige asked.

"Sorry. I wasn't talking to you," she said.

"You're really starting to scare me, CJ."

"Yeah. Me, too, baby."

She squatted down on the floor, staring at the bottom cinder block. She could see where the ground had been scraped clean. She pushed the block and it moved.

"I think I found something," she said. Before she could turn the block, the door started opening.

"So did we."

The door turned on a center pivot and three flashlights shined in.

"Thank you, thank you, thank you," she said with a grin as she pocketed her phone. She met Ice's frightened gaze. "Hey, baldy, glad you could make it."

"Let's just get the hell out of here," he said.

"Yeah. I need a little daylight myself," she said, pushing past them.

Feeling like she'd been freed from a prison dungeon, CJ hurried out, through the dining room and into the entryway, out the front door to the porch...and daylight. Even though it was dark and gloomy with a steady rain still falling, it took a moment for her eyes to adjust. She turned. The others were right behind her.

She looked at Paige and smiled. "Thanks."

"You want to tell us why the hell you took a dive into the chute?"

CJ shook her head. "I was pushed."

"We didn't—"

"It wasn't by you."

"So, the...the *ghost* pushed you?" Billy asked.

"Let's don't call her a ghost," she said. "It's not like Casper is there, dancing around. It's a...a voice. Not even an image. I don't know if the voice is in my head or what." She frowned. "And don't look at me like I'm crazy."

Billy held his hands up. "Hey, I'm just glad it's not talking to me."

"I just wish we could stop talking about it," Ice said. "Because it's crazy talk."

CJ opened up her palm, almost forgetting she still held the chalk. "So there's this," she said. Paige took it from her, inspecting it.

"I think we should request a forensics team," Paige said. "Dust the room for prints, see if there's any useable evidence."

"There'll be something," she said. Why else were they led to the room in the first place? Of course, acknowledging that some... some *spirit* or something was talking to her, telling her to open the doors, shoving her down the chute so that she'd find the piece of chalk was…well, it was damn near crazy. "Listen…there's no reason Howley needs to know about…well, about the…"

"The voices in your head?" Billy asked.

"Yeah. That."

CHAPTER TWENTY-SIX

Paige and CJ stood back, letting Ice and Billy handle things with Deputy Brady. Howley had suggested they solicit the sheriff's department to secure the house until the forensics team got there.

"I'm going to read over the file we got from Brady," CJ said. "See if something jumps out. I want to see if the old file from fourteen years ago and the new one mention anything about a locked door in the kitchen." She headed over to her truck, but Paige stopped her with a light touch on her arm.

CJ's words had been robotic. It was so unlike her, it caused Paige concern. "Are you okay?"

"No. Not really." CJ paused, then tried to smile. "I don't mind saying, as I was flying down that damn chute, I thought I was a goner," she said as she rubbed the back of her head.

"Sore?"

"Yeah. Got a little bump."

"When you fell?"

"Yeah. Banged my head on the floor. Thankfully, it was an earthen floor."

"So you think you were led to the shaft?"

"I know it sounds crazy, Paige, but yeah, I was."

"Not as crazy as it is to hear you talking to...someone," she said.

"I'm just trying to keep my sense of humor and not lose my fucking mind," CJ said. Then, quickly, "Sorry."

"It's okay. I've heard the word before." She grinned. "I've *used* the word."

CJ smiled too. "The beautiful and very proper Paige Riley has said *fuck* before?"

Paige blushed. "Thank you. Now go."

"You want to kiss me, don't you? Because I'm cute."

"Yes, I do. And yes, you are. Don't get a big head," she said as she went to join the guys.

"Too late for that, baby."

Paige laughed at her parting shot. Didn't take long for CJ to get her swagger back. Billy saw her walk over, and he stepped away from the others.

"CJ okay?"

"Yes. A little shaken, but she's...CJ," she said with a quick smile. "How are things here?"

"Oh, hell, Ice is having to listen to stories about how the house is haunted," Billy said with a quiet laugh. "Look how pale he looks."

Ice was standing by, wide-eyed, as one of the deputies was recounting a story from his high school years.

"Man, I about peed my pants when we saw a person looking out the window up on the second floor. Susie—she's my wife now— swore it was a young girl. Hell, I didn't stick around long enough to find out," the deputy said with a shaky laugh. "Gives me the creeps to be here now, you know, but hell, it ain't dark yet."

Paige walked closer, thinking Ice needed rescuing. "Special Agent Riley," she said, extending her hand to him.

"Deputy Carter, ma'am," he said politely.

Ice stared at her. "We got no damn business being in this house," he said. "Did you hear what he just said? A young girl in the window?"

"Yeah," Billy said. "She's friends with CJ, apparently."

Paige couldn't contain her laughter at the look on Ice's face.

"Glad you find it funny," he said.

Paige turned to the deputy. "Deputy Carter, where was the little boy found the other week?"

"Oh, around front there. In one of the few places where the undergrowth hadn't taken over. Could just barely see him from the road."

"So if whoever dumped him wanted him to not be found, they could have put him almost anywhere else?"

"Yes, ma'am. Like I said, kids still come out here. Someone would have seen him eventually. But where he was placed, I'm thinking whoever did it wanted him to be found."

"Why is that, do you think?"

He shrugged.

"Any luck finding the car?" Billy asked.

He frowned. "What car?"

"The sports car," Ice said. "Weren't you working this case with Brady?"

"Yeah, man, but we turned it over to y'all," he said. "He hadn't said anything to me about a sports car."

Paige watched as Billy and Ice exchanged glances. She knew neither of them liked Brady. And CJ had described him as a "prick."

"Carter, quit running your mouth and give me a hand over here," Deputy Brady yelled from the porch.

As soon as Carter was out of earshot, Ice turned to her. "I should have known the little bastard wouldn't take us seriously."

"We didn't really give him much," Billy said.

"He probably never even drove out to Thompson's like he said he would."

"Perhaps we should confront him," Paige suggested.

"Perhaps we should keep him out of the goddamn loop," Ice said instead.

"But Howley said we should—"

"Damn, Billy, I know what Howley said," Ice said.

Paige held her hand up. "Okay, let's wait and discuss this as a team," she said. "How about you show us where the window was broken from the inside? We can have them dust for prints on the pane."

"Yeah, okay," he said. "This way."

* * *

CJ rounded the corner of the porch, surprised they weren't there. She found the spot where the window was broken from the inside. She squatted down beside the glass, careful not to step on any of it. She listened, hearing a faint conversation and recognizing Ice's voice. She followed the sound, finding him, Paige and Billy out among the trees in the back. She stepped off the porch, the light rain of earlier only misting now.

"What's up?" she asked.

"Saw these ruins from the back porch," Paige said. "Looks like an old building of some kind. A garage maybe," she said.

The woods had overtaken it, and vines clung to the few remaining boards that still stood. A pine tree grew in what was probably the center of the building.

"Don't think it was a garage, though," CJ said as she stepped over a fallen tree. "Wow. Looks like lead pipes. They had plumbing out here. But didn't they stop using lead, like, back in the fifties?"

"So this would have been built back when the house was built," Paige said. "So maybe it was a guest house."

"The dude who built it, Spencer, was he wealthy? I mean, back in the day, this thing was probably a mansion," Ice said. "Maybe if he had servants, this is where they lived."

"Yes, that could be," Paige said. "I would assume he was wealthy to have built a house this size."

"Does it matter?" Billy asked. "I mean, fourteen years ago, this couldn't have been in much better shape than it is now," he said.

Paige smiled at him. "I think we were more curious about it than thinking it had anything to do with our case."

"Yeah, speaking of that," CJ said. "Howley called. Forensics should be here in about forty-five minutes. And I think we could have secured this place without getting the sheriff's department out here."

"Yeah, but Howley wants them involved," Billy said.

"They're going a bit overboard," she said. "They got crime scene tape up, which just calls attention. There were already four cars parked along the road watching. Next thing you know, there'll be a damn news crew out here." They left the damp woods and headed back to the porch. "I did read through the files, though," she continued. "Someone's definitely been in the house."

"How so?" Ice asked.

"The initial report, the one the sheriff's department did when they first found Paul Canton, said the door inside the kitchen went into a small room. They listed it as a storage room. Empty. The FBI's file also mentioned the door. They said it was a large pantry." She shrugged. "So, it was unlocked when they did their search."

"And the new case?"

"No mention of the door. Which leads us to believe that they didn't really check the house. We can check with Brady. It's his report."

"He said they checked the house. Nothing was disturbed," Billy said.

"And like we've already surmised, they probably opened the door, saw all the spiderwebs and crap and called it good," she said.

"So if the door leads to a storage room or a pantry, why lock it?"

"And it was locked from the inside," Paige said.

"Exactly. So was the room off of the dining room," she reminded them. "It was unlocked the first time I was down there. It slammed shut. I thought it was...well, I thought it was a damn ghost," she admitted. "But what if someone was in the house? They slammed it shut and locked it."

"From the inside," Billy said skeptically.

"Yes."

"So how did they get out?"

"We know that room has a secret door, it opens into what? I called it a laundry room, but was it? It had an earthen floor. Seems a little dirty to be a laundry room."

"What are you getting at?"

"Maybe there's a second door," she said. "It was dark. I couldn't tell. But maybe there was another door, one that opened into another part of the house. A trick door like the first one."

"And?"

"And maybe the room off of the kitchen is the same. Maybe it's got a secret door too. Maybe it opens into another room like the one I was trapped in."

Ice shook his head. "Now you're just making shit up, CJ."

CJ grinned. "Yeah. But it's possible."

"Come on. Secret doors, hidden rooms. Makes no sense."

"Well, it does make sense," Paige said. "We've seen it, Ice. There could very well be another one. But I think our main question should be, who would have known about it? As Howley told us in our first briefing, the house has been vacant forty years."

"Well, we do know one person who could have known," CJ said. "Edith Krause."

"How?" Billy asked.

CJ looked at Paige. "Remember what Lizzie told us? That Edie's mother worked here for the Underwoods. Edie was young, still living at home. Chances are, she came here with her mother."

Paige nodded. "She could have known about the rooms."

"Yeah. And when her son died, she took her revenge out on the boys who picked on him. We know Butch Renkie did. And Lizzie said Mark Poole did too," she said.

"Four boys went missing," Ice said. "How do we find out, now fourteen years later, if they were bullies or not?"

"We could ask Lizzie about the other two," Paige suggested.

"Or teachers," Billy said. "Small towns like this, teachers tend to stick around."

"Good idea," she said. "Of course, we're speculating Edith did this. We still need to account for her husband, who appears to have dropped off the face of the earth."

"She killed the boys, then killed him," Ice said.

"Sounds great," she said. "Only we have zero evidence of that."

"Maybe they'll find something in your…you know, the laundry room," he said.

"Yeah. Why don't you guys hang around for that? We'll head over and visit with Lizzie again."

Ice made a face. "I'm not going back in that house," he stated. "No way."

"There's nothing in that house that's going to hurt you," she said. After her little trip down the chute, she could say that. Whatever *thing*—spirit—that was talking to her, while unsettling to say the least, appeared to be helping, not hurting.

"You don't know that."

She knew there was no arguing with him. He had his own phobia. So she let it go with a slap on his shoulder. "See you guys later."

"You're coming back here, right? I mean, it's gonna start getting dark in a few hours. You think they're going to want to be in there then?"

"Don't tell them the place is haunted."

CHAPTER TWENTY-SEVEN

CJ drove the now familiar road back to Shady Pines. It was only a few miles from the Wicker house as it was, but she took her time.

"Are you okay?" Paige asked.

"Yeah. It's just been a crazy day." Then she laughed. "Probably shouldn't have used the word 'crazy,' huh?" She glanced at her. "What? Are you worried about me?"

"A little, yes."

CJ shook her head. "I know it's...yeah, crazy," she said. "But really, I'm trying not to think about it."

"So you're going to leave this out of your report?"

"The voices? Hell yeah. After what happened in Hoganville, Howley would most likely have me committed." CJ reached across the console and rested her hand on Paige's thigh. "You don't think I'm crazy, do you?" She asked the question with a smile, but part of her was afraid Paige was going to say yes. Paige seemed to consider her reply carefully, which made CJ even more apprehensive.

"I don't think you're crazy, CJ. I'll admit, I don't understand it. But I'll say it again, after all we witnessed in Hoganville, nothing really surprises me." She linked her fingers with CJ's. "I never shared this with you, but when Fiona was dying, she told me something, something she had no possible way of knowing."

"What?"

"She said, 'Don't run from CJ. Trust her.'" Paige squeezed her hand tighter. "She said, 'The awful things her father did to her, it makes her wary of others.'"

CJ felt her chest tighten. "How could she have known about my father?"

Paige shook her head. "That's what I mean. She shouldn't have known. Yet she did."

CJ pulled her hand from Paige's, clamping it around the steering wheel instead. Even though she'd shared everything with Paige, from her childhood beatings to her father's molestation of both her and her sister, it was still difficult to think about, to talk about. So how in the world could Fiona have known?

"The point I'm trying to make, CJ, is that some things we can't explain. We can't explain how Fiona knew that. And we can't explain why you're hearing the voices of...of a presence in the Wicker house."

"Ester Hogan was, as Fiona put it, quite mad," CJ said. "Yet she had powers. Powers that, you're right, we don't understand. Did Fiona have powers too? Could she sense things? Read my mind? Yours?" She pulled to a stop in front of Lizzie's trailer. "I'm a little scared, Paige." She smiled. "Okay, I'm a lot scared. I think whatever is in that house is trying to help us, not hurt us. But it's...it's almost more than I can comprehend. And if it gets out, to Howley, to anyone, that I'm hearing voices, then I think my career is seriously in jeopardy. Especially after Hoganville."

"We're working the case based on the evidence, CJ. You found chalk. We found locked doors where they should not be. We've got a forensics team coming. We're just working the evidence, that's all."

CJ opened her door and got out, the rain from earlier having stopped completely. She looked at Paige across the bed of her truck.

"We're both ignoring the real issue here," she said.

"What's that?"

"That I'm going into a haunted house and...and I'm not just hearing some young girl talking to me. I'm hearing running up the stairs. I feel cold air. I felt a touch on my neck, my face. I can hear—visualize—Mr. Wicker beating his daughter before throwing her to her death." She took a deep breath. "That is more disconcerting than a young girl telling me to open the door and look down the chute."

"I don't know what you want me to say, CJ. When this is over with, do you want to see a therapist or something?"

CJ snorted. "Oh, hell no."

"There's nothing wrong with seeing a therapist," Paige said.

CJ shook her head. "Been there, done that. After the thing with my father, after Cathy died, I had to go weekly for over a year. The school set it up. And all the kids made fun of me." She gave a quick smile, even though the memory was still painful. "I'd just as soon not have to relive all that again."

Paige nodded. "I understand."

"Come on. Let's go see what else we can get out of Lizzie."

After the rain, the temperature was bordering on cool and now Lizzie had her front door open again, letting in fresh air. CJ knocked on the edge of the screen door.

"Lizzie? FBI again," she called.

She heard the squeaking of Lizzie's chair and soon saw her shuffling toward them.

"Edie still hasn't come back," Lizzie said, then she broke into a smile. "You brought your pretty partner with you. Come in, come in."

CJ stepped back, letting Paige go in first.

"Sorry to bother you yet again," Paige said. "You must be getting tired of us by now."

"Oh, no, dear. I love company." She went back to her chair, her stooped shoulders seeming to weigh heavy on her today. "I do get lonely sometimes. But I have the TV."

"We've been at the Wicker house today," CJ said.

"Oh my. *Inside?*"

"Yes," Paige said. "And we saw no ghosts," she added with a smile.

"I've been told there's still furniture in there," Lizzie said.

"Some, yes," CJ said. "Listen, we wanted to talk more about the four boys."

Lizzie nodded. "Yes. So sad still. Why, I talked to Allen yesterday. Markie Poole's grandfather," she clarified.

"Yes. We interviewed him the first time we were here," Paige said.

Lizzie nodded again. "He said talking to you brought back memories of Markie, like it was only yesterday."

"We know Butch Renkie picked on Eddie Krause," CJ said. "And you said Markie Poole did to."

"Yes. Eddie was fair game. So small and frail he was."

"What about Paul Canton? Did he pick on Eddie too?"

"Paulie lived on the second loop, not too far from where the Pooles lived. Those four boys hung together. Butch was the ringleader, probably because he was so much bigger than the others. Bradley Simon, if I recall, was the same age as Butch. They were a grade ahead of the others."

"So all four of them picked on Eddie?"

"Oh, yes," she said. "But they weren't the only ones. Even some of the older kids picked on him. Why, I recall one time, some of the high school boys tied poor Eddie to a tree and left him there." Lizzie shook her head. "I've never seen Edie so mad. She called the sheriff's department out, but they didn't do anything. Little Eddie was too afraid to name names."

"And the accident when Eddie died, he was in the first grade?" Paige asked.

"Yes, I believe so. He was just six. Oh, Edie took it so hard," Lizzie said. "Like I said, she just wasn't the same after that."

"And you haven't seen her since yesterday?" she asked.

"No. Her car was gone when I got up this morning." Lizzie clutched her hands together. "I can't imagine where she'd go, what with the rainstorm and all."

"You mentioned her cousin before," Paige said. "I believe you said her name was Donna."

"Donna Parks, yes. Haven't seen her since she moved."

"And that would have been last year when Edith moved back here?"

Lizzie nodded. "Is Edie in some kind of trouble?"

"No, no," CJ said. "We're just trying to piece everything together. Fourteen years is a long time ago."

"Do you remember when you spoke to the FBI back then?" Paige asked.

"Sure do." She glanced at CJ. "Dressed in suits and ties, they were."

CJ smiled at her. "Doing fieldwork like we are, suits and ties aren't really practical," she said.

"They were handsome, if I recall," Lizzie added.

"What kind of questions did they ask you? Did they ask about the boys' relationship with Eddie Krause?"

"Oh, no. They never asked me about little Eddie. I don't know why they would have. He had already been gone a year by then. Why, they mostly wanted to know if I'd seen any strangers around and if I'd seen anyone acting peculiar." She nodded slowly. "They talked to nearly everyone in the neighborhood, I think."

"And after Bradley Simon went missing, that's when Edith and her husband left?"

Lizzie nodded. "Yes, I believe they left shortly after that. Edie said it was just too much for her." She folded and unfolded her hands several times. "It was a scary time here, that's for sure. Not just Edie and Herbert that moved. Lots of families packed up and left. Can't blame them, really."

"No. I guess you can't," CJ said. She glanced at Paige and motioned to the door. "We should probably get back."

"Yes." Paige stood, smiling at Lizzie. "Thank you for your time."

Lizzie pushed herself out of her chair. "You're not going back to that house, are you?"

"Yes, I'm afraid so," Paige said.

Lizzie's thin lips pursed together. "It's an evil house. It makes people do evil things," she said. "You should stay away."

CJ wanted to agree with her so she hoped her smile wasn't condescending. "We'll be fine. We just have a few things to check out." She paused before leaving. "You'll call if you see Edie?"

Lizzie nodded. "Yes, I will."

Back in the truck, CJ said what she assumed Paige was thinking as well. "I don't think Edith Krause is coming back, do you?"

"Maybe it's time for a BOLO on her car," Paige said.

CJ pulled away, shaking her head. "Why didn't they connect Eddie's death with the four boys?"

"I don't know. It seems obvious now, doesn't it?"

"They were looking for a serial killer," she said. "But with Edith Krause, she had motive, she had opportunity. She was exacting revenge for her son's death."

"We still have no evidence," Paige reminded her.

"And where the hell is her husband?"

"Maybe Ice is right. Maybe she killed him too."

"Why?"

"Maybe he had no clue she was the killer. Maybe he found out," Paige said.

"He found out, so she killed him. And then she fled to Midland. The disappearances stopped." CJ nodded. "I'll buy it."

"Yes. But her husband's disappearance makes no sense. I mean, surely he had family who would miss him. Parents, siblings."

"There wasn't anything in Howley's report about family. He just disappeared."

"So maybe he had no close relationships. Or maybe Edith contacted them, pretending to be Herbert."

"We have a hell of a lot of maybes," she said.

When they pulled into the driveway at the Wicker house, Ice jogged out to meet them.

"The team is already inside," he said. "Sheriff's department brought in some lights and a generator."

"Did you get the door opened in the kitchen?" she asked.

"Billy's in there now," he said.

CJ grinned. "You still want no part of it?"

"Well, it's not quite as scary with so many people in there, but yeah, I thought I'd supervise out here." He raised his eyebrows. "You get anything new?"

"Lizzie confirmed that all four boys were known to pick on Eddie," she said.

"Damn. So Edith was getting revenge?"

"That's our theory." She watched as Deputy Brady walked out of the house. "You get with him yet on the new case?"

Ice scowled. "Hell, I don't trust him. Said he took a trip out to the nursery, drove up the forest road. Said Thompson wouldn't talk to him."

"So it's obvious he's not working the case. Do we want to speculate as to why? Is he lazy? Doesn't care?"

"I put a call in to Thompson myself," Ice said. "His daughter said he was out in the back and she'd have him call me."

"We're all in agreement these two cases aren't linked, right?" she asked.

"Yeah. I talked to Howley while you were gone," he said. "Told him we're not getting any cooperation in this new case. I think he's so giddy that we might bust this cold case that he's willing to hand this one back to the locals."

"So the boy's killer will never be found," Paige said. "That sucks."

CJ and Ice stared at her, both smiling.

"What?"

"I think that's the closest I've ever heard you come to cussing," Ice said.

"Just because I don't have a potty mouth, doesn't mean I don't curse," Paige said. "I say 'hell.' I say…'damn.'"

CJ laughed. "'Cuss,' not 'curse.'"

Paige stared at her and smirked. "Damn. Hell. Shit." She arched an eyebrow. "*Fuck*."

CJ and Ice nearly howled with laughter, causing curious stares from the officers standing about.

"God, you're so juvenile," Paige said as she headed into the house. "I can't believe you made me do that."

CJ was still smiling. "Man, I needed a laugh," she said. "She's cute, isn't she?"

Ice nodded. "Yeah. Cute as hell. You're lucky."

"Luck has nothing to do with it. I'm charming. And I've been called cute myself," she said. "She couldn't resist me."

"Yeah. And you're so humble too," he said with a laugh.

"Yeah, I am pretty modest." She slapped his shoulder. "Come on, baldy. Let's go see what they found."

CHAPTER TWENTY-EIGHT

Paige stood back, watching as the forensics tech dusted the inside doorknob for prints. The kitchen door had been locked with a deadbolt, but it had only taken them a few seconds to unlock it.

"I've got to learn to pick locks," Billy said. "That was so cool."

She smiled but didn't take her eyes off of the work in progress. As the earlier reports had said, the room was a pantry of sorts, although there were only two shelves on one wall. The other three walls were bare. She was about to ask if he found a useable print when a commotion in the other part of the house got her attention. She and Billy headed in that direction, meeting an excited CJ in the process.

"They found another room," she said. "Come look."

They followed CJ through the dining room and into the small interior room where the trick door was. Inside that was CJ's laundry room. On the far wall, another trick door stood open.

"What's inside?"

"They just got it opened. And they've got some prints from

the tables. Who knows how old they are, but some are obviously children's," CJ said.

"Where's Ice?"

"Oh, he came in for a little bit. But one of the deputies started in on hearing screaming and stuff and he bolted again."

"Agents, in here," one of the techs called to them.

Whereas the laundry room was lit with the portable lights that the sheriff's department supplied, the interior room that the techs had found was black dark. They all clicked on their flashlights before going inside. What they found caused all of them to stop in their tracks.

The skeletal remains of three bodies—children—lay slumped against a wall, their clothes still amazingly intact.

"Damn," Billy whispered.

"Yeah. Damn," CJ said quietly. She flashed her light along the walls. "There's got to be another door," she said.

"Why do you think so?" Billy asked.

"Because the only entry can't be through the dining room, into the closet, into the laundry room and into here. That doesn't make sense. Whoever did this had to have another way inside."

"I agree," the tech said. "Looking at the layout of the house, I'd guess most of the interior of the first floor is hidden rooms like this."

Another tech stuck his head in. "Hey guys, you're going to want to see this."

"Now what?" CJ murmured as they followed him back through the house and into the kitchen. Inside the pantry, they'd found another door, like the others that opened on a center pivot. Inside wasn't anything as benign as a laundry room, however.

"Holy shit," CJ said.

"Is that…like an altar or something?" Billy asked.

Paige stepped around Billy, getting a better look inside. The altar itself brought back memories of Hoganville and the cave. But this altar made Ester Hogan's look like child's play. Eight skulls adorned this one, some animal, some human. There were knives of various sizes displayed on the altar. One glass jar on top contained eyeballs. She didn't know if they were human or not. There was a mortar and pestle, candleholders with the remnants of candle wax caked around them and four small, black dolls.

"Sacrificial altar," the tech said. "Black magic. We had a case in New Orleans one time." He shone his light on something. "Chicken feet."

"Voodoo?"

"Voodoo gone bad," he said. "The ancient practice of voodoo was not an evil concept. Today's movies depict it that way."

"It doesn't look like any of this is recent," Paige said.

"No. I don't think this was an active site."

Paige's light flashed across the altar again. "What's that?"

The tech went closer. "I'd guess it's a spell book."

"What?"

"You know, witchcraft, spells, black magic."

"Lovely," she murmured dryly, turning away from the book.

"There's another door," CJ said, her light shining on a doorknob.

"Yeah. It's locked. I was going to dust it for prints before I get Harrison to pick it."

"So bad voodoo? Or devil worship? What do you think this all is?" Paige asked.

"Does it matter?" Billy asked. "It's obviously meant for evil and not good."

"This could date back to when the Wickers lived here," CJ said. She glanced at Paige. "Makes Hoganville look tame," she said.

Paige nodded. "Yes, it does."

"Okay, let me process this. I'll let you know when we open the other door."

It was with relief that Paige stepped from the room and back into the kitchen. She noticed twilight was upon them as light no longer penetrated the cracks in the boards that covered the windows.

"Let me find Ice," CJ said. "He can keep Howley in the loop."

"Okay. We'll go see what they found with the three bodies," she said.

"So those are the boys, right?" Billy asked as they headed back into the dining room.

"We can assume," she said.

"I hate cases like this," he said.

"I know. We all do," she said.

They had moved one of the portable lights into the room where the bodies were. They were photographing the scene and Paige and Billy stood back, watching them.

"It's already dark outside," Billy said, his voice low.

"I know."

"How long are we going to stay here?"

She turned to him. "I think we'll be okay."

"Yeah, but we might want to start fresh in the morning," he said.

His wish was granted only a short time later when one of the techs came out of the back room.

"We can't see a goddamn thing in there. We're going to wrap it up for the night," he said. "Can we get some more lights brought in tomorrow?"

"Let me check with Deputy Brady," Billy said.

"What about the bodies?" Paige asked.

"The ME is coming in the morning. It'll probably take us all day tomorrow to process everything, so this place needs to be secured tonight."

Paige and Billy exchanged glances.

"You mean you want *us* to stay here tonight?" Billy asked.

The tech held up his hands as he walked away. "Hey, I'm just a forensics guy."

Billy turned to her. "I'm thinking the sheriff's department should secure the place. Right?"

"Let's go talk to CJ and Ice. But it's our case, not the sheriff's department," she said.

"Oh, hell," he muttered. "I *hate* this case."

CHAPTER TWENTY-NINE

CJ steadied Ice with a firm grip on his arm.

"Say what?" Ice visibly swallowed. "Stay *here*? Tonight?"

"Brady is going to have a patrol car parked at the road," Billy said.

"With all the comings and goings," CJ said, "the locals know something's up. Hell, they had crime scene tape up. We can't leave the house unattended."

"Oh, *man*," Ice groaned.

CJ glanced at Paige. "You want to take shifts or what?"

"We missed lunch," Billy reminded them.

"We could order pizza," CJ offered. "And all stay." She looked at Paige. "Sorry. I guess finding a vegan pizza around here might be tough."

"I don't care anymore," Paige said. "I'm starving. If we can find a veggie pizza with cheese, I'll take it."

CJ grinned. "I knew you missed cheese." She turned to Ice. "Is that okay with you?"

"Yeah, okay. I don't want to take shifts, though," Ice said. "I'm just saying, no way in hell I'm staying here alone."

"We'll all stay." She raised her eyebrows at Billy. "Pizza okay with you?"

He gave a shaky laugh. "Yeah. What address will you give them? Turn left on the cemetery road and then take a right at the haunted house?"

"Look," she said. "We're going to be fine here. It's just a house."

"With three bodies inside," Ice said. "And ghosts."

"And some kind of a voodoo altar thing," Billy added. "With a spell book."

CJ put her hands on her hips. "Are you guys just trying to freak us all out or what?"

"Just saying," Ice murmured.

"Fine. Then you guys take care of ordering the pizza. And the directions." She shook her head. "Babies."

Paige followed her back up to the dark porch and stopped her with a tug on her arm. "Are you okay?"

CJ nodded. "Yeah. Just tired of all the ghost crap." She stared into the house, listening to the hum of the generator in the far back room they'd uncovered. "They left us fuel if we wanted to run the lights all night," she said.

"I don't see the need to run the lights in the back rooms," Paige said. "Maybe out here where we're going to be."

CJ smiled gently at her. "Not crazy about this assignment either, huh?"

"What? Staying here all night? No." Paige moved closer, letting their hands brush. "I'd much rather be at the hotel."

"With me?"

"Yes."

"Naked?"

"Of course."

CJ rubbed Paige's hand with her index finger, then drew back when she heard footsteps approach. It was Billy.

"Ice is hiding in the truck," he said. "He's ordering the pizzas. I told him to just get water for everyone. Is that okay?"

"Yeah," she said. "Although I kinda need to pee. I'm not looking forward to squatting in the woods."

Billy laughed. "Yeah, well, we don't have that problem. Aim and shoot."

With Ice still hovering near the truck—waiting for the pizza, he claimed—the three of them managed to move the generator and the lights out near the entryway. The only evidence that their *ghost* was around was the closed front door.

"Did you notice that the door never once closed when everyone else was here today?" Paige asked.

"She didn't want to show herself," CJ said with certainty. How she knew this, she had no idea.

"Can we not talk about it?" Billy said as he got the generator started again. Soon, light flooded the lower level near the door.

"Much better," Paige said. "Do you think we can get Ice to eat out here on the porch with us? It's actually quite pleasant out."

"Yeah, it's nice. We just need a picnic table and some chairs."

"How can you two act like this is a normal house?" Billy asked. "Did you forget that voodoo room?"

"No. And I haven't forgotten about the three bodies lying beyond the dining room either," CJ said. "But it's a crime scene. We've worked many, many crime scenes, Billy. Some too gruesome to talk about. This is just one more."

They all turned when Ice headed their way, his phone held up to his ear.

"He must feel safe now that we've got the light out here," Billy said.

"Thanks for calling," Ice said before pocketing his phone. "Shane Thompson called me back," he said. "He said he hadn't heard from or seen Deputy Brady. He said no one from thes sheriff's department has contacted him."

"Why the hell would Brady lie to us?" Billy asked. "Why tell us he'd been out there? Why say Thompson refused to talk to him?"

"He must have known we'd follow up on that," Paige said. "Makes no sense."

"Maybe he thought we'd be too preoccupied with this case," CJ said. "Which we are. Howley all but said to dump it back in their laps."

"Yeah, but remember your stance on Howley's directives and rules," Billy reminded her. "Subjective, wasn't that what you said?"

"Oh, so now you want me to break course with what Howley said?"

"Something's up with this case and we all know it," Billy said. "Brady is intentionally dropping the ball on this one."

"Maybe Brady is protecting someone," CJ said.

"So let's call him on it," Ice said.

"When do you want to do that?" CJ asked. "We've got a house full of evidence and a forensics team to follow around tomorrow. We still need to find Edith Krause. If Brady shows up here tomorrow, we might be better served getting his help in locating her than questioning his performance on this new case."

"I tend to agree," Paige said. "Although I don't like the idea of letting the new case fall back to him. I say, if—*when*—we find Edith Krause and wrap this up, we then turn our focus on Juan and finding out what really happened to him."

"That's assuming we determine Edith Krause is our killer," CJ said.

"I don't suppose her prints are in the system, are they?" Ice asked.

"If we could get a warrant to search her trailer, we'd obviously find her prints there," CJ said.

"Do we have enough evidence for that? Everything regarding her is based on speculation and what Lizzie has told us," Paige said. "And a lot of that is opinion and observation, not evidence."

"I think Howley could get a warrant. We've got the whole missing husband thing too. And all four boys being bullies to her son," CJ said. "One of whom killed him."

"Not to mention, she appears to have fled," Billy said.

"Why don't I talk to Howley?" Ice suggested to her. "See if he'll go for it."

CJ nodded. "Yeah, okay. You do that. We need a BOLO out on her car too."

They turned as headlights flashed along the road and through the trees. Ice headed that direction.

"Pizza," he explained. "They thought it was a joke. They wouldn't deliver unless I paid in advance with a credit card."

As Paige had said earlier, it was a nice night. The four of them sat on the porch with their backs leaning against the wall. The rumble of the generator was a bit annoying, even though it was a small portable one. But of course it beat having no lights on at all.

"How's your pizza?" she asked Paige.

Paige grinned around a mouthful. "I didn't realize how much I missed cheese."

"I know. I've seen you coveting mine whenever we eat together."

"And how often is that?"

CJ laughed. "Oh, baldy, you getting brave sitting out here on the porch, are you? Now you think you can ask questions about us?"

"You think Howley is going to find out?" Billy asked.

"Not unless you tell him," she said. "We're careful at work. Right?"

"Careful enough, I guess," he said.

"He'd split us up," Ice warned.

"I know. That's why we didn't want to tell you two," CJ said. She looked at Paige. "But it is what it is."

Paige smiled and nodded but said nothing.

The conversation lagged as they continued to eat their pizza in silence. She was stuffed after four pieces but managed to scarf down a fifth before closing the lid on the box. She took a swallow from her water bottle, then closed it up too. She'd put it off as long as she could. She had to pee. She grabbed a napkin and stood.

"Gotta do a potty break," she said.

Paige stood too. "I might as well join you."

"No hanky-panky," Billy said with a laugh.

"Oh, yeah, we're going to make out next to a haunted house. Now that's my idea of sexy," CJ said. She picked up her flashlight and clicked it on, flashing it toward the back of the house. There were plenty of trees and bushes to choose from. She tore her napkin in half and handed part to Paige. "Not Charmin but it'll have to do."

"I can't believe we're doing this," Paige said.

CJ laughed. "You want to drive over to Lizzie's and ask to borrow her bathroom?"

"Can we?"

CJ took her hand and led her away from the porch. "Are you telling me you've never peed outside before?"

"I have never had the need to, no."

"Long road trip? Never peed on the side of the road?"

"Are you saying you have?"

CJ stopped when they came to the edge of the woods, flashing her light around the bushes and seeing nothing out of place.

"I have a time or two, yes," she said. "Squat and get it over with."

Paige's answer was to walk at least twenty feet away from her. CJ did her business and dutifully kept her light off until Paige was finished. She couldn't help but laugh as Paige came out of the shadows holding her napkin gingerly between her thumb and index finger.

"What should I do with this?"

"I buried mine."

"Buried?"

CJ dug a shallow hole with the heel of her shoe, then stepped aside. "There."

"This is disgusting," Paige said as she laid her napkin in the hole.

"No big deal." CJ covered it up, then stepped on it. "Pretend we're camping."

"And what makes you think I've been camping before?"

"Girl Scouts?"

Paige shook her head. "My mother wouldn't hear of it."

"No, I guess not. But speaking of your mother, have you heard back from her?"

"Not a word."

"You going to call her or avoid her?"

Paige smiled. "I'm avoiding her. In fact, it wouldn't surprise me if she's on her way to Houston now, planning on popping in unannounced again, hoping to find you there."

"Why don't you just tell her?" she suggested.

"And what would I tell her? This is the woman I'm having an affair with?"

CJ paused, wondering if now was the right time for this conversation. "Is that what we're doing? Having an affair?" It was too dark for her to read Paige's eyes, but she was nervous as she waited for her answer. Paige reached out, grazing her cheek, her fingers brushing the hair away from her face.

"I don't want to have an affair with you, CJ."

CJ swallowed, not sure what that meant.

"And you need a haircut."

CJ smiled, thankful that they weren't going to delve into a full-blown discussion on their relationship now. Instead she tugged Paige to her, leaning closer to kiss her. It was slow and light, just lips moving against lips, but it was enough to stir her senses, enough to make her want more. Rather than giving in, she stepped away.

"We should get back," she said.

"Yes. Because I'm very close to dragging you to the back side of the porch," Paige said.

"Oh, yeah?" She headed back toward the guys. "And what would you do if you got me back there?"

"My hand would already be inside your jeans."

"Why, Special Agent Riley, aren't you the fast worker?" she teased.

Paige grinned, but before she could answer, the lights went out. The sudden darkness and quiet as the generator came to an abrupt halt startled them. Paige grabbed her hand tightly and Ice and Billy bolted off the porch.

"What the hell?" Ice said. "What happened?"

"Maybe the generator's out of gas," CJ said.

"We filled it when we moved it," Billy reminded her. "They said it would run for at least six hours. Something else happened. Or *someone*."

CJ clicked on her light and headed toward the generator. She loved the guys, she really did, but their constant fear of this house was wearing on her. She leaned over the generator, surprised to find the switch in the "off" position.

"Out of gas?"

She shook her head. The front door to the house was still open. She turned to the others.

"Go ahead and get it started again," she said as she headed to the door. She stopped before going inside. "And stay out here."

She expected Paige to protest, but she did not, simply giving her a quick nod. She felt only a little fear as she walked inside the dark house. She wasn't surprised to hear a voice call to her.

"*Up here.*"

She looked up the dark staircase to the second-floor landing, imagining shadows moving about. She pushed her nervousness down as she slowly climbed the stairs. Halfway up she paused, expecting to hear the running of feet along the steps. She waited but instead of running, she heard crying. She looked around, trying to determine where it was coming from. It seemed to be all around her, as if the walls themselves were crying.

The sound was nearly deafening, and she couldn't make herself move any higher. She wet her very dry lips.

"Please make it stop," she said. The crying stopped as abruptly as it had started. "Thank you."

"Now come up."

She nodded, taking the final four steps slowly, her light slicing through the darkness. At the landing, she paused, waiting for instruction. Her light flashed up the stairs that went up to the third floor.

"Not up there. You're not safe there."

CJ turned, instead following the voice down the hallway. The windows weren't boarded up on the second floor and she glanced out, seeing the lights on again. She hadn't even registered the return of the generator's hum. She leaned against the wall, sliding down to the floor until she was sitting. On impulse, she turned her light off.

"I…I guess you know we found the bodies," she said, her voice sounding nervous to her own ears.

"Yes. That took you long enough."

CJ smiled before she realized what she was doing. So her ghost had a sense of humor. "Thanks for that ride down the chute. What is that thing?"

"We used it for soiled clothes."

"So…you know who killed them, I guess."

"Yes. So do you."

"Edith?"

"She committed the physical act."

"What does that mean?"

"He controls her."

"He? Her husband?"

"No. Her husband is up on the third floor."

"Dead?"

"Yes."

"She killed him?"

"With an ax."

CJ paused. "Is that why you say I'm not safe up there?"

"I can't help you up there. He is too powerful."

"Who is he?"

"He's always been here."

CJ closed her eyes for a minute, trying to grasp the fact that she was sitting on the floor in a haunted house having a conversation with someone—*a ghost*—as if it were the most natural thing in the world.

"How…how did he control Edith? Did she go up to the third floor?"

"When she was young, yes. He drew her back here many times."

"She knew of the secret doors then," she said. "How did she get in the house?"

"Through the root cellar tunnel."

CJ grabbed the bridge of her nose and squeezed. "And the tunnel is where?"

"You were there. You were so close."

"The ruins behind the house?" she guessed.

"There is a plank floor. She covers it with dead tree branches."

"And are there other secret rooms?"

"Yes."

CJ leaned her head against the wall, trying to remind herself she wasn't interviewing a witness. She did have one question that she wanted answered, though.

"Why me?"

"You have a gentleness about you."

CJ shook her head. "Paige is the gentle one."

"Yes. But you were injured as a child. Your scars still show. You still grieve for your sister."

CJ's heart tightened. "How do you know about that?"

"My father was evil like your father. I can hear your soul as you cry."

CJ clenched her jaw, feeling tears in her eyes. She almost thought that maybe she was talking to her subconscious this whole time and not some damn ghost.

"Damn ghost?"

"Sorry. It's easier to think I'm talking to myself rather than thinking I'm losing my mind," she said.

"I'm sorry you think you are not sane, but you are. Now, you should go. He senses your presence. He will make himself known. That, I'm sure, will frighten you."

CJ slowly stood. "We'll need to go up to the third floor," she said.

"It cannot be you. I have reached out to you. He will know. He will kill you."

"I'll keep that in mind."

She pushed up off the floor, getting to her feet again. She clicked on the flashlight, halfway expecting to see someone—*her*—but there was nothing in the shadows. She was about to head back down the stairs when she heard a thunderous howl above her. She swung her light up the third-floor stairs, then nearly stumbled as an unseen force pushed her hard against the wall.

"GET OUT! GET OUT OF MY HOUSE!"

"Holy shit," she muttered as she steadied herself. The deep voice roared in her ears, but she stood frozen, her gaze glued to the stairs that spiraled up to the third floor, expecting something to charge her, to grab her, to toss her over the railing. And yet she stood there, staring up at nothing.

"You must go. Hurry!"

She whipped her head around, the sound of the girl's voice nearly a whisper compared to the monstrous roar from above.

"GET OUT!"

This time she heeded his warning, darting down the stairs two at a time, nearly tripping as she reached the bottom. She ran out onto the porch and toward the lights. Three sets of frightened eyes stared back at her.

She was breathing hard and she grabbed her chest, trying to calm herself. She looked at Paige. "Water?" she said between breaths. Paige handed her a bottle, and she noticed her hand was trembling as she opened it.

"What the hell happened?" Billy asked.

CJ shook her head. "You wouldn't believe me if I told you."

She leaned against the wall and sunk down to the ground, much like she'd done upstairs. She stretched her legs out in front of her, blinking several times, the growled words "GET OUT" still reverberating in her mind. She was aware of Paige sitting down beside her, aware of Ice as he positioned himself at the edge of the porch, ready to make a run for the truck, if needed. Billy stood on the porch steps, still staring at her.

"There's a root cellar," she said. "With a tunnel that goes into the house. That's how Edith was able to get inside."

"Great. You know how much I love tunnels," Paige said.

CJ turned her head and tried to smile, but it was too much of an effort. "The ruins out back. That's where the entrance is. We can take a look in the morning." She decided not to tell them everything. She would tell Paige later, about Herbert, about the voice, but she would do that in private.

Paige leaned against her, resting her head on her shoulder. CJ captured her hand and held it tightly, slowly letting out her breath. No one said another word. Billy sat on the top step of the porch. Ice came back and sat down next to Paige. When Paige reached over and squeezed his hand, CJ managed a small smile, but it quickly faded as she heard the heartbreaking sounds of crying—weeping—coming from inside the house.

CHAPTER THIRTY

Paige woke with a start, blinking several times as she got her bearings. While the front seat of the truck reclined somewhat, it still was not the most comfortable place to grab a few hours of sleep. She rolled her head, finding CJ still asleep.

As the clock had ticked toward midnight, they knew they needed some rest. She and CJ had taken the first shift, letting Ice and Billy have a few hours of sleep. At three, they'd switched places and she fell asleep almost immediately.

Now, dawn was drawing near; she assumed it was at least six. The generator still ran and she sat up, seeing Billy and Ice slouched against the wall of the porch. She rolled her shoulders, trying to get the kinks out.

"Hey."

She turned, finding CJ's sleepy eyes on her. "Did I wake you?" she asked quietly.

CJ rubbed her eyes and sat up too, pushing the seat back to its normal position. "It's time" was all she said.

"Are you ready to talk yet?" Last night, even though they'd been alone, CJ hadn't wanted to share what had happened in the house. Paige didn't push her. But now, if they were to search for a root cellar and tunnel, she at least wanted to know how CJ knew this.

CJ cleared her throat, then gave her a half-smile. "I had a goddamn conversation with a ghost."

Paige nodded. "You want to tell me about it?"

CJ ran her hands through her already tousled hair. "Well, you know, there's the root cellar thing…and the tunnel," she said.

Paige reached across the console and took her hand. "Tell me, CJ. I'm not going to judge you."

CJ leaned her head back. "No. You never do, do you?"

Paige squeezed her hand. "Tell me."

CJ sighed. "I'm ready to go home."

She smiled at her and squeezed her hand. "Me too."

CJ squeezed back. "Herbert is somewhere on the third floor."

That statement wasn't exactly how she thought CJ would start. "You didn't go up there, did you?"

CJ shook her head. "No. She told me. Said Edith killed him with an ax."

"I see."

"She knew about my father. She knew about my sister." CJ pulled her hand away and ran it through her hair again. "She said… she said not to go up to the third floor. She said *he* controls the third floor."

"Who is he?"

"I don't know."

Paige had to remind herself that they were talking about a…a ghost, a spirit, *something*, and not a person. She didn't want to put too much weight into that for fear she'd start questioning— doubting—CJ. So she pretended it didn't bother her that CJ was apparently having conversations with a ghost.

"If you think there's a body on the third floor, then we need to go up there," she said.

"No. You're not going up there," CJ said.

"But—"

"No." CJ met her eyes, holding them. "Look, I know how fucking crazy this all sounds. I *know* it. I didn't want to tell the guys any of this, but…I heard him. It was this roar, this…I can't even describe it. Something pushed me against the wall. And he was yelling 'get out, get out of my house.'" CJ had a wild look in her eyes. "And I was just frozen in fear. I just stood there. I just stood there, until she talked to me again, told me to get out, to hurry. And I did. I ran down the stairs."

Paige tried to keep her face expressionless even though her mind was telling her, yes, this *was* crazy. She had no doubt that what CJ was telling her really happened. She could see the fear in her eyes.

However, it was CJ's expression that changed. "You doubt me."

Paige shook her head. "No, I don't doubt you, CJ. I don't understand it, but I don't doubt you." She chose her words carefully. "There are more people around here now, not just us. The forensics team, the sheriff's deputies. We have to decide how much to tell them."

"Tell them? We can't tell them anything about this," CJ said. "I'd just as soon not have to do a psych exam."

"So how do you want to play it?"

"Explaining the root cellar is easy. We've already been out there. We'll stumble upon the door, open it, see where the tunnel goes."

"And the third floor?"

"She told me I couldn't go up there. She said since she had reached out to me, he would kill me," CJ said matter-of-factly. "And I don't want you going up there. And we know Ice won't go. Billy? Maybe. But I don't really want to take a chance with him either."

"So who?"

"Let's get Brady to send up a couple of his guys. We're safe on the second floor. Let's check those bedrooms. We'll have his guys take the third floor."

"And you really think Herbert Krause is up there?"

"She said he was." CJ leaned back in her seat and let out a heavy breath. "And if he's not, then I really am losing my fucking mind." CJ smiled. "Sorry. Fuck is my favorite word when I'm upset."

"I've noticed," she said with a quiet laugh.

"Come on. Let's go start the day. I hope the forensics team shows up early."

Paige got out and stretched her arms over her head. "You think we could talk the guys into a coffee run?"

"Miss your morning coffee?"

"Yes. I miss my morning shower and clean clothes too."

CJ grinned. "I miss joining you for your morning shower."

CHAPTER THIRTY-ONE

CJ's gaze traveled up the stairs, and she paused only for a few seconds before heading up. Paige and Billy were behind her. And behind them were three deputies. Everything appeared to be normal as she heard none of the familiar sounds she usually did— no running on the stairs, no crying, no screaming, no bursts of cold air.

When they got to the second floor, she glanced at the deputies as she headed down the hallway. "You guys take the third floor," she said as nonchalantly as possible.

"What are we looking for?"

"Just see if anything is disturbed," she said. "Anything we need the forensics team to look at."

Paige opened one of the bedrooms, and CJ peeked around her shoulder. It was completely empty.

"This one's got furniture," Billy said from the next room.

A thick layer of dust covered every surface from the old chest of drawers to the bed's massive headboard. The window had a crack from top to bottom running diagonally through the pane. As the mid-morning sunlight filtered in, she could see particles of dust dancing in the room.

"No one's been in here in years," she said.

Paige opened one of the drawers. It was empty.

Back in the hallway, Billy pointed to the half-doors. "I don't suppose you want to take another ride down the laundry chute, do you?"

"I'll pass," she said. "Check the last—"

"Got a body!" one of the deputies yelled loudly from the third floor. "Been here a while."

CJ and Paige exchanged glances.

"You want me to go up?" Billy asked.

CJ felt like a coward, but she nodded. "If you don't mind."

"Hey, we found another room," a tech called up from the first floor. "You guys want to take a look?"

"Where's Ice?" CJ asked.

"He's on the phone."

"Go on," Billy said. "I got this."

CJ and Paige hurried down the stairs.

"They found another body—this one on the third floor," CJ said. "Can one of your guys go up?"

"Yeah. The ME is about through down here. I'll get him to go up there next."

They waited while he went through the dining room and into the secret rooms they'd found yesterday. He came back out quickly and motioned for them to follow. He led them into the kitchen and the pantry, then into what they called the voodoo room.

"The door in the back opens into a small closet. But it had a false wall," he explained.

They turned their flashlights on and followed him inside. It opened into a larger room, this one big enough for a table and shelves.

"Remind me to get new batteries," CJ said as her light started to dim.

"The thing about this room is, it's all false walls," he said. "It's like we're in the center of the house. Each wall opens into a small hallway, which ends at another false wall. Here, you can get into the kitchen." He pushed on one corner and the wall spun.

They followed him into the hallway and he pushed the corner of that wall. It opened next to the sink. He retraced his steps and they followed. "Over here, this goes into the dining room." He demonstrated again and the wall turned. "Back here, this just opens into a staircase."

"Where does it go?"

"Haven't been up there yet. But found the entrance into the room where the bodies are. Through this hall," he said as he again moved the false wall. "And one more thing," he said, lifting up a section of the floor. "Steps going down."

CJ stared into blackness down below. "What is it?"

"I haven't been down, just flashed my light around. It's a small room, it looks like. Maybe an old cellar or something," he said. "Be my guests if you want to check it out."

She glanced at Paige. "Let me take a quick look around."

"If you insist," Paige said with a quick smile, her gaze traveling into the dark underground room.

CJ tested the first step. It appeared to be intact. She went down the stairs, aware that her heart was beating a little faster than normal. She flashed her light into every corner. It was dark, damp and humid, the air still. The space was barely big enough for her to stand upright. It appeared to have indeed been a root cellar at one time. The wood used to reinforce the walls was mostly rotted, but some shelves remained and a wooden bin of some sort was built against the wall. Not far past the bin she saw the black gaping hole of a tunnel entrance.

She looked back to the top of the stairs, illuminated by both Paige's and the tech's flashlights.

"Got a tunnel," she said. "It's kinda crude. Nothing like Hoganville."

"Hoganville? Oh, that's right," the tech said. "You two were a part of that mass suicide thing."

CJ ignored him. "Paige, go out by the ruins. We can use our phones to find the entrance."

"Okay. Heading out now."

"I guess you want me to leave this door open?" the tech asked with a bit of a chuckle.

"If you don't mind," CJ said. "Smart-ass," she muttered under her breath.

* * *

Paige was glad to get outside into the daylight. She'd had enough of dark, secret rooms. She felt like they were digging into the very bowels of the Wicker house. She took her phone out, waiting for CJ to call. Ice hurried over when he saw her.

"Howley called. Got a warrant for Edith Krause's trailer," he said.

"That's great. Are you going to handle it?"

"I thought I'd take Billy with me."

Paige shook her head. "Found a body on the third floor. He's dealing with that," she said.

"A body? Herbert?"

"Don't know yet," she said.

"Where's CJ?"

"In what we think is a root cellar," she said.

"Damn. So there really is one?"

She nodded. "There's a tunnel too."

"You want me to hang around? Help you find the entrance?"

"No, I got it. You should head over to Edith's."

"Yeah. Okay. I'm going to see if I can get one of the techs to go too."

"You should get Brady to take you," she suggested.

"Yeah. And maybe I'll find out why he's giving us the runaround about Thompson," he said. "I'll let you know if we find anything." He paused, then smiled. "Have fun in the tunnel."

"Right," she said dryly. "I just hope there's no cave attached to this one."

"You better hope there's no big scary monster at the end of it."

"Thanks for reminding me."

He gave a quick laugh, then headed inside the house. She walked over to the ruins, looking for anything that seemed out of place, but the area was so overgrown, nothing appeared to be foreign. She was about to call CJ when her phone rang.

"Hey. I'm out here now," she said. "How far are you?"

"Far enough that I wished we'd switched lights," CJ said. "Mine is fading fast."

"How is it down there?"

"Spiderwebs are at a minimum," she said.

"Well, that's a plus. By the way, Ice heard from Howley. He got the go-ahead to search Edith's house. He's getting a tech to go with him and getting Brady to drive him."

"Okay. And I guess I'm at the end now. That tunnel was so narrow in places, two people couldn't have fit."

"But nothing, you know, jumped out at you?"

"Well, there was that ax," CJ said. "It was on a shelf."

"Maybe it's the murder weapon," she said as she stepped over a limb, hoping there were no snakes about. "I don't see anything that looks like a door."

"Okay. We can do the GPS thing again, if you want."

"Wait. This is odd," she said, staring at a mess of tangled vines.

"What?"

"There are vines that look like they've been cut." She moved closer, then nearly tripped as her foot caught a limb. She looked around, still not seeing anything odd, then noticed the pile of leaves. They looked like they'd been raked. With her foot, she moved the leaves, revealing what appeared to be a plank of wood.

"Sounds like you're standing on the door," CJ said. "I'm not sure how secure it is. You might want to step off."

"Sorry. I assume it opens outward?"

"Yeah. I've got an old leather strap in here. Used to pull it shut, I guess."

"Okay, let me get the debris off and we can try to open it."

Now that she knew where the door was, she could tell how staged the limbs and dead tree branches were. She moved them to the side and brushed at the leaves the best she could.

"Ready?" CJ asked.

"There's like an old brass ring on my side," Paige said. "The door looks fairly small."

"Paige, sweetheart, kinda getting claustrophobic in here," CJ said. "My light has barely a flicker left."

Paige smiled. "Okay. Sorry. Let's open it."

It opened with little effort, evidence that it had been used recently. CJ stepped back as leaves and dirt fell inside. Paige pointed her flashlight in. "Hi."

"Hi, yourself." CJ held her hand up, silently asking for help out. Paige took it and CJ tentatively climbed the stairs.

"These steps have seen better days," CJ said as she clicked her light off. "I wasn't sure they would hold me."

"So how was it?"

"Uneventful."

"So it's small? Short?"

"Compared to Hoganville's tunnels, yes," CJ said.

"That seems like so long ago, doesn't it?"

"Yeah. I think about that damn monster and it was almost like a dream." CJ turned to her and smiled. "Of course, there were some really good parts of that assignment."

Paige reached out and quickly squeezed her arm, letting her fingers linger only a second. "Yes, there were. Remember the night we went dancing?"

"The second time?"

"Yes. We kissed as we danced. And then you took me outside," she said, remembering how aroused she'd been after the dance. Outside, hidden in the shadows, she didn't care that others were about. She met CJ's eyes now, holding them, wondering if CJ remembered how she'd begged her not to stop.

CJ nodded. "Yes. It was the first time I got a glimpse of your naughty side."

Paige laughed quietly. "We should do that again."

"Dance?"

"That too."

CHAPTER THIRTY-TWO

Ice sat in the front seat of Brady's patrol car while the forensics' tech sat in the back. It was a short drive to Shady Pines, but Ice thought it was as good a time as any to bring up Thompson.

"So you haven't had any luck getting with Shane Thompson, huh?"

Brady shook his head. "He won't return my calls."

"Is that right? You couldn't go out there?"

"Yeah, I did. He wasn't around."

Ice shook his head. "Come on, man. I talked to Thompson myself. He said he's heard nothing from you."

Brady looked only slightly uncomfortable. "I talked to a woman. I believe it's his daughter. She was supposed to give him a message to call me." He shrugged. "Never heard from him. And I haven't been able to get back to it, since you guys have us at your beck and call over at the Wicker house."

"Well, maybe you can get back to it. Looks like we're about to wrap this one up," he said as they pulled into Edith Krause's driveway.

"Man, what a dump."

Ice glanced at the tech. "Yeah. Makes you wonder what the inside looks like."

He got his wish a short time later when their knock went unanswered. He was about to kick the door in when the tech stopped him.

"I can open it," he said as he pulled a small leather pouch from his pocket

Ice stepped aside. "Be my guest."

It took him all of twenty seconds to pick the lock and push the door open. They all covered their noses when they went inside. It was cluttered and dirty, but not overly so. The kitchen was an absolute mess, though.

"Smells like something died in here too," Brady said.

"It's not human decomp," the tech said. He went to the garbage and lifted the lid, turning his head quickly. "It's a chicken. And it hasn't been cooked."

Ice went over to take a look. "Feet are missing."

"Yeah. And it's been gutted."

Ice looked over at Brady. "Take a look around."

"What am I looking for?"

He shrugged. "I guess we'll know when we find it."

"You want me to take some prints, right?" the tech asked.

"Yeah. Hopefully they'll match the ones we found at the Wicker house."

While Brady pulled open drawers in the living room, Ice went down the short hallway to the bedrooms. The first room was immaculate. It was also a child's room. While the rest of the house could stand a good cleaning, this room appeared to be spotless. He went inside, seeing pictures of a young boy—Eddie. Ice could see why he'd be an easy target for bullying. He was small and thin and wore glasses. In one smiling picture, he had a pronounced overbite. Ice shook his head. The poor kid hadn't had a chance.

But it was in the second bedroom where he knew they'd found what they were looking for.

"Brady," he called. "In here."

It was obviously Edith's bedroom, but there was only a small double bed and one tiny dresser and mirror. The other half of the room was turned into a workplace. A long table was shoved against the wall and hanging above it was a large old-fashioned bulletin board—a cork board. And pinned to it were dozens and dozens of pictures and newspaper clippings of the four missing boys. Right in the center of the board was a small, brief article about Eddie's death.

"Damn," Brady murmured. "I guess she did do it."

Ice took a closer look at the table, then stepped back. "Oh, *man*."

"What?"

He pointed. "It's one of those…those witchcraft books. A spell book," he said.

"Was she into that?"

"You know they found that room in the Wicker house, right? The voodoo room."

"Yeah. I took a peek in there. It was creepy."

Ice turned to go get the tech but found him standing in the doorway, camera ready. They got out of his way, letting him process the room.

"Let me call my team," Ice said, moving back through the living room and outside. The stench from the kitchen was too much to stand. CJ answered immediately.

"What'd you find, baldy?"

He couldn't help but smile. At first he'd hated the nickname she started using when he'd shaved his head. Now, it had kinda grown on him.

"Found what I guess we'd call a serial killer's trophy room," he said. "She's got a wall full of school pictures of the four boys along with what looks like every newspaper story she could find on the disappearances."

"Good job. The tech got prints, right?"

"Yeah. But there was something else. First, we found a mutilated chicken. Feet were cut off and it was gutted."

"Gross."

"Yeah. The smell was horrendous," he said. "And in the room where the newspaper clippings were, there was a book. A damn spell book. Like the one in the voodoo room," he said.

"Old like that one?"

"Yeah. It wasn't a new purchase, in other words."

"So maybe there were two books at the Wicker house and she took one. We know she knew all the secret rooms," CJ said.

"This kind of shit creeps me out, man."

"I know, buddy. But it's almost over with."

"So the body? Is it Herbert?"

"Positive ID hasn't been made, but Herbert Krause's wallet in his pocket, so we can assume. Had forty-five bucks in there, driver's license and a family photo."

"So where the hell is Edith? You don't think she'd head back to Midland, do you?"

"I wouldn't think so. Her old neighbors have already alerted her that we were up there," CJ said.

"Okay. You already call Howley?"

"Yeah. He actually said he was proud of us," CJ said with a laugh.

Ice absently rubbed his hand across his slick head. "If we could find out what happened to Juan, then maybe we'd get off his shit list for good."

"Anything from Brady?" she asked.

"Excuses," he said. "Listen, do you think I should have Brady put up crime scene tape?"

"No. That'll just draw attention from the neighbors. Let's keep it as low-key as possible. You and Brady can secure it, right?"

"Yeah. But we need to get this evidence out. Can you spare any guys for over here?"

"Yeah, they're about done here. They're doing the third floor where they found Herbert. The ME has already taken the bodies. I'll see if a couple of guys can head your way."

"Okay. Thanks. I'll see you later."

He turned, feeling eyes on him. He only caught a glimpse as an old, white-haired woman went back inside her trailer. That would be Lizzie, he thought.

CHAPTER THIRTY-THREE

CJ shook hands with Mike Dupree, the lead of the forensics team. "Your guys did a great job," she said.

"Thanks. I must say it's one of the most unusual scenes we've done."

"Yeah. Tell me about it," she said.

"I'll let you know as soon as we get the results back. I'll have the fingerprints analysis from here and the suspect's residence first thing. I'll let you know," he said as he opened the car door.

"Thanks."

As soon as they drove off, CJ glanced over her shoulder at the house, the sun having slipped behind the trees, leaving long shadows in its wake. Paige came out of the house and walked over to her.

"Do we need to secure it again tonight?"

"Not for evidence, no. But we still haven't located Edith," she said.

"You think she's going to show up here?"

"I don't know. To me, this is kinda like her lair, isn't it? She's got secret passageways, secret rooms to hide her victims."

"BOLO's been out two days," Paige reminded her. "No sightings."

"Yeah. Maybe she did leave the area. But my gut tells me she didn't. Her husband's here. I think since she's been back from Midland, she comes here often to visit him."

Paige arched an eyebrow. "You *feel* this or…someone suggested it?"

CJ grinned. "I haven't had any little voices in my ear lately, no. In fact, nothing since last night."

"Okay. But I'm not sure how much good we're going to do here. We're all exhausted."

"I know we are. Ice got Brady to agree to post a couple of deputies here tonight. We'll lock up the house."

"And the tunnel?"

"Not sure what we can do about that. If they're parked in the driveway, hopefully they'll see her if she tries to enter it." She shrugged. "We'll just have to chance it. Like you said, we're all exhausted."

Billy came out of the house then and closed the door behind him.

"Lock it up?"

"Yeah."

"Man, I'm almost too tired to eat," he said as he came over. "But what's the plan for dinner?"

"I just want to crash," CJ said. "I'll pick up something and take it to the room. You guys go out if you want."

Paige shook her head. "No. Relaxing in the room sounds better than going out."

Billy smiled. "Yeah, you two head back to the hotel. I'm just glad we don't have adjoining rooms."

CJ scowled. "Bite me."

"You wish."

"What are you two bickering about?" Ice asked as he joined them.

"Nothing," Billy said. "You want to go out for dinner? The girls are going to pick something up and eat in their room."

Ice looked at CJ. "That's the plan, huh?"

"I'm tired, man. I would not be good company," she said.

"That's cool." He turned to Billy. "Steak? I'm starved."

"Yeah. Good with me."

Ice winked at her. "See you in the morning then, girls. Don't party too hard tonight."

CJ shook her head as they got in Billy's truck. "If I only had the energy."

Paige smiled at her. "Too tired for even that, tiger?"

"Afraid so."

"I'll have to agree with you. Chinese okay?"

"Sure. I'll try to stay awake long enough to eat."

* * *

Paige rolled over to her side, snuggling closer to CJ. CJ's even breathing never wavered. After they'd showered, they had eaten, but neither of them had come close to finishing their meal. They had literally fallen into bed and were asleep before words could even be spoken.

She reached out now, snaking an arm around CJ's waist, needing the closeness. While CJ had put on a brave front the last two days, Paige knew a lot of her bravado was forced. This whole situation with…with the house, with everything *in* the house, had taken its toll. They were all stressed, sure, but CJ was the only one who was…*hearing* things.

Paige closed her eyes and sighed. She believed her; how could she not? If they weren't as close, if they weren't lovers, she might have had her doubts at the beginning. But not after the other night. Not after finding Herbert Krause's body on the third floor, not after finding the tunnel and the root cellar. Those things, CJ couldn't have known unless someone had told her. Nonetheless, it was unsettling. She could only imagine how disturbing it must be for CJ.

She opened her eyes again when she felt CJ stir. Soon, a warm hand covered hers, fingers rubbing lightly across her skin. Such a simple, innocent touch, yet her pulse sprang to life. Would CJ's touch always do this to her? Those fingers moved higher up her arm, still softly touching. When CJ turned her head, Paige's mouth found hers. It was a slow, languid kiss, lips moving unhurried, just lightly caressing.

CJ rolled toward her then, and they lay facing each other. They both moved at once, their legs entwining. She heard CJ give a contented sigh and she smiled. But CJ's mouth was on hers again, this time just a little harder and she felt her heart flutter. She kissed her back, opening her mouth, moaning quietly as the tip of CJ's tongue met hers.

She rolled to her back, pulling CJ on top of her, spreading her thighs to give CJ room. Her hips rose up to meet her, her breathing labored now as their kisses turned heated. Her eyes slipped closed as CJ left her mouth and found her breast instead, her tongue twirling around her nipple, teasing it before closing her lips around it.

Paige's hands moved at will across CJ's bare back, then lower, cupping her from behind and pulling her harder against her. She nearly whimpered when she felt CJ's hand moving between them. No words were spoken as she parted her legs. CJ's fingers glided through her wetness, eliciting a quiet moan as Paige drew in a sharp breath. CJ entered her slowly, surely, drawing out each stroke before going back inside her, deeper and harder, but not faster. Not yet.

Paige let her set the pace, not rushing her, and she enjoyed the slowness of it, relishing each stroke, her hips moving as slowly as CJ was, letting CJ pause inside of her before pulling out again. It was so slow, so deliberate, that she was surprised when she felt the familiar build of her orgasm.

CJ's mouth still nuzzled against her breast, her tongue bathing her nipple as slowly as her fingers moved inside of her. The sweet, unhurried pace made her body melt under CJ's touch and she let her orgasm come, moaning quietly as it washed over her in effortless pleasure.

As many times as they'd made love before, it was this time… this simple, purposeful lovemaking…that pulled the words from her.

"I love you."

CJ's finger's brushed against her face, her eyes, her lips. Paige didn't care if CJ felt her tears or not.

"God, Paige...I love you too."

CHAPTER THIRTY-FOUR

CJ's eyes fluttered open, but she closed them quickly, willing sleep to take her again. Even though she knew she was alone, she reached for Paige, grabbing her pillow instead and hugging it to her. She heard the shower but couldn't work up the energy to join Paige there.

Or maybe she was simply feeling a bit shy this morning.

I love you.

She felt nearly dizzy as she remembered the words Paige had whispered to her, words that CJ had returned. They'd made love again after that, with an intensity that was meant to show exactly how much they loved. They'd fallen asleep immediately, still tangled in each other's arms.

And now the light of day was upon them. And she was feeling a bit exposed. And more than a little vulnerable.

She heard the bathroom door open and rolled over, releasing Paige's pillow. Their eyes met, held, both questioning. Paige finally gave her a small smile and CJ did the same.

"Do we need to talk?"

CJ hesitated, wondering if that was Paige's way of saying *she* wanted to talk. "Umm, I'm good," she finally said.

Paige stared at her for a moment, still holding her eyes captive. Then she nodded, releasing the towel that had been tied around her, giving CJ a wicked smile as she walked naked back into the bathroom.

CJ laughed, feeling the tension leave the room.

"Tease," she called.

"I'm not stopping you from coming in here."

CJ flung the covers off and hurried into the bathroom after her.

* * *

"They said all was quiet," Ice said. "Of course, I wouldn't doubt if they'd fallen asleep. They look like they've been napping."

"No hits on her car; I wonder where the hell she went," CJ said. She glanced at Paige. "Do you think there's a chance she went back to Midland?"

Paige shook her head. "Where would she go? Her mother's in a nursing home and they sold the house." She shook her head again. "I think *this* is home to her," she said, motioning to the Wicker house. "Her husband was here."

"A man she most likely killed," Billy reminded them.

A man she was most likely *forced* to kill, CJ thought, but she didn't voice it. She still hadn't told Ice and Billy everything that she'd learned that night in the house.

"So what's the plan? Continue to hang out here and hope she shows?" Ice asked.

"She has to get to the root cellar somehow," CJ said. "Maybe there's a trail through the woods."

"Oh, great," Paige said. "Let's take a trail through the woods. Nothing bad *ever* happens there."

CJ laughed. "I don't think any big, scary monsters roam these woods." She headed toward the ruins, then stopped. "That's okay with you, right?" she asked, looking at Billy and Ice.

Ice shrugged. "Sure. You know me, I love the woods," he said sarcastically.

"I won't let anything happen to you, baldy."

The area around the door—the wooden plank—did not look disturbed. After they found the tunnel yesterday, they'd covered it back up, much like they'd found it. CJ walked around it, her eyes scanning the area, looking for any sign of a trail.

"Here," Paige said. "Through the vines."

CJ looked where she pointed. It was another spot where the vines had been cut. Billy went first, moving limbs out of the way. It didn't take much of an imagination to find the trail. It had been partially covered in brush for the first twenty feet or so. After that, the trail was well formed until it reached the back fence.

"She must have used this trail a lot," Paige said.

"She's been back a year. Maybe she visited Herb regularly," she said, going closer to the fence. "Here's the break." The wire had been cut in a straight line but had been repositioned to look intact. She pulled it apart, revealing the gap.

"Do you think this is how she brought the boys in?" Ice asked.

CJ ducked under a low wire and to the other side. "Most likely, what with the gate being locked in the front. I can't see her driving them here."

"Listen," Paige said, and they all stopped. "Birds."

CJ nodded. "Yeah. I guess we're out of the dead zone."

"I hate that term," Ice said.

"It is what it is, baldy."

They walked on, single file, another fifteen minutes or so before they came to a fork in the trail. The one to the right looked well used. To the left, not so much.

"What do you think?" Billy asked.

"We need to check them both out, see where they go," CJ said. "You and Paige, take that one," she said, pointing to the right. "We'll take this one."

Paige looked at her questioningly for only a second. CJ offered her a quick smile. Yeah, she'd rather be partnered with Paige too, but frankly, she didn't trust the guys together. Paige seemed to understand and nodded.

When they walked off, she turned to Ice. "Ready?"

"So we're taking the one less traveled?"

She laughed quickly. "Yeah, I guess so."

"The other one is more likely to turn up something," he said.

"Maybe. But this one was obviously used at one point. And while it's not as well worn, it's been used in the last fourteen years. And I'd guess it's been used in the year she's been back. Besides, I got a feeling." She stopped, touching a small limb that had been recently broken. The leaves on the damaged end were still clinging to life. She pointed at it. "Recent break."

He nodded, his glance going to the woods behind them.

She moved on, slower now, looking for footprints, looking for signs. Leaves were starting to fall from the trees, covering the trail in spots. If they had been a month or two later, she doubted they would have even found this trail.

"Is this private property?" Ice asked.

"I have no clue. Maybe the county owns it. Maybe it's a greenbelt or something."

He laughed at that. "We're in the middle of the woods. I think greenbelts are reserved for the cities."

"Yeah, okay, so I'm a city girl now," she said, continuing along the path.

After a short while, he said, "Does this remind you of Hoganville?"

"No. Should it?"

"Well, we're in the woods on a trail," he said.

"And that is the only similarity. We were on that damn trail at night with your big scary monster chasing us. This is a walk in the park."

* * *

Paige let Billy take the lead, and she followed close behind, ducking under a low limb as he had done. She was glad she'd worn jeans today as a vine caught against her leg.

"So, you and CJ okay?" Billy asked.

"Yes. Why do you ask?"

"'Cause she's with Ice, and you're with me."

"Well, you and I *are* partners," she reminded him.

He stopped and turned. "Is this whole *ghost* thing getting to her?"

She tilted her head. "Wouldn't it get to you?"

He shrugged. "I'm not entirely sure I believe it all."

"I know it's farfetched. For me too," she admitted. "But how else can you explain how she knew about the tunnel? Or about Herbert being on the third floor?"

He frowned. "What about Herbert?"

She bit her lip. She'd forgotten CJ had not shared that with them. "That night when she went in the house, when she told us about the root cellar, about the tunnel. She told me that we would find Herbert on the third floor."

"Are you serious? So she's like…psychic or something?"

"CJ's not psychic, Billy," she snapped. "How do *you* think she knew about it all?"

"So you believe a ghost is talking to her? Telling her all this?"

"You were there," she said. "You saw her take a dive down the laundry chute." She arched an eyebrow at him. "Or are you forgetting that?"

"Maybe I've had a chance to sleep on it," he said. "In broad daylight, it all sounds a little crazy."

She wanted to be angry with him, but she couldn't. Because yes, in broad daylight, it did seem a little crazy.

"Let's just follow the trail," she said, giving him a gentle push.

CHAPTER THIRTY-FIVE

Paige stopped up short. "Are we where I think we are?"

"Shady Pines?"

Paige bent down, peering under the limbs of a thick cedar, shocked to find herself staring at old, shabby trailer homes.

"Do you know which one is hers?"

"I don't know that I'd recognize it from this direction, but I could find Lizzie's," she said, moving along the trail again.

A short time later, the trail disappeared into a pile of brush. She looked at Billy with raised eyebrows.

"She hid the trail at both ends," he said.

They were still a good forty or fifty feet away from the break in the woods and the nearest trailer. She could hear a dog barking off in the distance but other than that, all was quiet. They started moving the brush out of the way, exposing the trail. It took a sharp turn to the left, leading them away from the trailer houses they'd seen. The limbs and brush covering the trail now were scattered haphazardly, and they could easily make out the trail until they came to another large pile of brush. Paige grabbed Billy's arm as he went to move it.

"That must be hers," she said. "Lizzie's home is across the street."

"I don't see a car," Billy said. "You think she'd come back here?"

"Probably not. Let me call CJ."

* * *

The ringing of her phone pierced the silence of the woods. CJ answered it immediately. "What'd you find?"

"You won't believe where the trail leads," Paige said. "Back to Shady Pines...and Edith's trailer."

"You're kidding? I didn't think the Wicker house was that close." She glanced at Ice. "The trail led back to Shady Pines."

"Her car's not here," Paige said. "We're going to take a quick look around, make sure she hasn't been here."

"Okay. I don't know where the hell we are," she said, looking around them. "We're still in the woods. If we don't come upon something soon, we'll turn around."

"Be in touch."

"I will."

She pocketed her phone again and started walking. "Makes sense it goes back to Shady Pines, doesn't it," she said.

"Easy for her to come and go without being seen," he said.

"Man, but I saw her. She just doesn't look the type. I mean, she's overweight, kinda frumpy looking. I can't see her taking this trail through the woods," she said.

"It's been fourteen years. People age."

"I suppose. But that trail has seen use recently." She stopped, seeing what looked like stones. "Look. What's all that? Big rocks?"

He followed her gaze. "There's chain-link fence," he said.

They walked closer, then she stopped again. "Whoa," she said. "Headstones."

"Oh, shit. We're at the cemetery."

"Yeah. This must be the back side. Look how old the headstones are." The trail ended at the fence, and she didn't see any evidence of a breach. "I know damn well she didn't jump this," she said as she leaned over, looking for anything disturbed.

"Over here," Ice said.

She followed him as he made his way through the brush and around the corner of the fence. Through the trees, they could just make out the road. She grabbed his arm as she saw the sun reflecting off of glass...or maybe chrome.

"What?"

"There's something in the woods," she said.

He turned pale. "Something like what?"

She laughed. "Relax, baldy. I mean I saw a reflection. Could be a car. Come on."

She hurried now, dodging low-hanging limbs and stepping silently over dead, fallen trees. The car was well-hidden from the road. She held her hand up, signaling for him to stop. She pointed in the other direction, motioning for him to take the flank. He nodded, and they pulled their weapons from their holsters. She waited until he was in position, then started walking toward the car.

As he circled from the back, she walked directly toward the driver's side. It was hidden in shadows, but she saw no movement inside. She waited again, letting Ice draw nearer.

"Trunk is open," he said quietly.

She nodded, then reached for the door handle. It was locked. She leaned closer, peering inside.

"Empty."

She joined him at the back, then stood aside as he lifted up the trunk. They both took a quick step back.

"Jesus Christ," Ice murmured.

"Oh, God, no," CJ said, reaching inside.

"Who is it?"

"Lizzie." She was bound and gagged, and CJ was shocked to find a weak pulse. "She's alive. Call Brady, get an ambulance," she said quickly.

She pulled the duct tape from her mouth as gently as she could. Lizzie groaned but didn't open her eyes.

CJ slowly lifted her up, seeing the dried blood on the back of her head, marring her snow-white hair.

"I'm so sorry," she whispered. And she was. They had no business asking this ninety-year-old woman to assist them, no business leaving cards and asking her to call them if Edith showed up. *Damn.*

"Brady's on his way. Ambulance too."

"Looks like she got whacked on the back of the head," CJ said. "Why do you think she left the trunk open?"

"Edith has probably known Lizzie most of her life. I imagine she couldn't bring herself to kill her." Her gaze went into the woods as she held Lizzie's thin, frail body. "So if Edith isn't here, where the hell is she?"

CHAPTER THIRTY-SIX

"Should we knock?"

Paige pulled out her weapon. "I'm going to say no."

He nodded, then turned the doorknob. It wasn't locked. "Wonder why they didn't lock it up when they left yesterday."

He went inside and she followed, both of them covering their noses immediately. Ice had told them the stench was bad, but this made her eyes water. It was dark inside and she flipped on a light switch. Nothing happened. Her eyes darted around the room. Something wasn't right. She could feel it.

"Ice didn't say anything about there being no power. He did say there was a raw chicken in the garbage though," Billy said. "He wasn't lying about that. You'd think—"

"Shhh," she said. "Did you hear that?" she asked in a whisper.

He shook his head.

She glanced down the dark hallway, seeing nothing in the darkness. "I left my flashlight in CJ's truck," she said quietly. "You?"

He shook his head again.

The hair on the back of her neck stood out, and she knew they weren't alone. Adrenaline kicked in and her heart pounded in her chest. Even then, she had no time to react. Edith Krause leapt up from behind the sofa, lunging at them. Paige cried out in pain as her arm was smashed, knocking her gun from her hands. Billy spun around, only to take a bat to the jaw, dropping him in his tracks. Paige fell to her knees, scrambling for her gun along the dirty carpet. Just as she reached it, just as her fingers wrapped around it, the back of her head exploded in pain and her world plunged into darkness.

* * *

After seeing Lizzie safely inside the ambulance, CJ and Ice caught a ride with Brady back to the Wicker house. It was already after one and CJ's stomach rumbled. She looked at Ice.

"So I'm hungry," she murmured.

"Me too."

Brady stopped his patrol car at the gate. "You want me to hang around?" Brady asked.

"No, we got it. I'd rather you make sure her car gets impounded so we can have our guys go over it," she said as she got out.

"I can do that. I guess you're going to want us to have a patrol car here again tonight, right?"

"If you can, yes. Until we locate Edith Krause. We'll hang around here until then."

Brady tipped his hat at her and smirked. "We aim to serve the FBI, ma'am. We'll come around about five or so."

He spun his tires a bit as he pulled away, and CJ shook her head. "Prick." Then she reconsidered. She shouldn't be so hard on him. He was helping them out, after all.

"Hey," Ice said, holding up his phone. "Billy's still not answering."

The smile left her face, and she pulled out her own phone again. She'd tried calling Paige earlier but hadn't gotten an answer. She'd blamed it on a weak signal. But Paige and Billy should have checked in by now. Or else have made their way back here along the trail. She punched Paige's number, her eyes scanning the woods behind the house. It was still several hours before the shadows would become thick, before the woods turned dark, but it would happen all too soon. She locked gazes with Ice as the phone continued to ring, unanswered.

"Let's get over there," she said as she broke out into a run for her truck.

The five-minute drive from the Wicker house to Shady Pines seemed to take an eternity. She skidded to a stop in Edith's driveway, and they pulled out their weapons as they crept closer to the door. Nothing appeared disturbed.

Ice went up the cinder block steps and tried the door. It was locked. CJ glanced at the windows, but blinds covered each one.

"Knock," she said and Ice pounded on the door.

"FBI," he called loudly.

CJ tilted her head, listening. "Did you hear that?"

"I heard movement, yes. Stand back," he said.

It took three kicks before the lock gave way and the door slammed open. The stench hit them immediately.

"Jesus Christ," CJ murmured as she covered her nose. "What the hell?"

"Dead chicken," Ice said quietly as he went inside first, gun in the ready position.

CJ went in behind him, eyes scanning the room. Her heart caught in her throat when she saw them on the floor, tied together. *Oh God.* Her first instinct was to go to them, but her training took over.

"Secure the trailer first, Ice."

He went into the kitchen, and she headed down the hall, pausing to squat down beside them. She pulled the duct tape from Billy's mouth first, then Paige's.

"Is she still here?" she whispered.

"Don't know," Billy mumbled, his eyes still closed.

She touched Paige's face, seeing her eyelids flutter open, then closed again. CJ went down the hallway, pushing open each door carefully.

"Clear," Ice called.

"Clear back here," she said as she hurried back.

Ice was already untying them, and CJ stood by helplessly, her eyes drawn to Paige's face, waiting for her eyes to open and show those baby blues.

Ice looked up at her. "Looks like Paige took a whack to the back of the head too."

Billy groaned and sat up, holding his face. A dark bruise covered his jaw. CJ kneeled down beside Paige as they rolled her over to her back.

"Hey, can you open your eyes?" she asked gently.

Paige squeezed her hand tightly, but her eyes remained closed. "This carpet is filthy."

CJ grinned. "Yeah, it is. I'm afraid to move you, though. What hurts?"

"What doesn't?" Her eyes finally opened. "Billy?"

"He's okay." She glanced at Ice. "Baldy is calling an ambulance."

"Don't need one. Just have a little headache," Paige said as she reached behind her, only to wince in pain.

CJ noticed the swelling and bruise on her arm. She wouldn't be surprised if it was fractured. She turned Paige's head, seeing blood on the back of her neck. She gently moved her hair aside, revealing a two-inch gash at the base of her skull.

"Oh, baby," she whispered.

"Baseball bat," Paige murmured.

"Okay, just lie still." She looked at Billy. "What happened?"

"We should have known, I guess," he said, his words mumbled as he barely moved his mouth. "The door was unlocked when we got here. Power was off. She was hiding behind the couch," he said. He held his jaw lightly. "She's quick with that bat, man."

"She was possessed," Paige murmured.

"Possessed?"

"Like Spiderman. A ninja Spiderman."

CJ frowned and glanced at Billy. "*What?* Spiderman?"

"She flew over that couch. Quick as lightning," he said, then groaned again as he held his jaw.

"Quick as lightning? Edith Krause? Are you sure it was her? I mean, I've seen her. Come on," she said.

"A ninja," Paige said again.

"And she swung a mean bat. I feel like my teeth are falling out."

"You probably have a broken jaw, man," Ice said. "You're damn lucky. You both are."

Yeah. Damn lucky. CJ took a deep breath and let it out slowly. She didn't care that Ice and Billy were watching. She sat down beside Paige, her hand touching her cheek lightly, just needing some contact. Her beautiful face was etched in pain, the blond hair she loved to run her fingers through was caked with blood. Yet Paige still clung tightly to her hand. Her eyes opened again, enough for them to make contact, and CJ held her gaze, wanting so badly to tell her she loved her. Last night seemed so long ago. But Paige's eyes slipped closed again, and CJ let out a frustrated sigh.

She looked across the room, finding Ice watching her. She gave a weak smile.

"It stinks in here," she said.

"No shit."

"God only knows what's on this carpet," Paige murmured, causing them all to laugh.

* * *

CJ and Paige's gazes locked together until the slamming of the door cut them off.

"Two ambulances in one day," she said as they watched it drive away. "Some kind of record for us, huh?"

"Yeah. Usually it's the coroner's van," Ice said. "They said she's okay. Not even a concussion."

CJ nodded. "I know. It's just...scary." She met his eyes. "I know, our line of work, there are risks we take. But now...hell, Ice, she told me she loved me." She was certain she was grinning like a teenager. "She said she loved me."

"Well, I hope you told her too and didn't freeze up like some guy."

CJ laughed. "I am *so* not some guy."

"Does that mean you did?"

Her expression turned serious. "I did. And it was...so special, that moment. I'll remember it always."

He surprised her by pulling her into a tight hug. "I'm happy for you, CJ. You deserve some love in your life."

She clung to him tightly, this man who was her partner, her rock. Then it occurred to her—and probably him too—that this was the first time they'd ever hugged like this. They separated, each looking a tad embarrassed.

Ice cleared his throat. "So…where do you think Edith is?"

"The only place she can be. The Wicker house."

"Yeah. I was afraid you'd say that."

"Come on," she said, heading to her truck. "Let's put an end to this. You want to call Brady? Get some backup?"

"What? You think we can't handle her?"

"Well, Spiderman and all," she said as she pulled away. "I'm more worried about you, actually."

"Why?"

"Because I'm going to need you in the house with me," she said with a quick glance his way.

He nodded. "We're partners. I'm with you." He paused. "There's just one thing. They took the generator and the lights."

"Yeah…it's going to be loads of fun."

CHAPTER THIRTY-SEVEN

CJ stared at the sky, watching in disbelief as dark, ominous clouds gathered, hiding the early afternoon sun. Shadows were already creeping in from the forest, the tall pines out back of the house looking sinister and threatening. The dead sentinels standing guard nearest the house were but skeletons, their bony fingers sprawling out as if protecting it from unseen forces. She pushed the front door open slowly, listening. All was quiet.

"Stay here," she said.

"Where're you going?"

"Up to the second floor."

"What the hell for?"

Telling him she was going up to see if a ghost was going to talk to her—help her—seemed a bit, well, irrational. But what the hell?

"I'm going to see if there are any friendly ghosts around," she said.

"Jesus, CJ, I'm freaked out enough," he said. "Do you have to talk like that?"

"I'll be right back." She paused. "I think maybe you should give Brady a call after all."

"Yeah. Okay."

She hurried up the stairs, cringing as the fourth step squeaked with her weight. She paused, halfway expecting to hear running feet beside her along the stairs and was actually disappointed when she did not. The only sound she heard was her own breathing... and the pounding of her heart.

"Now would be a good time for some help," she murmured. She waited. Nothing.

She walked up to the landing, looking into the shadows. Outside the windows, it was nearly dark. She didn't dare put her flashlight on for fear someone—*something*—would see it from the third floor.

"Come on," she whispered. "Where are you?"

She waited. Thirty seconds. Ninety. Still nothing. *Damn.* Had she been imagining everything this whole time? She shook her head in frustration, then retraced her steps, finding Ice still standing in the doorway.

"Well?"

"Nothing," she said.

"Okay. Now what?"

"Now we search the house."

"Look how dark it got," he said, his voice crackling with nervousness. "It's still early. What is it? Two? Three?" He looked behind him as dark clouds blanketed the woods around the house.

"I know. Brady?"

He shook his head. "I got no service."

She frowned. "We've had service out here all along." She pulled out her own phone. Nothing. She looked at him, eyes wide.

"Don't look at me like that," he said.

"Like what?"

"Like you're thinking some damn ghost or something is blocking our signal."

She tilted her head. "You got a better idea?"

"Yeah. You know, maybe the cell tower...maybe it's—"

"What? On the fritz or something?"

"It's a possibility."

"Sure it is," she said. "But regardless, we're cut off."

He shook his head slowly. "Oh, man. I got a bad feeling, CJ."

"Yeah? Well, fuck it. We can do this." She clicked her flashlight on, glad she'd remembered to grab Paige's instead of her own dim light. "Let's start in the kitchen."

"I hope you know what you're doing."

Ice followed close behind her, their lights crisscrossing along the floor and walls as they entered the kitchen. They stopped, their lights shining on the closed door to the pantry.

"They left that door open," Ice whispered.

CJ nodded. She walked slowly toward it, reaching out to grab the knob. It was locked. She glanced back at him and shook her head.

"Oh...*man*," he murmured.

She turned him around, pushing him out of the kitchen.

"Dining room. Let's see if the door to my laundry room is locked too."

"We should wait for backup," he said.

"I thought you said we could take her," CJ replied.

"Yeah, that was when we were outside in the daylight," he said. "Ninja Spiderman, remember?"

"I'm more worried about what's on the third floor," she murmured.

"What are you talking about?"

She shook her head. "Nothing. But any backup we're going to get isn't coming until five. That's when Brady said he'd send someone. So come on. It's just us."

The dining room door stood open, as it had been. Being an interior room without windows, it was completely dark inside. Their flashlights did little to brighten it. CJ walked purposely toward the door to the small closet. As with the kitchen door, it had been left open. It too was now closed. She wasn't surprised to find it locked as well.

"I think it's safe to say she's here at the Wicker house," she said in a near whisper.

"Yeah. But where?"

"She's on the third floor," she said. Oh, Edith could be hiding in one of the secret rooms, sure, but CJ didn't think so. Whatever was going to happen, it was going to happen on the third floor. How she knew this, she couldn't be sure, but she knew it with certainty.

She reached out, grabbing Ice's forearm and squeezed. "Be ready for anything," she said.

"We...we should wait for some backup," he said again.

"It isn't Edith Krause I'm worried about," she said, walking past him.

Back out in the foyer, she was almost disappointed that the front door remained open. It was yet another sign that she was on her own. But she kept hearing that voice in her head, that voice that told her not to go up to the third floor.

I can't help you up there. He is too powerful.

She didn't mind admitting she was afraid, if only to herself. She pushed down her fear and headed up the steps. She felt Ice behind her even though he hadn't said another word. She could tell by the shaking of his light that he'd rather be anywhere other than here. She stopped, listening. Nothing.

"It's quiet," she whispered. "Too quiet."

Ice touched her back, and she jumped, startled. "Sorry," he murmured.

She took a deep breath, then went up another two steps, her weapon held out in front of her. She was nearly embarrassed by the pounding of her heart. It was so loud in her ears, she imagined Ice could hear it as well. She glanced back at him, but his gaze was fixed on the second-floor landing. Though he appeared a little pale, his face was etched with a look of determination that wasn't foreign to her. He may be afraid of this house, afraid of whatever ghosts might haunt it, but the look on his face told her he was ready to do his job. That was comforting, although it did very little to ease her apprehension as she slowly inched up another two steps.

What was left of the remaining daylight barely illuminated the second-floor windows. Nonetheless, she clicked off her flashlight and shoved it inside her jeans at the waist. She held her weapon with both hands now, stepping into the hallway, her glance immediately going to the third floor. She peered into the darkness, but nothing seemed out of the ordinary.

"Let's check these rooms," she said quietly, even though she doubted Edith would be hiding in them.

Ice slowly pushed open one of the bedroom doors. This was the empty room, and there was no place for her to hide. They went to the other room, the one that was still furnished. It faced west but even then, there wasn't enough light left in the sky for them to see without their flashlights. CJ felt perspiration on her neck as she squatted down and looked under the bed. She saw movement and nearly screamed.

"Shhh. She'll hear you."

"Son of a bitch," she muttered as she grabbed her chest in fright.

"What?" Ice asked urgently. "What is it?"

CJ shook her head as she stood back up. "Go out in the hall, Ice," she said.

"What?"

"Give me a second."

His eyes widened, and he nodded, backing out of the room and closing the door. CJ took several deep breaths, trying to tell herself she did not just *see* something under the bed. She clicked her flashlight off, plunging the room into near darkness.

"You hiding?" she finally asked.

"He is angry with her. She was supposed to kill them."

CJ didn't know if she meant Lizzie or Paige and Billy. Probably all three. She felt a tightening in her chest. "Are you afraid of him too?"

"This is the safe room" was all she said. Then, *"You mustn't go up there."*

"Is Edith up there?"

"Yes. She has the ax. She's to use it on you."

"Nice to know," she said.

"If you go up there, you will not return."

CJ blew out her breath. "Guess we'll have to see about that." She turned to go, then stopped. "Did I really see you there under the bed? Because if I did, I may need to get into a new line of work." She gave a quick, uneasy laugh. "Okay. Never mind."

"She...is the key."

"The key?"

"To unlock the evil."

CJ frowned. What the hell did that mean? She shook it away, needing to focus on the task at hand, not try to decipher the words of a ghost. Back in the hallway, Ice was pressed against the wall, his eyes darting around.

"Well?"

She slid her gaze up the stairs to the third floor. "We go up."

She walked to the bottom of the stairs, then paused, glancing back at Ice. Their eyes held for a long moment, both of them finally nodding. As she took the first step, she heard it. Boards creaking overhead. They looked up at the ceiling, as if they could see through it. Footsteps moved over their heads, walking faster now.

"She's up there," CJ said quietly. "She...she may have an ax."

"Yeah? Bring it on. My nine-millimeter trumps her ax," Ice said. "Let's get this over with. I want to get the hell out of here."

CJ wasn't sure what she was expecting, but she was expecting *something*. But after five steps, then six, there was still no sign of... of anything. She barely had time to register those thoughts when a ferocious roar rumbled down the stairs, bouncing off the walls around her. Ice's eyes widened and his mouth opened but no sound escaped. He heard it too.

"What...what the fuck is that?" he finally managed.

Before CJ could even think of answering, she was thrown against the wall, her head slamming back, and she nearly sunk to her knees. Feeling as if an iron hand circled her neck, she struggled to draw a breath.

Ice grabbed her, trying to pull her down the stairs, but something...some force held her back.

"Come *on*," he yelled, wrapping an arm around her waist.

Her head was spinning, and she was afraid she was going to pass out. She held tight to Ice, squeezing her eyes shut as the pressure in her head magnified.

Just when she thought they'd made it, Ice was flung away from her, down the stairs, landing in a heap against the far wall.

"GET OUT OF MY HOUSE!"

The grip around her neck disappeared, and CJ fell like a ragdoll. She sucked in deep breaths, her chest heaving. The roar down the stairwell was as loud as a jet engine during takeoff. She tried to cover her ears, but the sound penetrated. She got to her feet, glancing back at Ice. He shook his head from side to side as if to clear it. Instead of going to him, she took another step up, looking for movement, looking for Edith.

"GET OUT!"

A blast of hot air took her legs from her, and she fell, face first, on the stairs. The force knocked the gun from her hand, and she snatched it back up, seconds before she was picked up and thrown down the stairs. She landed against Ice's solid chest, and he steadied her, holding her tight.

"What the fuck is happening?" he yelled, trying to be heard above the roar.

It suddenly became clear. Yes, Edith was the key. He needed Edith to do his dirty work. If he could kill them, he would have already done so. She grabbed Ice's arm and tugged him into the bedroom...the safe room. As soon as the door closed behind them, the roar in the hallway ceased.

They looked at each other, breathing hard. The shadows in the room were chased back by the glow of their flashlights.

"This is a safe room," she said.

Ice raised his eyebrows questioningly.

"Because she told me it was. I know now what she meant when she said Edith was the key."

"What the hell are you talking about?"

"Just listen to me," she said impatiently. "He can't touch us. Not that way. Not in a way to kill us," she said. "He can toy with us. He can try to scare the hell out of us. He—"

"Yeah, that's working so far," Ice said. "Because I about shit in my pants."

"He needs Edith to do his bidding. He knew we would go to her place. He sent her there to wait."

"How the hell do you know that?"

"Because Paige said she was possessed. I've *seen* Edith Krause. No way she goes all ninja Spiderman on them. She's a frumpy, overweight, middle-aged woman," she said.

Ice shook his head. "Something had a hold of us. Some dude yelling to get out of his house. Something picked me up and threw me down the stairs. Something picked you up and tossed you down the stairs."

"Yes. Something had a grip around my throat," she said, touching it. "But I'm still here, breathing," she said. "He needs Edith." As they stared at each other, it finally occurred to her that Ice was hearing the same things she was. Her eyes widened. "You *heard* everything," she said. "Not just me. But you heard it too."

Ice nodded. "Yeah, I heard the son of a bitch."

CJ grinned broadly. "Oh, thank you," she said. "I was so tired of being the only one."

"Glad you find it funny. And here we are, hiding in a safe room," he said. "If we wait a little longer, Brady's guys might show up."

"Yeah. And how do we explain everything to them?"

He stared at her, dumbfounded. "*That's* what you're concerned with?" He paced across the room. "Jesus Christ, CJ, there's a goddamn ghost or something out there," he said loudly, pointing to the door. "He's flinging us around like dolls and you're worried about explaining it? Hell, explain it to me," he said, pointing at his chest.

"Okay, calm down," she said, holding up her hands. "Just calm down."

"I will not calm down," he snapped. "I want to get the hell out of here."

"Yeah? Well our suspect…our *murder* suspect…is up there. You want to just leave her be? Maybe give her a pardon or something?"

He rubbed his bald head with his hands, back and forth, finally letting out a deep breath. "You're right. We're fucking FBI agents." He walked to the window where dark clouds seemed to be so close, they could almost touch them. "What the fuck is happening, CJ?" He pointed out the window. "It's like we're in a goddamn horror movie."

She walked over to him and leaned against him, resting her head on his shoulder as both of them looked out into the ever-darkening woods. She sighed heavily and he did the same.

"Come on. Let's go get her."

CHAPTER THIRTY-EIGHT

The hallway was completely dark, and they flashed their lights around the walls and floor. It was quiet. CJ looked to the ceiling, hoping to hear Edith overhead, but there was no sound.

"Jesus, what the hell is that?" Ice whispered. His light shone against the wall near the base of the stairs, then slowly moved higher.

CJ went closer, staring in disbelief. "It's…it's blood."

"Whose?"

"I'm guessing it's not recent." It seemed to be growing as she watched, the dark stain crawling along the wall up to the third floor.

"What do you mean? It looks fresh. It's still wet."

"Lizzie said Wicker killed his two remaining children and his wife with an ax. She said the walls were covered with blood. I imagine this is where it happened."

"Oh, *man*," Ice murmured.

She pulled her eyes away from a droplet of blood as it ran down the wall beside her. "Ignore it. It's not real," she said as she edged past it, taking one step at a time. Her light flashed up the stairs, but she saw no movement.

Then, as before, a thunderous roar came rolling down the stairs, engulfing them. As she was doing with the blood on the wall, CJ tried to ignore the sound. She pushed through it, going higher, six steps, now seven. She nearly dropped her flashlight when an invisible iron fist pushed against her face, slamming her into the blood-soaked wall. She felt the wet stickiness against her cheek, belying her assertion that it wasn't real.

"Edith?" she yelled. "Edith Krause?" She doubted Edith could hear her; the roar was so loud, her words were lost as soon as they left her mouth.

She pushed away from the wall, wiping at the blood on her face. She glanced back at Ice, who stood frozen in place, his eyes wide.

"Come on," she yelled.

His light was shaking as he came closer, but he never took his eyes off the stairs above them. He was just one step below her when he was literally picked up and flung down the stairs, landing on his back. His light and gun both went scattering when he fell.

"GET OUT OF MY HOUSE!"

"Ice?" *Goddamn.* She retraced her steps, bending over to check on him. He was struggling to catch his breath, and she helped him sit up. "You okay?"

"GET OUT!"

"Are you seriously asking me that question?"

Despite it all, she gave a quick laugh. "Yeah, what was I thinking?" She moved to pick up his light and gun, handing them to him. The roar suddenly stopped, leaving complete silence in its wake. "Can you get up?" Her words seemed loud in the now quiet house.

"What the fuck are we doing, CJ? We can't see a goddamn thing. We can't even get *up* to the third floor."

"So what do you want to do? Wait for the goddamn sheriff's deputies to show up? Then what? Have them try to get up here?"

"I don't know."

She stood up straight, facing the stairs. "Edith?" she yelled. "You're under arrest!" She looked at Ice and grinned. "That always works, right?"

"Yeah, right."

She waited and was actually surprised to hear footsteps overhead once again. It sounded as if Edith was pacing, back and forth above them.

"If he wants Edith to kill us, why won't he let us get up there?" she asked.

"What are you talking about?"

"I think he gets his power by the killings," she said. "It started with Spencer. Then the Wickers. Then the Underwoods. After that, nothing. Not until Edith brought the boys here and killed them. And then killed Herbert."

"This isn't some goddamn movie, CJ."

"Don't you think I know that? Hell, I lived through the Hoganville nightmare. Nothing would surprise me anymore," she said.

"Okay. Okay. So he gets his power by killing. What's your point?"

"I don't know what my point is," she said. "Unless he's afraid of us."

"Why would he be afraid of us?"

"Because Edith is the key. If something happens to Edith, he's lost his power."

He stared at her and shook his head. "Are you just making this shit up or do you really believe it?"

"Just play along with me, baldy." She held out her hand and pulled him to his feet. "Come on."

She stood at the bottom step, staring up. She took two deep breaths, then raced up the stairs, not stopping until she'd reached the landing on the third floor. Hot air surrounded her, and she felt pressure against her chest, much like that day in the café in Hoganville. She shook it off, telling herself it wasn't real.

"Ice?"

He headed up the stairs, slower than she did. He made it to the sixth step before he was pushed against the wall.

"Fight it," she yelled at him. She looked into the dark hallway of the third floor. "Edith? Edie Krause? Come on, goddamn it. Show yourself." She glanced back at Ice, who was still pressed against the wall. His flashlight fell from his hand, and she watched as it bounced slowly down the stairs, one step at a time, coming to a rest against the wall on the second floor. She took a step down, intending to go to his aid, then stopped. She heard a rustling down the hallway, and she whipped around, shining her light into the shadows. Nothing.

Her heart was pounding loudly and sweat beaded up on her face. She took quick, shallow breaths, trying to see into the darkness, looking for any movement. Even then, she still wasn't prepared when Edith Krause leapt toward her from seemingly out of nowhere. She ducked, dropping to her knees as Edith swung the ax, embedding it in the wall above her.

CJ scrambled back to her feet, only to be slammed against the wall by an unseen force. Her eyes widened as Edith swung again. Everything slowed to a crawl as she was held in place, unable to move. She tried to raise her hands, but they were locked to her sides, her light and gun ripped from her fingers. She opened her mouth, trying to speak, but her throat closed completely.

The sound of a gunshot pierced the silence. Edith staggered in mid-swing, her fixed gaze going from CJ to Ice. She stopped, hissing as an angry animal would when she glared at Ice. In the dim light, all CJ could see were red, glowing eyes as Edith turned to Ice, the ax held high over her head. When Edith charged Ice, the force holding CJ disappeared, and she dropped to the floor. She scrambled to find her gun, wincing as Ice fired again.

Edith kept going, oblivious to the gunshots, brandishing the ax as it swung back and forth over her head. She let out a scream, something primal—loud and hideous, and it echoed up and down the stairwell.

"Drop the goddamn ax," Ice yelled, pointing his gun at her. Edith ignored his warning as she stumbled down the stairs toward him.

"GET OUT OF MY HOUSE!"

The loud, thunderous roar that had subsided picked up again, filling the staircase. CJ's hand was shaking as she watched the scene unfold in the small beam of her flashlight. Ice looked like he was prepared to fire again when his legs were knocked from him and he fell to the stairs, rolling down to the landing again. Edith charged and took a swing at him and CJ fired her weapon, hitting Edith in the back. Ice rolled out of the way only seconds before the ax hit.

Lying on his back, he fired again, twice. The blows only served to stagger her. She picked the ax up again, taking aim at him as he scooted away from her.

CJ ran down the stairs, grabbing the ax from behind as Edith attempted to swing. She pulled hard on it only to have it slip from her hands. Edith spun around, quick as a cat, pushing CJ against the wall. She opened her mouth and growled, and CJ was hit with a repugnant smell, so foul and putrid that she nearly vomited. Edith's eyes glowed red, and yes, she was indeed possessed by something evil. Blood dripped from her wounds, yet she showed no signs of weakness as her hand tightened around CJ's neck.

CJ raised her knee, hitting Edith in the groin. Edith hissed again, and CJ brought her hand between them, pressing her gun against Edith's chest. Their eyes locked together, and CJ saw nothing but pure evil. She fired twice in quick succession, and Edith finally loosened her grip, her eyes rolling back in her head as blood spewed from her heart. In what may have been a last attempt, the ax was raised, taking aim at CJ's head. CJ braced herself against the wall and, with as much force as she could muster, she kicked Edith in the stomach, sending her flying backward, the ax falling from her hands and bouncing down with a thud.

Again, everything seemed to slow as Edith hit the railing of the stairs, teetering precariously against it until her weight forced her over. CJ watched helplessly as Edith tumbled out of sight, falling over the edge. It seemed like an eternity before she heard the unmistakable sound of her body hitting the floor down below them. She went to the railing, shining her light down, seeing Edith's crumpled body lying on the first floor.

A loud, ferocious scream engulfed the stairwell. So intense was the sound that CJ covered her ears as she staggered back down to Ice. He too winced at the sound, his eyes wide with panic.

"Let's get to the safe room," she yelled against the sound.

But before they could move, the scream lessened, turning into a deep wail. The air around them turned scorching hot, and she felt pressure build, pulling at her clothes, her hair. She fell to the floor beside Ice, tugging him closer.

As if there was a giant vacuum above the house, the air was sucked from the room, threatening to take them with it. They held tight to each other. CJ swore she could actually see the air as it raced past them, streaming up the stairs to the third floor.

There was a flash of light and then a deafening boom; they heard the windows on the third floor shatter. The explosion was loud enough to shake the house. CJ buried her face against Ice as plaster from the ceiling fell around them.

And then, as if it had never happened at all, silence filled the house. She glanced past Ice to the window. The beam of sunlight grew brighter as the dark clouds that had surrounded the house faded, leaving clear, blue skies in their wake.

She stood, holding out a hand to Ice. He took it, letting himself be pulled up. He reached out and touched her face.

"Blood," he said.

She held up her hands, both stained with Edith's blood. "Hell of a day's work."

"I hope we never *ever* have to do shit like this again," he said. Then he blew out his breath and smiled. "Damn, CJ. That was some ride, wasn't it?" He raised his hand to high-five her. "Ghostbusters."

She laughed and slapped his hand. "Oh, now he thinks it was all fun and games."

He laughed too and they reached for the other, taking the time for a quick hug.

"Thanks for having my back," she said.

"I think I should thank you. She was about to chop me in half."

She looked up the stairs to the third floor, seeing sunlight streaming in. The house was just a house again. If not for all the blood that was splattered on the stairs, there was no evidence that a fight just took place.

"I'm going to check it out," she said.

He took his phone out. "Got a signal again."

"Yeah, imagine that," she said.

"I'll get Brady over here."

She nodded, then walked up the steps, taking care to avoid the blood. She stepped over the ax and headed up. She was no longer afraid. Whatever had been plaguing this house now seemed to be gone. She pushed open a door, looking into one of the bedrooms. The room was furnished with only a bed, nothing else. Both windows were blown out and a pleasant breeze rustled the curtains.

CJ stared for a moment as they swayed back and forth. She walked out and opened another room. This room was fully furnished. Judging by the mess in the bed, this is where they found Herbert Krause. The windows in this room were also blown out. She went inside, going to one of the windows and looking outside. She smiled as a ray of sunshine touched her skin. Then she heard something that had been missing. Birds. She nodded as she watched a male cardinal fly into one of the dead trees that stood close to the house. Soon another joined him.

"Yeah. Everything's okay now," she said as she turned to go.

She heard Ice talking on the phone, and she paused on the second floor, her glance going to the safe room. She pushed the door open, again smiling as sunlight filled the room, so different than earlier when she and Ice had taken refuge there.

"You still here?" she asked.

She waited, listening, but heard nothing. She was oddly disappointed.

"Oh, well," she murmured. She took one last look around then shrugged and headed out, closing the door behind her.

It was darker down on the first floor, the boarded-up windows preventing the sun from streaming inside. Her gaze landed on Edith's crumpled body, but she turned away from it quickly, going out to the porch where Ice was waiting. She raised her eyebrows.

"Yeah, Brady's on his way. I called Howley too. Paige had already called him, so I guess she's doing better." Ice smiled. "Oh, and Howley said Billy's jaw wasn't broken, but he lost two teeth. I was hoping they'd have to wire his mouth shut."

CJ laughed. "What? Did you and Billy have too much togetherness on this case?"

He nodded. "Yeah. I'll stick with my current partner, thanks."

She clapped his shoulder. "You got it."

"So listen, if you want to head over to the hospital, you can. I'll wait here for Brady," he offered.

"You'd stay here by yourself? What the hell's wrong with you?"

"I'm guessing there's not a damn thing in this house anymore. Not after all that," he said, pointing to the scattering of broken glass on the ground. "How in the hell are we going to put all of this in our report?"

"Oh, we'll make some shit up," she said. "If you're sure you're okay here…"

"Yeah. Go," he said, waving her away. Just when she opened the door to her truck, he called out. "Hey. You better clean off that blood before you get to the hospital. They might just admit you on sight."

CHAPTER THIRTY-NINE

Paige tugged at the removable splint on her arm, tightening it just a bit. Then she reached behind her head, feeling where they'd shaved her hair so that they could stitch up her wound.

"Quit messing with it," Billy said.

She glanced at him. "It's noticeable, isn't it?"

He rubbed his jaw. "At least you still have all your teeth."

"At least your hair is still even."

He shook his head. "Sometimes you're such a girl."

"Really? A girl? Because I'm concerned that they shaved part of my hair?" Was she really that vain? She touched the back of her head again, cringing as her fingers touched her scalp. "Men," she muttered. "It wasn't like it was life or death. I mean really, couldn't they have worked around the hair?"

"Are you afraid CJ is going to say something about it? Because I think you could be bald and CJ wouldn't care."

Paige laughed. "You could be right. That's one thing I love about her."

"Yeah. And shouldn't she be here by now? I'm ready to get out of here."

"She had to go by the hotel first," she said. CJ had been really noncommittal about why, but Paige could only assume it had something to do with the brief "battle" with Edith, as CJ called it. All CJ would tell her was that Edith had ended up falling from the third-floor stairs.

Paige got up and opened the door, taking a glance in both directions down the hallway. Two nurses were chatting with an older man, but other than that, the hallway was empty. She thought about going to check on Lizzie again, but the doctor had warned her Lizzie would be kept sedated. She was likely hit with the same bat as Paige. Whereas Paige had escaped the ordeal without any damage other than the ten stitches required to close her wound, Lizzie had swelling and bleeding around her brain. She knew from the deputies that Lizzie's sister and brother-in-law were on their way up from Conroe. At least she would have family with her. Paige tried not to blame herself for Lizzie's injuries, but she knew if she and CJ had not gotten her involved, Edith would have had no cause to harm her. But as it was, without Lizzie, they probably would have never solved this case.

She was about to go back into the room when she saw a familiar sight. She smiled as CJ walked confidently down the hallway toward her.

CJ grinned. "Hey."

Paige smiled with relief. "Hey."

CJ apparently didn't care that they were in a small-town hospital. She pulled her into a hug, and Paige wrapped her arms around her neck, pressing close to her.

"Are you okay?" she whispered into her ear.

CJ squeezed her tight, then stepped back, inspecting the arm that had the splint on it. "I was about to ask you the same thing. Broken?"

"Hairline fracture," she said, tugging CJ with her into the room.

CJ walked over to Billy, shaking her head. "I would have sworn your jaw was broken, Billy Boy," she said. "What did they say?"

"It's everything *but* broken," he said as he rubbed it. "Lost two damn teeth. Got another they think I can salvage if I get to a dentist for a root canal."

"Did you get lots of fun drugs?"

"Oh yeah. So I can't operate any heavy machinery. That probably means I shouldn't use my weapon either," he said around a yawn.

CJ turned back to her, motioning for Paige to turn around. "Let me see."

"They…they kinda had to shave my hair to stitch the wound," she said.

CJ lifted the hair away from her neck gently. "It looks fine," she said. "Any damage?"

"No, just a little swelling."

"Headache?"

Paige nodded. "Killer."

"Concussion?"

"No."

"Great. So you can leave?"

"Yes." Paige sat on the edge of the bed Billy was lounging on. "But first, tell us what happened."

CJ shrugged. "Edith was in the house. Third floor. She…she was possessed or something. Like you said, a ninja. She had an ax." CJ looked at them both. "There was some…some *force* or something there." She smiled quickly. "Get Ice to tell you that part. Anyway, Ice shot her four times. I shot her once in the back as she was taking a swing at Ice. It didn't even faze her." CJ took a deep breath. "I was pinned against the wall, she had the ax. I shot her point-blank in the heart. Twice. She was still trying to take a swing at me," she said with a shake of her head. "I…I kicked her. She fell over the railing, down to the first floor."

Paige went to her, giving her a quick hug but not knowing what to say.

"It's okay," CJ said. "She wasn't Edith Krause then. She was possessed by…by something. But whatever was in that house is gone. All the windows on the third floor blew out." She laughed quietly. "And get Ice to tell you about that too."

"So the bald man hung in there?" Billy asked with a grin.

"He was a trouper, yes." Her phone rang and she pulled it out of her pocket. "Speaking of Ice," she said. "What's up, baldy?"

CHAPTER FORTY

Shane Thompson was waiting for them when they pulled up to the office. He shook their hands firmly.

"Thank you for coming so quickly." Then he looked at Billy's bruised and swollen jaw. "What happened to you?"

"Baseball bat."

"Ice—Special Agent Freeman—said you saw the car," CJ prompted.

"Yeah. Well, some of the kids did. They alerted me," he said. "We were working the elm trees in the back pasture. The kids sometimes tag along and help when we're running irrigation lines," he explained. "It was a red Mustang. It went on up the forest road."

"How long ago?"

"I called Freeman as soon as the kids said that it was the car that hit Juan," he said. "We've been watching. It hasn't come back out."

"Where does the road go?" Paige asked.

"Up in the forest. There are logging roads back there. But if they're coming back to Cleveland, they've got to come back down this way," he said.

CJ nodded. "Okay. We'll go take a look." She turned to Billy. "You up for it? Or do you want to stay here and wait for Brady?"

Billy rubbed his jaw. "I think I better hang out here. Those pain pills, you know."

She then looked at Paige, knowing what her answer would be before she even asked. "You?"

"I'm fine," Paige said. "Let's go find the bastard."

CJ laughed as they got back in her truck. "You have turned into such a potty mouth."

"It's the company I keep."

When they pulled out of Thompson's driveway, CJ glanced at Paige. "Are you sure you're okay? I mean, your head, it wasn't that long ago that—"

"I'm fine, CJ. I have a little headache, that's all."

CJ eyed her skeptically. "I thought it was a killer headache."

"It's nothing I can't handle," Paige said. "I'm not letting you go after him alone, if that's what you're thinking."

"Okay. Then I won't worry."

"Good. Now what about you? You had quite an ordeal today too."

"I wouldn't call it an ordeal," she said.

"No? You have bruises on your neck and arms," Paige noted.

CJ glanced quickly at her forearms, seeing the telltale sign of hands squeezing against them, leaving a bruise. And they weren't from Edith Krause.

"Yeah, it was like Ester Hogan all over again," she admitted. "Ice and I were picked up and tossed around like ragdolls," she said. She met Paige's eyes for a moment. "I wasn't sure we were going to make it out of there alive."

Paige reached over and rested her hand on CJ's thigh, squeezing slightly. "You left that part out of your story earlier," Paige said.

"Yeah. It was some kind of scary," she said. "And Ice hung in there the whole time." She smiled as she turned onto the forest road. "When we're back home and you spoil me with one of your expensive bottles of wine, I'll tell you the whole story."

"Deal."

She slowed as they reached the back part of Thompson's property. She could see the rows of trailer houses that skirted the greenhouses and rows and rows of trees. She stuck her head out of her open window while she drove, noting the tire tracks on the dirt road.

"I'm going to bring up the satellite GPS. At least we'll know where the roads are," Paige said.

They drove for ten minutes or so before the forest opened up and revealed a logging road. The tracks they were following did not turn there, however. CJ kept going.

"There's another road coming up on the right," Paige said. "Looks like maybe a mile or so."

CJ nodded and kept going. Before too long, they found the second road. She slowed as they approached it. "He turned here," she said, still following the tracks.

"It doesn't look well used," Paige said.

"Old logging road. Probably just dead ends, right?"

Paige handed her the phone. "It goes a ways back, but yes, it just ends."

CJ studied the map. There was no way out other than this road. The satellite image was obviously taken shortly after the area had been logged. The new growth of trees there now were missing from the image.

"So what would our guy be doing out here?" she asked as she handed Paige's phone back to her.

"What are you thinking?"

"After this area's been clear-cut and the loggers pull out, I wouldn't imagine there's much traffic down this little logging road," she said.

"Marijuana?"

"Why not?" She drove on, slower now, the road extremely bumpy.

"They patrol areas like this by helicopter," Paige said.

"True. At the request of the local sheriff's department, though."

"Okay. You obviously have a theory. What is it?"

* * *

"So Shane Thompson saw a red sports car go down the forest road, and he thinks it's the one who ran down the kid?" Brady asked.

Ice nodded. "He said some of the kids saw it and told him it was the same car." Ice looked at the speedometer, noting Brady's slow pace. "Shouldn't we be in more of a hurry?"

"I thought your people were out there?" Brady gave him a smug look. "What? The FBI can't handle it?"

"Two of them just got out of the hospital," Ice said. Damn, but this guy got on his nerves. "So can you speed up a little bit? We're to pick up Special Agent Calhoun at Thompson's," he said.

"You guys are so formal. Calhoun is Billy, right?"

Ice sighed. "Yeah. Billy."

"So, those two women, are they, you know…queer?"

Ice narrowed his eyes at him. "What did you just say?"

Brady laughed. "Yeah, I thought so. Now the blond one, Paige, I would have never guessed. She's hot. But the other one, CJ, she's cocky and arrogant." He nodded. "She's kinda cute too, but I thought she was a dyke all along."

"Look, man, that's none of your business. Can you just get me to Thompson's please?"

"Yeah, yeah. We're almost there."

Prick. Ice slowly shook his head. If CJ had been in the car, she'd have probably shot him. That thought, of course, made him smile.

When they got to Thompson's, Billy was outside and waiting. He got in the backseat of Brady's patrol car.

"They're on an old logging road," he said. "I told them to wait, but you know CJ."

"Man, that's some bruise," Brady said. "Broken?"

"No. At least that's what they tell me. I can't imagine it hurting any worse," Billy said. "So if you'd take it easy on the bumps, I'd appreciate it."

"How long have they been out there?" Ice asked as Brady pulled away with a jerk, causing Billy to wince.

"They left here about twenty minutes ago," Billy said.

Yeah, plenty of time for CJ to get into trouble, he thought.

CHAPTER FORTY-ONE

"There's a black truck parked in the trees," CJ said, handing Paige the binoculars. "You can just barely see the red car."

They had pulled off of the logging road and parked next to a stand of young pines. Not exactly hidden.

"We should wait for the guys," Paige said. "If it is a marijuana farm, we have no idea who all might be out here."

"I'm telling you, Brady's involved," CJ said again. "It all adds up."

"As much as I appreciate your gut feeling, CJ, that's reaching. Even if he's involved in the drug business, I can't see him turning a blind eye to a murder. He was nothing but helpful to us at the Wicker house."

"All I'm saying is, it makes sense. He ignored calls made by Allen Poole when he complained about his neighbors. He wasn't all that happy with us for doing a bust. He didn't follow up on leads, he never contacted Thompson, never worked the case. That tells me he's involved somehow."

"Are you sure you're not implicating him simply because you don't like the man?"

"He's an obnoxious prick," CJ said. "And if he's a dirty cop, it'll be a pleasure to take him down."

Paige loved CJ's passion, but her theory that Brady was involved in the local drug trade—and possibly the murder of a little boy—was pure conjecture. She herself hadn't had any dealings with Brady so she wasn't quite as biased as CJ was. Could it be possible? Sure. And she would be prepared. He was bringing Ice and Billy to the scene. CJ's speculation would be put to the test very soon.

Suddenly CJ snatched up the binoculars. "I think we've been spotted," she said. "I count four guys."

"The only way out is this road," Paige reminded her.

"One took off on foot," CJ said. "The other three got into the black truck." She again handed Paige the binoculars before starting her truck. "Gonna try to block the road. Check in with Billy and see how far out they are."

Paige quickly called Billy, waiting impatiently through three rings before he answered. "Where are you?" she asked.

"Bouncing down this damn forest road," he said. "What's up?"

"We found the car. There's a black truck here too. Four guys that we can tell. One has fled. The black truck is heading our way."

"We should be there soon," he said.

"Tell Brady it's the second logging road, to the right. We're about three or four hundred yards down it," she said. She listened while he conveyed the message.

"He said he knows the road," Billy said.

Paige's eyes were glued to the fast approaching black truck. "Tell him to hurry," she said before disconnecting.

CJ's truck was parked sideways across the road, blocking access. Dust flew up behind the black truck as it came closer.

"Surely he's not going to hit us," she said.

"Fucker," CJ muttered. "Come on. We need to get out."

Paige opened the door quickly and followed CJ to the edge of the woods. They snapped open their holsters and withdrew their weapons. The truck's engine seemed loud to her and her eyes were riveted upon it as it slowed, now some fifty feet away. She could make out three men squeezed in the front seat. The passenger door opened and a guy stood up.

"Move your goddamn truck out of the way," he yelled.

CJ immediately held up her credentials. "FBI," she yelled back. "Get out of the truck."

He laughed at her. "Yeah, right."

Paige heard a twig snap behind her, but before she could turn, she was grabbed. She cried out as the back of her head hit a solid chest. As a strong arm circled her neck, she lashed back with her elbow, hitting him in the stomach. Just as she was about to twist out of his grasp, his hand clasped around the back of her neck, pressing hard against her wound. The pain was enormous, but she raised her hand intending to swing at him, only to have him hit the splint that was protecting her fractured arm. She winced in pain and her weapon fell uselessly to the ground. Before she could recover, she felt the cold metal of a gun barrel as it was pressed to her head.

CJ spun around too late, her eyes wide as she raised her weapon. "Damn, but you run fast," she said. "Don't be stupid. We're FBI agents."

"Drop your gun," the man said. "I got no problem with shooting her."

"And I got no problem with shooting you," CJ said.

Paige felt herself being dragged backward and her eyes searched CJ's, trying to determine their plan of attack. She looked past CJ, seeing the three men from the truck approaching.

"Behind you," she said, but CJ never turned. All her attention was on the man who held her.

"Special Agent Riley, did I ever tell you I was a sharpshooter?" CJ asked, her voice calm, a contradiction to the desperate look Paige saw in her eyes.

Paige tried to swallow as the arm around her neck tightened.

"Look, lady, drop your gun already," one of the three said from behind CJ. "You ain't going nowhere."

"Lady? *Lady?* I'm a goddamn FBI Special Agent and if I had a mind to, I'd have already shot all three of you," CJ said without looking at them. She moved to the side, circling Paige and the man who held her.

"We ain't looking for trouble," he said.

"Is that right? Then why is this dickhead holding a gun to my partner's head?"

"Come on, Scottie. They're FBI, for God's sake. Let her go."

"Shut up," the man holding her yelled. "Why do you think they're here? Chuck said they were looking for me. Because of the damn kid."

Paige's headache was blinding, but she was cognizant enough to know that Chuck was most likely Chuck Brady. Apparently CJ's gut feeling was right after all.

"I told you we should've taken the boy to the hospital."

"I said to shut up. Let me think."

"So what, Scottie?" CJ asked. "When you mowed down the kid and he didn't die, you had to kill him? Had to strangle him? He was only six years old."

"I don't give a fuck," Scottie said. "They were all out in the goddamn road. It wasn't my fault."

"That's right. It wasn't. And had you called an ambulance, maybe the kid doesn't die," CJ said. "But you didn't do that, did you?" CJ turned to the other three. "Which one of you was with him?"

The man who stepped forward appeared to be in his early twenties. "I was."

"Was it Scottie's idea to put the kid in the trunk and drive off?"

"Yeah."

"Shut the hell up," Scottie yelled as his grip tightened around Paige's neck. She was having a hard time breathing, and she was afraid she was going to pass out. She met CJ's eyes, trying to hold on. She heard the sound of a car approaching and assumed it was Brady. Thankfully, the grip around her neck loosened.

"Is that Chuck?" one of them asked.

"Yeah," Scottie said. He laughed at CJ. "My cousin is with the sheriff's department. They don't take too kindly to outsiders."

"Deputy Brady is your cousin, huh? Well, that makes me no difference, seeing as how you're still holding a gun to my partner's head."

"Jesus Christ, Scottie, what the hell are you doing?" Brady asked as he walked closer.

"They came snooping around here, man."

Paige looked at Billy and Ice, who had their weapons out. Brady held his hands up. "Everybody just calm down."

"Calm down? I'm about to shoot his ass if he doesn't let her go," CJ said.

Brady shook his head. "I swear, Scottie, this is one mess I can't get you out of. You need to let her go."

"No! I'm not letting her go. I'm getting out of here."

"And where are you going to go? You got four FBI agents here, Scottie. Now let her go."

"Fuck you," he spat as he jerked her hard against him. "They know about the kid. Get out of my way," he said as he drug Paige with him.

"I'm afraid I can't do that. I've turned a blind eye to your drug dealings but not this," Brady said with a shake of his head. He slowly pulled out his own weapon and held it up. "Now you let her go, Scottie."

"You're not going to shoot me."

"I will if I have to. But probably one of these FBI agents will beat me to it."

"Yeah? Well, she's going with me if they do." The gun to her head pressed harder, and she closed her eyes.

"Paige."

She opened them, meeting CJ's steady gaze.

"Remember last year? When that homeless guy had me?"

"Shut up! No talking."

Homeless guy? Paige ran the scene through her mind quickly. The homeless guy had a broken beer bottle held to CJ's neck. Ice had his gun on him when she and Billy had run into the alley. CJ had tried to talk to the guy, but he wouldn't let her go. "I'm about to bust your balls, man," she remembered CJ telling him. What was CJ suggesting? That she attempt to disable this man who had a gun held to her head? The pain in her arm was intense, but it didn't nearly match the pain in her head. God, did she even have the strength?

She nodded. "I remember," she said.

"Shut up," Scottie yelled and jerked her back against his chest. "Quit talking. I swear I'll blow your head off."

"Scottie, stop it right now," Brady said. "They're not messing around. They're going to shoot to kill."

"So am I."

Paige held on to CJ's eyes, seeing the subtle nod of her head. She knew all CJ needed was a clear shot. With as much strength as she could muster—and praying Scottie didn't pull the trigger—she made a fist and swung back, hitting him high in the groin as hard as she could. He yelped in pain, losing his grip on her. She fell to the ground instantly, rolling away as gunfire shattered the silence. The pain in her head became nearly unbearable, and she wondered if she'd been shot.

Then CJ was there, gently brushing the hair from her face, her eyes doing a quick inventory of her body.

"Okay?"

"I think so," she said. She rolled her head, seeing Scottie lying on the ground. She didn't know how many shots he'd taken, but blood covered his plaid shirt. Brady stood over him, staring at his lifeless body.

"When we were younger, we were like brothers," Brady said, his voice thick with emotion. "I was two days older than him. I went into law enforcement. He went in the opposite direction."

"What the hell was he protecting out here?" Ice asked.

"Marijuana farm," CJ said. She glanced at Brady. "Right?"

Brady nodded. "I let a few things slide as far as he was concerned. I didn't think he hit the kid, though. When you came back and said it was a sports car up on the forest road, I went around to see him. He said it wasn't him." Brady turned away from the body. "I took a look at his car. There wasn't any damage," he said with a shrug. "I guess deep down I knew it was him."

"You should have taken yourself off the case, Brady," Ice said.

"Is that why you let the drug house slide? The one out in Shady Pines?"

Brady nodded. "Yeah. The guys worked for Scottie."

CJ helped Paige to her feet, keeping an arm around her to steady her. Billy had the other three men leaning against CJ's truck.

"You got yourself in a little bit of trouble, Brady," Ice said. "Obstructing an FBI investigation is only part of it."

"Like I said, we were like brothers." He looked over at the other three. "Lou? Were you with him?"

Lou nodded. "He was driving too fast. It was almost dark. I kept telling him we were going to hit a deer or something. We came upon those kids, he couldn't stop." He shook his head. "I told him we needed to call an ambulance, told him we should call you. He wouldn't listen. When we got to his house, the kid was still alive, man. I got the hell out of there."

"The kid was strangled," CJ said.

"I had nothing to do with that. Scottie told me the next day what he'd done."

"Why dump him at the Wicker house? How is it significant?"

Lou shrugged. "I think he just found an abandoned house and dumped him. Scottie never thought that house was haunted anyway."

Paige looked around her. Billy was resting against CJ's truck, rubbing his bruised jaw. The three men were all staring at Scottie's body. Brady had a look of shock on his face as Ice held out his hand. Brady handed over his service weapon without protest. She turned, meeting CJ's watchful eyes.

"Quite an eventful day," CJ said.

"Yes. And I remember now. I was pissed at you that day in the alley," Paige said as they headed to her truck.

"The homeless guy? Why were you pissed?"

"You showed up that morning with a hickey on your neck." Paige was surprised to find CJ blushing. "I may have chastised you a little. So you proceeded to go into great detail as to how you got the hickey," she said. "She was a redhead, I believe."

"Okay, okay," CJ said. "Let's drop it." She lowered her voice to a whisper. "You can give me a hickey later tonight if you want."

"Yes. I think I will mark you." Paige met her eyes. "Only it won't be on your neck."

CHAPTER FORTY-TWO

Howley looked at them skeptically. "And the windows blew out?"

CJ and Ice nodded.

"And the reason for this is…internal pressure? What the hell is that?"

CJ cleared her throat. "Well, I looked it up on the Internet. It sounded good."

"Look, your recount of what happened is bare bones as it is. You want to tell me what really happened? Then you can go revise your report to something a little more feasible."

CJ glanced at Ice. "You want me to tell him, baldy?"

"Sure." He tried to keep the smile off his face as their eyes met.

"Okay."

CJ stood and paced behind him. It was a plan they'd come up with that morning over coffee. The truth was just too farfetched for anyone to believe. So they'd pretty much left it as Howley had said: bare bones. Now CJ would throw out some of those unbelievable facts and let Howley make the call. CJ predicted he would leave it at bare bones once they mentioned *ghosts*.

"See, the house was really haunted," CJ said. "And there was this ghost. Well, there were two that we know of. One was kinda like Casper. The other, not so nice. Anyway—"

"CJ, what the hell are you talking about?"

"Ghosts. It seems like the good ghost was helping us. Pushed me down the laundry chute so I'd find the chalk. Led me to the root cellar and the tunnel. Told me—"

"Seriously? This is what you want to go with?"

"You wanted more than bare bones," CJ reminded him. "Anyway, the ghost—the bad ghost—must have possessed Edith. At least, that's what we think. I mean, she took out Paige and Billy like that," CJ said, snapping her fingers. "So when Edith attacked us with the ax and we had to shoot her seven times, it was like he lost his energy when she died. All of the air was sucked out of the house, up to the third floor, causing the windows to blow out."

Howley stared at her, slowly shaking his head. "So you're saying the place was haunted?"

"Yeah."

"And there was a ghost?"

"Yep. At least two of them."

He glanced at Ice with raised eyebrows.

Ice nodded. "Yeah, a ghost. And the air got sucked out."

Howley let out a heavy sigh. "Okay. So we'll go with…internal pressure then."

CJ grinned. "Yeah, that sounds good."

"And really, I don't think you need to mention *ghosts* to anyone," Howley said. "I'm still trying to explain your report on Hoganville. You know, big scary monster and all."

"I understand," CJ said.

Ice shifted nervously as Howley turned his attention to him. "If I find out you two are just blowing smoke up my ass because you didn't want to do a thorough report, I'll—"

"No, sir," Ice said. "It really happened."

"Okay." He glanced at the door. "Take off. Billy and Paige are going to be out a few days with their injuries. You should take some time too. You did a damn good job on this case."

"Thank you," CJ said. "Does that mean we're back in good graces after the Hoganville debacle?"

"It means I thoroughly enjoyed telling Larry Figures my team busted an old cold case of his while still working an active case. Damn good job."

Ice nodded. "Thank you. I don't mind taking a few days off."

They closed the door behind them, then CJ slapped Ice's shoulder. "See? Told you it would work."

"And days off too. Can't beat that."

CJ grinned. "I guess you know where I'll be."

"No doubt."

"I'm going to do nothing but sleep and make love."

"I don't need to know your plans, CJ."

"What about you? Just going to crash?"

"Oh, hell, I told Billy I'd go by his place. I'm supposed to bring him soup and ice cream. I've never heard a grown man whine so much about a little toothache."

"Well, you have fun, baldy." She winked. "I know I will."

Ice smiled as he watched her head out. She had a spring in her step and a light in her eyes that told him how very much in love she was. He was happy for her. He was happy for both of them.

CHAPTER FORTY-THREE

CJ still nuzzled her breast long after Paige's orgasm had ripped through her. She ran her fingers across CJ's bare back, then lower, cupping her and bringing her closer still. CJ's mouth returned to hers, their kisses slow and tender now after their fiery lovemaking.

"I love you," she murmured against CJ's lips.

CJ lifted herself higher, enough to meet her eyes. "I love you, Paige. I'm...I'm so scared, but I love you."

Paige touched her cheek. "Why are you scared?"

"I'm scared you're going to break my heart."

"Oh, sweetheart." Paige rolled them over, and she now rested her weight on CJ. "What we have is beautiful. And it's new and it's growing," she said. "You can't go into this thinking it's going to end, or that I'll grow tired of you, or whatever other thoughts you have." She kissed her gently. "What I feel for you is so...so different for me, CJ. And so unexpected. I mean, there was always an attraction between us, but I never thought it would turn into this. But when I look into your eyes, when you touch me, when I touch you—it's all so beautiful. Beautiful inside and out," she said. "This feeling I have is almost too amazing for mere words." She kissed her again, slowly. "You're in my soul now, CJ. And that's where I want you to stay."

CJ had a hint of tears in her eyes, but Paige didn't call attention to them. For all her bravado, CJ was never afraid to show her vulnerabilities to her. That was yet one more thing Paige loved about her.

"So…we're okay?"

CJ nodded, then smiled. "We're in love."

Paige grinned. "Yes, we're very much in love."

"So we're good," CJ said. "And I'm starving."

"The pizza will be here soon enough," she said. "And you're such a bad influence on me. Pizza is very bad."

CJ rolled them over, now on top. "You got the veggie. I'll slap your hand if you try to steal a pepperoni off mine."

Paige smiled dreamily at her. "I want Mexican food. Fish or shrimp tacos. Take me somewhere this week?" she asked.

"I know just the place. We'll have a date." Then CJ's face turned serious. "I've never really been on a date before."

She didn't have to elaborate. Paige knew what she meant. So she said nothing, just pulled CJ down for a kiss.

"Then it's a date. And when we get home, we'll treat ourselves to some dessert."

CJ smiled at her. "I think I'm going to love your dessert."

The doorbell interrupted their playful kissing, and CJ rolled off her.

"Pizza. That was quick."

She got out of bed, pointing at Paige. "Stay put. I'll bring the wine."

"Pizza in bed?"

"Unless you want to sit at the table naked. You're not allowed to put clothes on." CJ held up Paige's robe. "Can I borrow this?"

Paige laughed. The robe was *so* not CJ, but she nodded, laughing again as CJ tugged it closed and nearly danced out of the bedroom.

"God, she's adorable."

* * *

CJ grabbed some cash from her jeans, which were still lying on the living room floor. Paige had tossed them there earlier in her haste to get CJ naked. The doorbell rang again, and CJ hurried to the door and yanked it open.

"That's the fastest pizza delivery we've—" Her mouth dropped open. *Oh fuck.*

"Why is it that when I visit my daughter, I find you here?" She glanced at CJ's bare legs and then at the robe that was barely closed. "And nearly naked. Again."

"Mrs. Riley," CJ said. She looked away from her intense stare. "Paige is…she's…well, she's…she's in the…let me…let me go get her."

CJ spun around and nearly ran down the hallway and into the bedroom. She closed the door quickly and leaned against it, her heart caught in her throat.

Paige was sitting up in bed, naked, the sheet scarcely covering her. CJ's eyes were drawn to the curve of her hip and she had to shake her head to clear it. Paige's *mother* was here, for God's sake.

"Are you okay?" Paige asked with a tilt of her head. "Pizza?"

CJ slowly shook her head. "No. Definitely not pizza." She swallowed down her nervousness. "Your…your mother is here."

The color drained from Paige's face as they stared at each other. Long seconds passed by without a single sound, then Paige smiled. Then she laughed. And then she buried her face in her pillow as a fit of giggles overtook her. CJ stared at her in disbelief. She was *laughing*?

CJ walked closer to the bed. "Paige…I mean, I'm glad you find this funny, but she's like…right out there," she said, pointing to the door. "We can't exactly hide in here."

Paige uncovered her face, her eyes still twinkling with amusement. "You opened the door—naked, wearing my silk robe—and it wasn't pizza. It was my mother." She laid her head back as laughter again bubbled out. "Is that not hysterical?"

CJ grinned. "Well, okay, *now*. But not so much when I was standing there, no."

Paige finally stood up and held her hand out. "Give me the robe." CJ's gaze traveled over her body, lingering on her breasts. "Easy, tiger. We have Mother to face."

CJ stripped the robe off and handed it to Paige. Paige wrapped it around herself, then reached for the removable splint they'd taken off earlier. "Help me with this, would you?"

CJ strapped it to her arm, then looked around for her own clothes. Her jeans, of course, were still in the living room. She found her T-shirt but couldn't find her bra. She looked at Paige. "Where did you fling my bra?"

"Don't worry about it. Just put your T-shirt on. I don't expect she'll stay long." Paige came closer, pausing to kiss her lightly. "I'm sorry. I guess I should have already told her about me, about us."

"It's okay. We'll be fine." She arched her eyebrows. "We will, right?"

Paige smiled. "Yes, sweetheart. We'll be fine." Paige stared at her bare legs. "Let me guess. Your jeans are out there," she said, pointing to the door.

"Afraid so."

Paige started laughing again. "God, it just keeps getting better. Come on."

* * *

For all her earlier merriment, Paige was actually terrified of having this conversation with her mother. Yes, she should have told her years ago that she was gay. But it was a little late now for that revelation.

She was surprised, however, to find her mother lounging on her sofa with a bit of an amused expression on her face. Paige tugged the robe tighter around her waist.

"Hello, Mother."

Her mother's gaze slid from her to CJ, who was trying to inconspicuously slip on her jeans. Paige covered her mouth to hide her smile as CJ triumphantly pulled up her zipper.

"Funny, but earlier I could have sworn that *she* had on that robe," her mother said.

Paige gave a quick smile to her mother. "You remember CJ," she said.

"Of course. The last time I was here, if I recall, she was naked, wearing only a sheet." Her mother stared at CJ. "I do believe, after a rather awkward introduction, you nearly fled from the apartment."

CJ's laugh was quick and short. "Yeah. And I've got a mind to do the same right now."

At that, Paige did laugh, having to contain the giggles that wanted to return. "Okay, Mother, enough of this," she said with a smile. "I guess it's obvious what's happening here."

"What's obvious is that this is something you've intentionally kept from me."

Paige eyed her mother, wondering why there was no outburst, no protest. "You're taking it well."

"What? The fact that you have a girlfriend instead of a boyfriend?" Her mother glanced at CJ. "That is the proper term, isn't it? Girlfriend?"

"We have been...seeing each other for a while, yes," Paige said. "But I'm assuming you already knew that."

"It took a very expensive dinner and a two hundred dollar bottle of wine to get Seth to talk."

At that, Paige laughed. "Did he make you promise not to tell his mother?"

"He did. And I called her immediately. Seth goes through their money like it's candy."

"Mother, surely you could tell that Seth and I...well, that there was nothing between us."

"Yes. But you kept dating, so we assumed there *was* something. Why did you feel the need to pretend?"

"You both nearly had a stroke when I joined the FBI. I could only imagine your outburst had I told you I was a lesbian."

Her mother cringed. "I'm not quite used to that word yet. Not when it applies to my daughter."

Paige nodded. "Of course. I'm sorry. Now, why are you here?"

"You wouldn't take my calls."

"I was working. We had a case," she said.

"Well, I thought you were avoiding me." She turned her attention to CJ, who had been standing by quietly. "Are you living here?"

CJ shook her head. "I have a place. It's—"

"Mother, don't try to intimidate her." Paige linked an arm through CJ's. "She stays here most nights."

Her mother appeared to only then notice the splint on her arm. "What happened?"

"It's a slight hairline fracture is all," she said.

"Someone hit you?" She looked at CJ suspiciously.

"Yes, a crazy woman with a baseball bat," Paige said dismissively. "Now, we're having pizza for dinner. Would you like to join us?"

Her mother paused. "Well, it's been a while since we've visited. You will put some clothes on, won't you?"

"Yes."

Her mother stood. "I'll choose the wine. I assume you have some decent bottles?"

Paige sighed and gave an apologetic smile to CJ. "Yes, I have decent bottles of wine. That is one thing you taught me."

Her mother seemed pleased by that statement, and she gave Paige a genuine smile. "Go change, dear. CJ can keep me company." She turned to CJ. "Tell me about your family. What business are they in? Law enforcement like you?"

CJ looked at her helplessly. "Well, kinda. More like...in the prison system, though."

Paige hurried back to her bedroom, feeling a swell of affection for CJ, loving her sense of humor. She knew that was one thing that CJ was most worried about—her upbringing. If CJ was in her life, then her parents would want to know more about her. And as well as her mother was taking the news that she was a lesbian, she doubted she'd be as understanding if she knew that CJ's father was in prison.

But they would deal with that later. Right now, she was just trying to wrap her mind around the fact that her mother was here, chatting with CJ, about to dine on pizza and very likely her most expensive bottle of wine.

After pulling on jeans and one of CJ's FBI T-shirts, she left her feet bare as she hurried back to the kitchen. She paused when she heard her mother's question.

"So what exactly are your intentions with my daughter?"

"Intentions? I don't know what you mean. I'm madly in love with her. I know that."

Paige smiled as she entered, her eyes meeting CJ's.

"The feeling is very mutual," she said, ignoring her mother as she placed a light kiss on CJ's lips.

CJ blushed profusely and was saved by the ringing of the doorbell. "Pizza. Finally. I'll get it."

CHAPTER FORTY-FOUR

"Stop apologizing. It wasn't that bad," she said.

"She interrogated you for most of the night," Paige said as she handed CJ her plate.

"It was fine. I actually like your mother." She looked at the plate. "Do I want to know what's in it?"

"It's quiche."

"Right. And do I want to know what's in it?" she asked again with a smile.

"Well, it's very healthy. No eggs."

CJ made a face. "Is it possible to make a quiche without eggs?" She took a bite. It was very good. She nodded. "I see broccoli and mushrooms. So what's not normal about it."

"It has blended tofu instead of eggs."

"You didn't have to tell me that."

"You asked."

CJ grinned. "I'm teasing. It's really good. Thank you."

"More coffee?"

CJ nodded and pushed her cup closer. They were having brunch on Paige's terrace. It was large enough for a table and four chairs and ever since the weather had cooled, they used it more.

"Tell me again why you invited my mother to go out to dinner with us tonight?"

"I told you, I like her."

"I'm going to say you tolerate her."

"Well, she's a little uppity. Now I know where you get it from," she teased.

"Funny."

"No, I just thought, since she's in town, you might like to spend some time with her. And it wouldn't hurt for her to get to know me better."

Paige touched her arm and squeezed gently. "That's very sweet of you. If you're not careful, she'll invite us to Dallas for the holidays."

"Oh, hell, I didn't say I wanted to meet your father," she said with mock horror.

Her phone rang and she wanted to ignore it. It was her day off. But it was Ice's ringtone so she answered it.

"What's up, baldy?"

"Hey. Is this a good time? I don't want to, you know, interrupt anything."

She laughed. "Well, if you were interrupting something, I wouldn't have answered. We're having brunch. What's up?"

"Got a call from Cleveland. You remember that young deputy? Carter?"

"Yeah. He worked the case with Brady, didn't he?"

"Yeah. He called. Had a couple of pieces of news." Ice paused. "Lizzie Willis is out of ICU. I thought you and Paige would want to know."

"That's great news." She turned to Paige. "Lizzie is out of ICU," she repeated.

"And there was one other thing," Ice said. "They found Brady. Dead."

CJ sat up straighter. "What the hell?"

"Self-inflicted gunshot wound to the head."

"Jesus," she murmured. She glanced at Paige. "Brady shot himself," she explained to her. "Did he leave a note or anything? I mean, he screwed up, sure. Probably wasn't going to do any jail time though."

"No note," Ice said. "But that's not all. Guess where they found his body?"

CJ swallowed. "The Wicker house?"

"Yeah. Up on the stairs. Third floor."

"You have *got* to be kidding me."

"No. And I don't care what happens, but I ain't going back there."

CJ shook her head. "But we were there. We *saw* the damn air sucked out of the house. The windows blew out. The house was *clean*," she insisted. Hell, she'd gone up to the third floor. The sun was shining, the birds were singing. It was just a house again. Or so she thought.

"Maybe it wasn't clean. He shot himself right where you shot Edith."

"Coincidence?"

"It's a damn scary one if it is."

"Yeah. But I got no answers," she said. "Maybe he was trying to get the last laugh."

"If he's in a state of mind where he's about to off himself, I doubt his lasts thoughts were about messing with two FBI agents."

"I like that thought better than to think he was somehow drawn to the house. But I don't want to think about it now. We'll talk about it later. Okay?"

"Sure. Listen, you guys want to go grab a beer tonight?"

"How about tomorrow? Got dinner plans tonight. Paige's mother is in town."

Ice laughed. "It must be serious if you're having dinner with Paige's mother."

CJ smiled as she met Paige's gaze, locking eyes with her. "Yeah. It's very serious."

Bella Books, Inc.

Women. Books. Even Better Together.

P.O. Box 10543
Tallahassee, FL 32302

Phone: 800-729-4992
www.bellabooks.com